D1414383

Murder in Megara

Books by Mary Reed and Eric Mayer

The John the Lord Chamberlain Mysteries
One for Sorrow
Two for Joy
Three for a Letter
Four for a Boy
Five for Silver
Six for Gold
Seven for a Secret
Eight for Eternity
Nine for the Devil
Ten for Dying
Murder in Megara

Murder in Megara

A John the Lord Chamberlain Mystery

Mary Reed and Eric Mayer

Poisoned Pen Press

First Edition 2015

10 9 8 7 6 5 4 3 2 1

Library of Congress Catalog Card Number: 2014958049

ISBN: 9781464204067   Hardcover
       9781464204081   Trade Paperback

Poisoned Pen Press
6962 E. First Ave., Ste. 103
Scottsdale, AZ 85251
www.poisonedpenpress.com
info@poisonedpenpress.com

Printed in the United States of America

Prologue

"Exiled or not, the emperor's Lord Chamberlain camped at Megara's gates means trouble!"

"Former Lord Chamberlain, remember. The way you speak you'd think he'd brought an army with him instead of those two servants." The speaker nodded at an elderly man and a woman—half her companion's age—who were inspecting the tuna, mullet, and eels displayed on a marble slab on the opposite side of the marketplace. A cloth awning over the fish merchant's stall cast a reddish shadow. The woman had tawny skin and black hair. The man maintained a military bearing, but his step was hesitant.

The group of townspeople, partly concealed by stacked cages full of live chickens, had watched the pair as they moved around the square, filling the woman's wicker basket with figs, a pot of honey, three fist-sized melons. The chickens clucked despondently, already half-boiled by the late August sun of southern Greece.

"Black as a Nubian, isn't she?" remarked a middle-aged woman, dressed too well for a dusty market in an insignificant city. "And you notice they speak with different accents. The senator's estate has turned into a regular Tower of Babel."

"Egyptian, so I hear. And that's her husband with her," someone else said.

"Not her husband. Grandfather, surely!"

The city square smelled of fish, goats, and produce that had gone unsold for too many days. People haggled noisily:

"Ah, there you are. I'm sorry I was detained. Business. Let's find a quiet spot to talk."

"Grilled fish, here! Buy your grilled fish! So fresh it'll leap into your mouth!"

"How much did you say? Is that what you think my fine cloth is worth? Does it look like I stole it off a beggar?"

A dog barked. A baby cried.

The observer, lounging against a column in the colonnade at the edge of the marketplace, couldn't make out every word of the conversation from beside the chicken cages.

But enough to be of interest.

A man with a beak-like nose and eyes as round and black as pebbles spat in the dirt. "What do you expect from a bunch of dirty foreigners? Foreigners and pagans, every one of 'em."

"First you see an invisible army, now you see foreigners. The Lord Chamberlain—John, his name is—grew up hereabouts, as we all know."

The beaked man turned his dark eyes toward the speaker. "Who are you to be defending him? Do you expect he'll pay all the back taxes? We don't need a new landowner, especially one who'll actually live on his estate, meddling and upsetting things."

"That's right," put in a shrunken, clerkish fellow. "What does an official from the court at Constantinople know about how things are in Megara?"

"My oracular fowl refused their feed this morning," the beaked man continued. "One flew away. That's a sure sign of disaster."

This prophesy was met by a general murmur of assent.

"You and your oracular fowl! We've all had them for dinner. Once they're past egg-laying days they predict they'll bring a good price at market. It's the only prediction they get right." The speaker tapped one of the cages, eliciting agitated squawks from within. "That's what you all sound like, terrified of one miserable exile and a couple of servants."

A tepid breeze slithered through the shadows in the colonnade, bringing the smell of the sea but no relief from the heat. The chicken seller—and oracle owner—was pointing out the whole empire knew about Justinian's fickleness. He'd shown his Lord Chamberlain mercy on a whim and he'd change his mind just as easily. Assassins could well be stepping off a ship at the docks right now.

The observer couldn't suppress a grim smile at the thought.

Before the former Lord Chamberlain's defender could reply, the clerk barged in, warning that powerful officials have powerful enemies, as if this were something of which he had personal knowledge. Every one of the new arrival's enemies would be furious he hadn't been executed, and more than one might decide to rectify the imperial error. Before long the city would be swarming with hired murderers. Innocent people were bound to be caught in the bloodshed. It was intolerable. What were the authorities going to do about it? The clerk's strident voice rose to a higher pitch.

The two servants under observation turned away from the fish and walked out of the awning's red shadow into the brightness of the square. Other market-goers kept their distance, eddying around the two, only moving their heads to gawk after they had passed.

The observer barely made out the well-dressed woman's words. "The chamberlain's not a proper man, you know."

The chicken seller spat again.

The woman looked as if she would like to do the same but instead made an obscene gesture. "Eunuchs! Unnatural creatures! Greedy, scheming, all of them! You can't trust them. What unhealthy intrigues has he bought from the court? He'll doubtless be conniving to get back into power, and whatever bloody plan he hatches, we'll pay for it!"

"What are we going to do about it?" Perhaps the clerk meant to issue a challenge but the effect was ruined by the quaver in his voice.

The observer stepped away from the column and strode toward the group, hearing low cursing from several who had remained silent until then.

"What's the matter with all of you?" asked the former Lord Chamberlain's lone defender. "He's nothing more than a farmer now."

"Does the crab ever learn to keep his legs straight?" asked the observer.

The two servants came abreast of the stacked cages. The old man made as if to examine them, but the young woman, glancing quickly at the people gathered there, tugged at his arm, and they continued on past instead.

As she looked back over her shoulder a stone flew from behind the cages. The observer couldn't have said who threw it. He saw the woman step protectively in front of her companion and kept on walking out of the marketplace.

Chapter One

Peter limped grimly through the courtyard gates just as John and Cornelia emerged from the house. He might have come straight from a battlefield. Blood speckled his sleeves; a smear of red ran across his forehead.

"Master, Hypatia was attacked by a mob and…and…"

Before he could gasp out the rest of the sentence Hypatia, looking pale, intervened. "Don't bother the master, Peter. It was just a few stones, most of them wide of the mark. You put yourself in worse danger by trying to catch the perpetrators." Directing a fond smile at her husband, she continued. "I had to insist we return immediately or he'd still be fighting!"

"I wish I'd had a weapon," Peter told John. "They crept up on me, the cowards. They hurt Hypatia." His voice quavered.

"It's just a lump on the back of my head."

Cornelia peered at the injury and pursed her lips. "It's going to be a very big lump, Hypatia. Why would anyone do such a thing?"

"The whole town hates us. We're despised foreigners, if you'll pardon my saying it, mistress," Hypatia replied.

"She's right," Peter said. "We're not safe here. I should like to be armed next time we go to market."

John, who had looked on silently, shook his head. "I don't want you fighting a war over every basket of melons and turnips. How did this happen?"

Peter gave a colorful description of the visit to the market-place. Hypatia stepped in occasionally, softening the more lurid details. "Please don't worry," she concluded. "As soon as we put these purchases away I'll make a poultice to take down the swelling."

She carried her basket off in the direction of the kitchen, with Peter trailing, still looking grim, swinging one arm as if he carried a sword.

John and Cornelia departed for their walk in a somber mood. They followed their already familiar route along the low ridge overlooking the sea. Unkempt meadows ran into fields, and fields became rocky hillsides without any clear demarcation.

They passed through a meadow watched over by a fig tree so massive and gnarled it might have been older than the empire. Their tunics rasped faintly against sharp, stiff blades of tall grass, brown and crisp at the end of the dry summer.

Worried by Peter and Hypatia's experience, John studied Cornelia. Was she distressed by it all? Had his sentence of exile widened the gray streaks in her dark hair, or was it merely that the unforgiving sunlight called attention to the gray, causing it to glitter like frost when she moved her head to look at the sea or the hills or down at a yellow flower in the grass? When she bent to pick it John took the chance to let his fingers fondly brush her small shoulder.

"Don't ask me its name," he said. "Hypatia might know, especially if it has medicinal value."

Cornelia turned the flower about in her fingers, narrowing her eyes to examine it in the glare, accentuating the fine wrinkles in her deeply tanned skin. She paused thoughtfully, then resumed walking. "I'll take it back to the house. Back home. And see what Hypatia has to say. Do you know, I had the urge…but then, it would look foolish for me to come back with flowers in my hair like a silly young girl or one of those nymphs the gods were always chasing about, wouldn't it?"

"When did you stop being a young girl? I hadn't noticed."

"You are an old silver-tongue!" She strode off through the meadow, the shape of her slender, well-muscled legs outlined under her thin, pale green tunic.

"No, I meant it," John called after her, immediately realizing he sounded like a feckless, lovestruck boy. He watched her move away. The gray in her hair, like the wrinkles in her face, were nothing more than bits of strange adornment. Cornelia was no different to him than ever.

He caught up to her with a few strides, took the flower from her hand and threaded it, clumsily, into the gray strand that fell across her temple.

She smiled up at him and then said, quite unexpectedly, "John, why can't you be happy here?"

He withdrew his hand. "It isn't that I'm unhappy, Cornelia. It's just that everything is in such disarray." He nodded in the direction of a field down the slope between where they stood and the sea. "That should have been plowed by now, there's harness in need of mending, the fish pond requires cleaning and restocking."

Cornelia beamed and adjusted the flower in her hair. "There speaks the farmer! You're recalling these tasks from when you were a boy?"

John took her arm and helped her over a dry weed-choked ditch. "As to the fish, at least we can be certain Peter won't follow the example of the cook who deceived his master, a certain Bithynian king, with slices of boiled turnip shaped like anchovies when none were available."

"You could have changed the subject more subtly! I know we're in a difficult situation. Perhaps a dangerous one, judging from what happened to Peter and Hypatia in the marketplace. When the townspeople get to know us they won't be afraid. They'll stop hating us."

John thought it better to say nothing.

They passed along a rutted path leading to a field dotted with sheep. From behind a knoll rose a column of black smoke.

"The blacksmith is at work in his forge again," John observed, "but there's no evidence of his labors anywhere. There are broken rakes and hoes in the barn. A farm with equipment left in that state has either been neglected for too long or run in a careless fashion. Since there are signs of some work being carried out, I am inclined to suspect the latter."

"There were worse things than broken rakes lying in wait at the Great Palace, John."

"But I understood Justinian's court and its intrigues," John pointed out.

"Only after spending many years there."

He squeezed her arm lightly. "I begin to feel guilty for bringing you to this place."

"Oh? Did you force me to accompany you? I recall I came of my own accord. It's what we've both wanted, John. To live in the country and farm."

They approached the remains of a small temple—several columns, portions of three walls, a part of the roof. It was a place they had visited before. From the slight rise where the ruins stood, the land sloped downward allowing a vista of the sea, enticing them with its offer of relief from the honeyed heat coating the landscape. Between the sea and where they stood lay the vineyards and gardens of a monastery. The buildings of the monastery were near the sea, in the direction they had just come, not quite opposite the temple. Close by the monastery, farther back in the direction of their house, sat the blacksmith's.

The temple occupied the furthest corner of the farm once owned by John's family. Perhaps the monastery's founder had purposely drawn the boundary there.

"Is today the day you will finally show me the farmhouse where you grew up?" Cornelia asked.

"Why would you want to see it? It's like any other farmhouse."

They walked on to the temple. Heaps of earth lay here and there, evidence of recent excavations.

"It appears that shoring up the foundation has received attention at least," Cornelia observed.

"Perhaps old beliefs remain stronger than many realize," John replied. "Rather risk the new owner's displeasure than the wrath of Demeter. However, I don't think that man sitting inside is there to worship or wield a spade."

A figure had moved in the shadowed interior, a gray-haired man seated on a fallen column. He pushed himself to his feet as they neared. Once he had been a big man; now he was merely tall and stooped, with knobby wrists protruding too far from the sleeves of a shabby tunic. He was almost completely bald. Beads of sweat ringed his sunburnt head in a crown-like way and ran down into his watery faded-blue eyes. He gave them a crooked smile, his few remaining teeth all clustered on one side of his mouth.

"John! What's the matter? Aren't you happy to see your father again?"

Chapter Two

"Don't call yourself my father, Theophilus."

Cornelia sensed a suppressed fury in John's quiet voice of
a depth she had never heard before. It was so shockingly cold
and unexpected it made the skin on the back of her neck tingle.

"Get off my estate," he had continued, "and stay off it."

The intruder was John's stepfather. That was all Cornelia
learned during their strained, mostly silent march back to the
house. She had known John hated his stepfather, but the depth
of his hatred she would never have guessed until now.

She knew John well enough not to question him when, as
they came to the courtyard gate, he made a vague excuse about
having matters to look into and wandered off toward the back
of the house. Matters to think through was what he meant, and
he needed solitude for that. It was his nature. She would have
liked to have offered comforting words or listened until he had
unburdened himself, but that was not John's way. Perhaps he
would walk to the other end of the estate until he had reasoned
himself out of his anger, or it might be he intended to return to
the temple and make certain Theophilus had gone.

How little she knew of John's past. He rarely spoke of his
family, had instead been almost secretive about them over the
years. When questioned, he would tell her they were part of
a different life and then change the subject. All she knew was
that he never returned to them after he ran away from Plato's
Academy as a young man to take up the life of a mercenary.

No doubt he had good reasons.

She crossed the courtyard and went into the kitchen, a big room with stairs in one corner leading up to the owner's quarters. The air was humid from pots steaming on the brazier. Hypatia sat at a well-scrubbed wooden table stirring a yellow mixture in a ceramic bowl.

"You've accomplished wonders in a short time, Hypatia." Cornelia glanced around the tidy, clean room with pans, bowls, and utensils arranged along the shelf by the brazier, remembering the sour-smelling rats' paradise that had greeted them at their arrival.

"Peter can't abide a dirty kitchen and neither can I, mistress. But when there are no women in a house, such matters often get neglected."

Drawing up a stool, Cornelia leaned her elbows on the table and asked what Hypatia was preparing. "Is it a sauce? Shall we have chicken tonight?"

"Oh no, mistress. Peter insists on overseeing all the cooking and I am uncertain what he plans." Her face clouded. "I'm making chelidon to treat his eyes. They're causing him distress and I'm afraid he may lose his sight. It is said that swallows dropped chelidon juice into the eyes of hatchlings born blind and it's certainly a wonderful cure for eye problems. It really should be cooked in a brazen pot, but the only one I could find needs repair. I don't suppose it makes much difference, providing the ingredients are mixed to the correct proportions. That's the vital point."

Cornelia expressed concern for Peter. She started to ask Hypatia about the poultice she had mentioned, then stopped. She felt awkward. Hypatia and Peter were servants, it was true, but had become more or less members of the family. How would the estate workers perceive such a state of affairs? Might it encourage lax work if they saw the mistress of the house chatting companionably with a servant? Or to be more accurate, would it encourage them to be more lax? As John had indicated, even a brief glance around the estate revealed they had not been closely attending to their duties while it was in the hands of the previous absentee owner.

As if summoned by the thought of estate workers, a big, bare-armed young man in a short laborer's tunic thumped into the kitchen. Tanned almost black, he was broad in the chest. His inky hair hadn't been cut for a long time and then badly. Yet his features might have been sculpted by Praxiteles.

He set the wooden stave he carried beside the door, cheerily asked Hypatia if there might be bread and cheese for a hungry watchman and, without waiting for a reply, helped himself to what was sitting on the nearest shelf.

"I see you've been hurt, Hypatia." He spoke through a mouthful of bread. "Obviously you can't rely on your grandfather for protection. I'd be happy to accompany you next time you go into town." He clapped a powerful hand around the stave and inclined it in Hypatia's direction, showing its wickedly sharpened point. "A taste or two of my stout friend here always persuades ruffians to be polite."

Hypatia glared at him. "How did you know Peter and I have been to town? Did you follow us?"

"I'm one of the master's watchmen, so it's my business to notice comings and goings. At least think about my offer, Hypatia. I wouldn't want to see you come to further harm." He took a bite of his cheese and addressed Cornelia. "Now, mistress, would you send a young woman into town with no escort but a tottering old man?"

"I think it is time you returned to your duties," Cornelia snapped.

Philip bowed awkwardly, grabbed his weapon, and fled, muttering apologies.

Hypatia looked at the ceiling and let out an exasperated sigh.

"That young man seems to be on very familiar terms with you," Cornelia observed.

"Philip's the tenant farmer's son. He's in and out of the kitchen constantly. Just a growing boy, always hungry."

"A growing boy? He must be in his mid-thirties. Your age."

"Well, he doesn't seem to recall it, mistress. Men have a habit of being younger than their age." She made a show of measuring out a spoonful of honey from the terra-cotta pot next to her mixing bowl.

Cornelia left shortly thereafter in a thoughtful mood.

Perhaps Hypatia tended to see men as younger than they were. That would explain much. On the other hand, she doubted that bread and cheese were the only attractions the kitchen held for Philip.

Chapter Three

John stepped into the courtyard as the dazzling edge of the rising sun appeared over the barn roof. Wisps of fog steamed from the tiles. There was a chill in the air of the type that often presages a hot day. The front of the massive barn across from the house delineated the far side of the open space. House and barn were joined by extended wings housing servants' quarters, storage rooms, and animal pens.

John shaded his eyes from the glare and looked around.

The blacksmith, a short, powerfully built man with a good-natured face and snub nose had already arrived. He was enveloped in a leather apron reaching past his knees, as if he were working at his forge rather than lounging in front of the pigsty. His punctuality impressed John.

"Petrus, sir, my name is Petrus. How may I be of assistance?"

"I want you to deal with these first." John indicated the equipment piled next to the barn door.

The blacksmith strolled over and hunkered down over a broken plow, taking a closer look with his hands, tapping and fingering, knocking off bits of dried dirt. He raised his eyebrows and shook his head. "I'm surprised the fields could get tilled at all." He stood, slapping his soiled hands on the leather apron. "I can take care of these, but it might be better to simply replace them."

"Have you spoken about this to the overseer?"

"No, sir. Diocles hasn't consulted me about repairs for months."

"Has he ordered any tools from you? Pitchforks, spades, hoes? Much of what I've seen needs replacing or is in short supply. I've only found a single pruning hook for the olive trees."

"It's been a year since I've made any farm tools, sir, and I could certainly use the work. Not to speak ill of a fellow laborer, but Diocles doesn't run the estate as he should. A workman is only as good as his tools, that's what I always say. A dull sickle makes a hard harvest. A pitchfork with no handle is worse than a hammer with no head, for a nail can be pounded with a brick but what can replace a pitchfork?"

John concealed his surprise at sensing neither enmity in Petrus nor wariness of his new master. Hadn't the town's opinion of John and his family come to the blacksmith's ears? Had he heard the rumors and dismissed them? Or was he merely being polite to the owner of the estate on which he lived as a tenant?

"Certain items for the kitchen are needed. Consult Peter on that. I understand a large bronze pot needs repair, for a start."

Petrus smiled. "You know what the thrifty say. Make whole your pot and save more than just a cooking vessel."

Before John could reply he was interrupted by Cornelia calling urgently from an archway leading into the courtyard.

"John! Come quickly!"

"What is it?"

She had vanished back inside. He found her standing beside a large amphora in the enclosure where the olive oil was stored.

"A mouse, John! A dead mouse floating in the oil!"

John patted her shoulder. "Since when are you afraid of mice?"

"I'm not, but it gave me a shock and…" she paused, composing herself, "Do you think someone was trying to harm us? Was it put there on purpose…?"

"I've never heard of anyone being poisoned by a mouse."

"No, but we aren't in Constantinople now. Everyone here hates us. Can we trust the estate workers? The mouse might have been tossed in there just out of malice."

John looked down at the half-submerged rodent. Small glassy eyes stared back. He noticed Petrus looking on from the archway, hiding a smile behind his hand.

The blacksmith let out a stifled chuckle. "I beg your pardon, mistress. I know it must be difficult for a city person to come to grips with country ways. You've got to try and see the humor in them. He who smiles at ill fortune will conquer it, you know."

Cornelia glared at him. Obviously he had misunderstood the cause of her discomfiture.

"Don't worry about it spoiling the oil," John said "On such occasions my mother would add a handful of some plant or other and it purified the oil."

Cornelia gave him a puzzled look. "I thought plants didn't interest you."

"You can hardly avoid them completely when growing up in the country. This plant, if I remember right, was quite tall and branched out. It had white flowers."

"I'm sure Hypatia will know what it is. I'll get a ladle and fish the poor beast out."

John returned to Petrus, who apologized profusely for his comments.

"No doubt you find us amusing? A strange family perhaps?" John replied.

"No, sir, I wouldn't call it strange. Some in Megara...well... but never mind...I don't find it strange. Not at all."

"Very well," was the curt reply. "Before you bring your wagon for these plows, find Diocles and send him to me. I'll be in the triclinium."

Chapter Four

Diocles was late. As sunlight falling through narrow windows crept across the triclinium floor, John shifted irritably on the edge of a dining couch with faded red upholstery, one of three around the long marble table.

No one had kept the emperor's Lord Chamberlain waiting.

Finally he got up and examined the wall paintings. He hadn't taken much notice before because he and Cornelia ate their meals in the second-floor living quarters which extended over the back of the house except for the triclinium. It surprised him to see, here in the countryside, bucolic scenes, not unlike the mosaic on the wall of his study in the capital. Why would a visiting owner need to look at a painted countryside when he could see the real thing simply by stepping outside or looking through a window?

Not that Senator Vinius had visited his estate very often.

Looking more closely, John realized the fresco landscape was not of the present time but rather that of classical Greece, with pagan temples on the hilltops and satyrs leering from behind intricate, stylized foliage. Here and there he spotted apparent additions, which might have been drawn by a child. A cow, or was it an overly large cat?

A crudely rendered waterfall descended in one corner. The ceiling directly above it showed water stains and peeling plaster.

"I see you are admiring my little repair job," came a voice from the doorway.

Diocles entered, a tall, dark haired man of saturnine appearance, whose eyebrows met above a long nose. In soft boots and a green tunic decorated with a large bronze fibula in the shape of an eagle, he was dressed for a banquet.

"Repairs?"

"I like to put my hand to creative works from time to time, sir. And I thought, why not take advantage of such a golden opportunity? The waterfall becomes very realistic when it rains. I found it striking to contemplate while dining. Besides, a daub of paint is so much less expensive than replacing a roof and the former owner was ever careful of his finances."

"I see." John went back to his couch and gestured Diocles to join him at the table. From the way the overseer's long nose wrinkled it appeared he didn't like what was being served—several courses of accounts spread out in codices and scrolls. "Then you have been using the triclinium for your meals? As you used the owner's quarters rather than the overseer's quarters?"

"Senator Vinius gave his permission, naturally."

"I should like to see that."

"Impliedly permitted it, I mean," Diocles replied.

"Much may be implied in a person's absence." John pushed a codex over to Diocles. "To proceed. According to the entry here the roof was replaced only last year. The expenditure was, in fact, considerably more than the cost of what you called a daub of paint."

"Oh. Yes. That was the barn roof. As you will learn, sir, a farm needs a dry barn."

"Thank you for enlightening me. You have much experience in overseeing a farm?"

Diocles nodded.

"Then you should be able to explain some of the discrepancies I've found in your records."

"I will be glad to explain whatever small matters you don't understand, sir."

"First, there is the small matter of the lack of maintenance. The estate has the appearance of having been pillaged by the

Goths. I hold you, as overseer, responsible for the neglect. What is your explanation?"

Diocles' gloomy countenance darkened until John thought a storm was about to break out over the man's head. However, only a few drops of sweat ran down his overseer's creased forehead. "Residing here less than a month, sir, you might not realize—"

"It's been enough for me to observe the sorry conditions. Explain."

"Yes, certainly." Diocles' shoulders slumped but John could see defiance in his eyes. "For one thing, it has been a bad year in general for everyone. Very dry, all year, and an outbreak of sickness a month or so ago meaning lack of laborers and subsequent delays in completing the tasks needing to be done then. We're still endeavoring to accomplish the last, ditches to be cleaned out and tools needing repair, for example."

"The blacksmith tells me it's been months since you asked him about repairs."

"There were so many other tasks to be accomplished first, sir."

"Indeed. I have also noted the meager income recorded for this past year and by contrast the luxurious furnishings in the owner's quarters. I particularly notice very few sales of the wool and oil produced here. Further, I have established that most of the storage jars for the latter are empty."

"Easily explained, sir. The olive crops last year were very disappointing, and with fewer sales we have had to consume much of our own produce rather than buy such as was needed. As for the other matter: The previous owner was very fond of his comforts. I suspect that is why we rarely saw him."

"Rarely? He hadn't visited in a decade, if not longer."

"True, he preferred to stay in Constantinople. However, there was always the possibility he might suddenly decide to visit. It was my responsibility to ensure all would be as he wished if he should. I also laid in a stock of expensive wine for him and kept it near me, to ensure the estate workers didn't take advantage."

"Expensive wine is more important than patching the roof of the dining room where the senator would drink the wine! And how did you know of the former owner's tastes? Whence came the money to pay for these comforts?"

"It was sent by his agent, who reported his master's requests that these tasks be undertaken."

"I see. These instructions were conveyed merely by word of mouth?"

"How did you guess, sir?" Diocles nervously fingered his bronze eagle. He looked as if he wished he could fly away. Dark patches of sweat blossomed down the sides of his green tunic.

John thought of his other estates, now confiscated, but seldom visited during his residence in the capital. Had they been mismanaged into ruin? If so, Justinian would be disappointed when the proceeds of their sale were added to the imperial treasury.

He pulled a codex over to him. "This purports to be the tax record. Regarding the blacksmith and the tenant farmer, there is no indication of their required tax payments. It is your job to see they are properly collected and turned over to the authorities promptly when due."

"They were certainly collected, sir. But in these hard times it can be impossible to come up with the required sums all at once, and thus I am given last year's taxes, which include part of the year before, along with this year's, but part of this year's needs to be credited to last year, leaving part of last year's to make up for any deficit this year, which can be accounted for next year, so that it all adds up eventually."

"One needs to be Pythagoras to grasp your accounts, Diocles."

The overseer made no reply. John saw his eyes move, and then narrow, as he looked from one end of the codex strewn table to the other.

"Apart from these accounts, " John said. "I notice the tenant farmer Lucian appears to have cultivated more land than he is entitled. I refer to several fields that are supposed to be dedicated to grazing the estate's livestock. Why have you allowed this?"

Diocles licked his lips. "This sickness I mentioned killed off many sheep, so I suggested some of the lost income might be made up by growing produce, until the flock could be replenished." There was an edge to the overseer's voice.

John judged him to be one of those men who become angry when their lies are not readily accepted. "Further, remind Petrus that a condition of his tenancy is giving priority to what needs doing on the estate, for which he is well paid. He told me he needs work but I've seen smoke from his forge every day."

"He has regular commissions from Halmus, one of Megara's wealthiest and most respected men," Diocles offered. "And a hard worker like Petrus is always interested in more work."

"I'm glad to hear it. He will have all he wants. And the estate workers. Do they live in Megara?"

"All of them live here, in the workers' quarters."

"You aren't employing paid workers from the town or elsewhere?"

"We have lost some farm workers lately, because—"

"I shall now inspect their quarters."

They crossed the courtyard and went through a doorway not far from the barn. The interconnected buildings and wings here were a warren rivaling the interior of the Great Palace in confusion if not extent. Rather than wandering inadvertently into a perfumed hall full of decorative court pages, however, visitors were more liable to end up amongst the cows.

"You see I insist on cleanliness and order," Diocles said, gesturing around a large whitewashed room akin to a barracks, lined with mats.

"The door at the back?"

"More workers' quarters."

Diocles opened the door with obvious reluctance to reveal a flight of stairs. John followed the overseer down into darkness and a strong smell of unwashed humanity. As his eyes began to adjust to the meager light seeping in through two high, tiny windows in the stone walls, he saw the forms of men sitting or lying in heaps of straw. They were all shackled and chained to the walls. There was no sound save for the loud buzzing of flies.

"These are workers who are recalcitrant," Diocles gave John a challenging look.

"This is a prison, Diocles. It isn't legal to keep farm slaves under such conditions."

"Technically speaking, I agree, but there is a difference between the laws in the making and the laws of practicality. Slaves are necessary. They are less expensive than hired workers and can be pawned off on unsuspecting buyers if they become ill."

By the time the two men returned to the triclinium John had ordered the men to be freed. "It's clear to me you're an incompetent liar who was robbing Senator Vinius for years. Not only that, you have been disregarding Roman law."

"If you would allow—"

"Count yourself fortunate that I am not having you arrested for maintaining an illegal farm prison. You are relieved of your duties immediately. Remove your possessions and be gone before dark."

"But I have been here for—"

"Too long."

Diocles stared at John, then as if realizing John's decision was final, he forced words from between tightened lips. "You don't understand Megara. You will be made to understand. You will be gone soon and I will still be here, of that you may be certain."

Chapter Five

The rocky track from John's estate to Megara could be covered in less than an hour on foot and John took half the time,
striding along like a soldier on a forced march, working off his
anger. Back in Constantinople, he would have shrugged at the
overseer's insolence, even though he could have had the man
thrown into the imperial dungeons for it. The fact that he was
no longer in a position to mete out punishment made him wish
to do so. Recognizing this made John angrier still, both with
Diocles and himself.

It was just as well he had an excuse to walk. He wished to inform
Halmus the businessman that he would not be dealing with Diocles
any longer. The overseer's negligence had at least spared John the
dilemma of what task to assign his son-in-law once John's daughter,
Europa, and her husband, Thomas, arrived to assist at the estate.
Thomas had been managing an estate not far from the capital and
John was anxious to hand over day-to-day operations to him.

The sun felt unusually hot, as if it were closer here than in
the capital. There was a different quality to the light. It seemed
to draw the color of everything up to the surface. Not that there
was much to see, only vineyards and olive groves surrounded
by decayed stone walls and beyond, rugged hills speckled with
sheep and low thorny shrubs.

John hadn't been this way before. This was the first time he'd
ventured into the city. There had been no particular reason for

him to visit and he'd been busy with the endless chores that
always accompanied settling into a new place. He reflected that it
was ironic that the great metropolis of Constantinople had ages
ago, according to legend, been colonized by Megarians, led by
Byzas, a son of Poseidon. Now John, a native of Megara and once
a high official in the capital, was returning to Constantinople's
origins as well as his own.

Making his way through the grounds of the Great Palace in
Constantinople and the crowded square of the Augustaion John
had been perpetually alert, instinctively scanning faces, sensitive
to any movement in his vicinity, instantly aware if there were
eyes focused on him. Hadn't John wished often enough that he
could let down his guard? Why did he feel strangely enervated
rather than relieved?

Halmus lived in a curiously nondescript two-story house domi-
nating one corner of Megara's main marketplace. The facade of his
home was brick and a thick confusion of dusty branches visible
above high walls behind it provided ample evidence of a garden.

Residents and farmers extolling their produce thronged the
square, all talking at the tops of their voices as if to compete with
the stentorian tones of the man in rags standing atop a column
beside Halmus' house.

"Demons! Yes, my friends, beware, I say, beware as you value
your immortal souls! The filth of hell is among us! Don't leave
your homes after sunset! There are dangers hiding in the night!
For certain persons we know of have been busy loosing demons
who lurk in the darkness, waiting to possess the unwary."

John looked up once more at the voice of doom, then rapped
on the iron-studded house door sporting a brass knocker in
the shape of an angel. The stylite's flow of impassioned words
reminded him of addresses from similar holy men in Constantinople. He had not expected to find one of their fellow ranters
in residence in Greece, but there he stood in full cry outlined
against the sky.

A passerby had pointed out Halmus' house, pausing long enough to inform John that the stylite was referring to the hellish newcomers at an estate overlooking the sea who were conducting unspeakable rites in a ruined temple to Demeter.

John waited impatiently for his knock to be answered, trying to shut out the stylite's ravings, staring at the angel who stared back at him, looking angry at being put to such demeaning work.

"Beware unholy shapes that haunt the darkness!" the stylite advised everyone within earshot. Sunlight flashed from a length of chain draped over one shoulder.

John wondered how a wealthy man like Halmus felt about a noisy pillar-sitter for a neighbor. Halmus' rooms must ring with religious diatribes.

Despite the angel's frown, he knocked again. Recalling the enmity encountered in the marketplace by Peter and Hypatia, he half expected a rock to fly at him. John had carefully dressed in a plain tunic, which would not call attention to its wearer, but no doubt many of the townspeople had heard about the tall, unnatural, ascetic-looking exile who had recently taken over the estate. Perhaps his appearance was not as grotesque as that of the devil they expected to see.

The angel flew backward suddenly as the door opened. Halmus' servant, a severe-looking man, stared at him silently.

"I wish to speak to your master," John said, adding, "if he is available" after a pause. He recalled he no longer held a post whereby he could demand entrance and be granted it without protest.

"The master is not available at this time, sir." He pointed to the stylite. "As you can see, he is attending to his penance. The whole city knows that he was, and I say it as his devoted servant, sir, saved by the good words of the saintly Paul to our neighbors the Corinthians. The admonitions of the apostle diverted my master from following the path leading to the fiery pits of hell."

He looked John up and down with suspicion as if he expected to see scorch marks on his clothing. His master was now addressing passersby with advice on avoiding certain colorfully detailed sins of the flesh.

"The body is the temple of the Holy Spirit," John replied, remembering a phrase he'd heard from Peter, or had it been Justinian? It appeared to allay the servant's fears.

"Ah, I see you understand, sir. So you will appreciate that my master is atoning for the awful deeds of his youth." He did not enlarge on what these transgressions had been. "Why, men come from miles around to hear him!"

"It must be difficult for your master to stand up there and still run his business concerns."

"With the Lord all things are possible, sir. The penance you observe isn't the half of it." The servant grew confidential. "At times he becomes a hermit and retreats to a cave. Not in the mountains. He had one constructed in the garden. There he will sit alone for days taking bread and water, and little at that, meditating on his sins and praying for all in Megara."

John observed Halmus was certainly a very pious man.

"His fame is far-flung!" The servant, becoming enthused, stepped out into the sunshine and peered up reverently at Halmus. "He does not boast, but everyone knows he's friends with the bishop. Imagine that, sir, to count a bishop among your closest friends! Of course, he does conduct a great deal of business with the church and turns an excellent profit."

"With the Lord all things are indeed possible," John observed, thinking the servant rash in revealing details of his master's affairs to a stranger. He asked when Halmus was expected to return to the house and was told it would be an hour or so, depending on how much penance he intended to do that day.

"Very well. I will visit again."

"At times he speaks in tongues, sir, and it is a wondrous thing. Do you not wish to linger and benefit from my master's teaching?"

"I shall not be far off, so I will be able to hear your master and mark his words."

The servant offered a respectful bow.

The wealthy and well-fed stylite continued to loudly explore sins of the flesh with the relish of a patron describing the wall paintings in a brothel. "We must all struggle against the temptations offered by our devilish members," he declared. "And some must struggle harder than others."

"True enough," John muttered, turning away and starting back across the square.

As he passed the column he looked up and for an instant Halmus' gaze seemed to focus on him. Perhaps it had been an illusion or an accident, but as John crossed the marketplace the stylite's diatribe turned once more to the evil that had come to dwell nearby.

How to pass time in a place like Megara? John considered the question as he ate the grilled fish he'd bought in the marketplace.

The emperors had done an excellent job of constructing baths, administrative buildings, a theater, a colonnaded main thoroughfare, everything required of a proper Roman municipality. He'd glimpsed all these trappings on his way to the square where he now stood. But while marble could be shipped in, it was not possible to supply a large, boisterous, and variegated population. The marketplace was crowded, but the surrounding streets were empty—compared with those of Constantinople—and John imagined the baths and theater would be sparsely attended. There was something missing, some feeling of excitement, a subtle, invigorating tension created by the presence of many people going about their lives in close proximity, as in the capital. By contrast Megara looked like a city but it had the soul of a small town.

John finished the fish and tossed the skewer aside. The vendor offered a different type of fish than the vendors near the docks in Constantinople.

Halmus continued to thunder doom from his airy perch. Could he really address the populace in that fashion for hours? John didn't wish to return home before speaking with him about whatever estate business he conducted with Diocles and discussing future prospects. Provided of course that Halmus had any voice left.

Suddenly, he felt uneasy and exposed, standing in the middle of the open square. As if he were being watched. Yet he had noticed no signs that anyone had recognized him. There had been no sideways glances, no quick turnings of heads.

The square sat at the base of twin hills, each crowned by an acropolis. John decided to explore the nearest, the easternmost. He had barely set out, however, when the ruins of a monumental temple caught his eye. A few upright marble columns and crumbling walls sat incongruously amid streets of tottering wooden tenements. It appeared as if the temple had fallen from the sky and crushed whatever it landed on, largely disintegrated, and caved in, scattering broken columns and blocks.

As he climbed the steps to what remained of the entrance he saw the outline of a giant knee, covered in the folds of a crudely rendered robe. This then must be the unfinished statue of Zeus, Megara's chief claim to fame. He wondered if Halmus, whose voice he could still faintly make out without being able to discern the words, ever demanded the destruction of this remnant of paganism. The part-time stylite was a full-time businessman and would doubtless appreciate the fact that Zeus brought a constant stream of visitors. And visitors spent money on lodgings, food, and other necessaries, not to mention temporary companionship.

That was the theory, but today the temple looked deserted except for a short, gap-toothed fellow squatting in a shadow near the entrance. He leapt to his feet and sidled up to John.

"Honored, sir, my name is Matthew and I can see you are interested in Megara's most famous antiquity. Now, it happens I have the sad history of the great unfinished Zeus at my fingertips, having studied it for years. For a small consideration I would be happy, as the saying goes, to speak of things older than parchment, that you may appreciate this most wonderful artifact all the more when you view it."

"Would not this history be more effective given before the sculpture?"

"Its custodians refused me further entrance some time ago because my fee to recite the history is less than theirs," his would-be guide confessed. "Even though they knew I had five children crying for bread, a sick wife, and elderly parents to support! Fortunately, those who make their way to Megara to see this wonder are generous, sir, always generous."

John handed him a couple of coins. He had read of the history of the colossus but hoped to gather more useful information about the city and its residents by questioning the short man with the large family after he concluded his remarks.

Matthew plunged into his lecture immediately. "The image is work of Theocosmos, a native of this region. The god's visage, as soon you will see, is of ivory and gold but the rest remains nothing but clay and gypsum. The work remained unfinished because the Peloponnesian War so reduced public revenues."

John decided Matthew's knowledge of the statue came not from a lifetime of study but rather from a quick perusal of Pausanias or some other ancient travel writer, although where he would have found such a source in Megara was hard to say. However, it was better to listen to the man chatter on than go back to the marketplace and subject himself to Halmus.

John glanced toward Zeus' knee as Matthew rattled on. Perhaps he should stop the lecture and go in to get a better look at this wonder.

His guide stopped in mid-sentence, muttered "It's Georgios, the City Defender," and had slipped away as unobtrusively as a shadow fleeing the sun by the time a contingent of men armed with spears reached the temple steps.

John took stock of their leader, a tall, broad-shouldered man. Georgios' strong, square-jawed face would have looked well on a nomisma. From his expression and the way he carried himself, he struck John as a man who demanded immediate obedience. A formidable opponent, if that is what he was destined to be.

Ordering his men to a halt, Georgios strode up the steps alone, hand on the sword at his side. "You are the newcomer known as John," he stated rather than asked. "I intended to visit your estate, but since you are here in my city I will seize the opportunity to warn you now."

"Warn me? Do I have something to fear?"

Georgios ignored the question. His lips were locked into the taut smile of a man looking forward to a grim task. "I am aware of a certain incident involving your servants. I am concerned for their safety as well as that of you and your family if you continue to visit Megara."

"That is necessary, given where we live."

"I hope it will not be necessary in the future. I have been advised by prominent citizens that public sentiment is against you. I do not have a palace guard at my disposal and I cannot offer you special protection. My men cannot be everywhere or see everything."

"It appears you are expecting trouble."

"It is my duty to anticipate the worst, and also to keep public order. Incidents such as the one caused by the presence of your servants here threaten the public welfare."

"I appreciate your concerns for my family, but if you are suggesting we stay out of Megara...that is not possible."

"Not as long as you live nearby. Which is why you might consider whether you should eliminate the necessity for putting yourself and your family in danger."

"You mean leave the area?"

Georgios looked thoughtful, as if considering the question, before responding. "Regrettably, that may be the wisest course. It is difficult enough that I cannot protect you adequately within Megara's walls, but remember that your estate lies entirely beyond my oversight yet is still within easy reach of anyone who takes a disliking to you, or any of your family. It would be best if you left the area entirely while you are still able."

Chapter Six

"You aren't considering bowing to threats." Cornelia was not asking but stating the obvious. She and John sat on a length of ruined stone wall resembling a bad tooth jutting out behind the house. They watched chickens scratch in the gravel of an empty area that should have held farm wagons.

"Not that I am at liberty to flee, even if I were inclined to do so."

"What could the emperor do if you departed for Egypt or Bretania?"

John pointed out Justinian's reach extended to the borders of the empire and beyond.

"But he isn't as vindictive as Theodora, and she's dead now and can't influence him," Cornelia argued.

"You said I shouldn't bow to threats. Do you think I should consider leaving?"

Cornelia frowned and kicked irritably at a hen pecking near her sandals. "No, it's just the situation. It's maddening being… well…"

"Being in prison, essentially. Which is what exile amounts to, though it is a very large prison to be sure, unlike the one where Diocles had those men chained up."

"They're gone?"

"Peter said they took to their heels as soon as the blacksmith struck off their shackles. They were free to stay on as hired men and continue working here but they must have feared the overseer would return or I would change my mind. I can't blame them."

"That's what enrages me, John. We're don't have as much freedom as slaves."

"They were freed slaves."

"Yes. I know you refuse to employ slaves."

"As were Hypatia and Peter once. And I was one myself, remember. After the Persians captured—"

She placed her hand on his where it pressed lightly against the warm stone. "Let's not talk about that."

"It's hard to avoid the past when you're forced to look at its landscapes every day."

"You've managed to avoid much of it, John. We haven't visited the farmhouse where you grew up yet and you've told me nothing about your stepfather. You've been no more forthcoming than you were during our years in Constantinople."

John lifted his gaze to the sky above the distant hills, not staring into the past but looking away from the farmyard that reminded him too much of the past. "He treated our slaves cruelly."

"Boys always hate their stepfathers, John."

"It was more than that."

"Theophilus came back looking for you while you were in Megara."

John jerked his gaze away from the sky to look with unconcealed concern at Cornelia. "What did he want? I clearly ordered him to stay away! Did me make any threats?"

"No. He just said he wished to see you."

"About what? Did he say why?"

Cornelia's expression clouded. "Well, he did mention he's fallen on hard times. He wondered if he could borrow some money to—"

John offered her a bitter smile. "You see? I have the measure of the man, don't I? He dared come around here begging, from me of all people!"

"You are his son by marriage, John, and I suppose he was hoping to trade on that."

John squeezed her hand. "Doubtless you noticed that scar on his cheek? I put it there, during a fight—our last fight—before I went to Plato's Academy. I was sent to Athens largely to get me away from Theophilus."

"But surely your mother wanted you to have an education?"

"She did, but Theophilus wouldn't have paid for it if he hadn't been afraid of me. I should never have gone. I don't know how my mother managed to deal with him on her own afterward."

"He mistreated her?"

John released her hand and stood abruptly. "Enjoyable as it is sitting here with you, I've lingered too long. I must continue going over the estate records."

Cornelia got up slowly, smoothing her tunic. A couple of wispy chicken feathers wafted into the air. "You've always been mysterious about your family. Perhaps it would be helpful to talk about it."

"So people say. It isn't. Talking about one's problems just creates a new burden for the listener. Besides, I would have to remember things I would far rather forget."

"Young men become angry, leave home, and vow never to see their families again, but then they grow up and often change their minds."

"The man I am now was never young. The youngster who ran off to become a mercenary was another person altogether, living a different life. The man who arrived in Constantinople as a slave and rose to hold the post of Lord Chamberlain was not the youth who left Plato's Academy."

"But, John, that's not true. I knew the young mercenary and I know the former slave. They are one and the same." She kissed his cheek lightly. "And both of them are maddeningly obstinate."

Chapter Seven

So the City Defender was of the opinion they should leave Megara before they became the target of something worse than a few thrown stones?

Cornelia stamped into the bedroom she shared with John. Her gaze fell on the mummified cat they had brought back to Constantinople after a visit to Egypt years earlier.

"Well, Cheops," she said to it, "you must be the most well-traveled cat in the empire. I wish we could take you back to your home and stay there. But we can't leave, whatever the City Defender thinks."

And now, she thought, here I am talking to an inanimate object, as John used to talk to the girl in the mosaic on his study wall.

"How will he manage," she asked Cheops, "now that he has no one but me to confide in?" The polished glass eyes in the shriveled feline head protruding from the bandage wrappings regarded his inquisitor with disapproval.

"No," Cornelia agreed, "it wasn't fair to ask that."

She sat down at a table made of citron wood inlaid with silver. The late senator's wife might have kept pots of cosmetics on it, if she could have been persuaded to leave Constantinople temporarily for what would doubtless have seemed very poor quarters in Greece.

"I blame myself for bringing John to this place," she informed Cheops. She took up a kalamos from a silver tray that also held an ink pot, and began to compose a letter to Anatolius, John's younger friend, the lawyer who had arranged for the purchase of the estate several years before, at a time no one could have foreseen John being exiled.

She had no one to speak to here about subjects John did not want to discuss. Her inclination was to confide in Hypatia, but that was improper. Not that Cornelia intended to share confidences with Anatolius. Rather, she thought he should be apprised of the situation. After all, he had paid them a visit just after their arrival and related the news from the capital. She also held on to the hope that as a former secretary to Justinian he might still have the emperor's ear and speak on John's behalf.

Philip, the farmer's son who had been pestering Hypatia, reminded her of Anatolius. He was a rustic version of the classically handsome patrician lawyer. She supposed every time she saw Philip now she would be reminded of Constantinople, and all that she and John had left behind.

"I don't want to return to the city," she murmured, "but if John is going to be unhappy here, and if we are going to be in danger…" She didn't finish the sentence. Cheops knew what she meant.

She dipped her kalamos in the inkpot and then scratched out the usual salutations.

She paused, deciding what to say. She stared at Cheops, who offered no suggestions. She turned the kalamos around, examining it, as if there might be some words hanging to its point. Finally she got up, opened the chest at the bottom of the bed, and dug through clothing and ornamental boxes until she found the note Anatolius had sent her some years before. Returning to the table she sat and read part of it again:

> "I made inquiries after you mentioned wanting to buy an estate near Megara and discovered the heirs of the recently deceased Senator Vinius are eager to rid themselves of his holdings in that area of Greece. I only mention this because by chance the land

includes the farm where John grew up, according to the information you gave me. It may therefore be of sentimental value to you with your hopes of retiring to Greece, although I would not count on John to share such sentiments. The report I obtained from the agent I sent indicates the estate includes the usual rocky fields and meadows, mainly suitable for raising sheep although there is a vineyard and several olive groves. The main buildings are not particularly large. There is no villa, only a few rooms set aside for temporary visits by the owner. As an investment the land is useless. It includes a few tenants. The place has been allowed to go to ruin since the senator rarely visited. I believe the heirs are selling it for a pittance because they want to shed its taxes. Although I feel duty-bound to mention the estate to you because of its location, I strongly advise against purchasing it."

Good advice as it turned out. Cornelia bit her lip, angry with herself.

Why had she insisted on looking for an estate where they could eventually retire, away from the intrigues of the court? John had often voiced that desire to her privately, at least at times of frustration or when he felt she might be endangered. Then again, he had consented to her search and to the purchase. He had—or used to have—estates scattered around the empire, thanks to his high position, but he never paid much attention to them or even to the income they produced. He preferred to live in austerity, so difficult for a man of his wealth. Now the task was easier.

She resumed writing:

"You were correct about the estate being in disrepair. You were also correct about John's lack of sentimentality. Thus far he has not visited his family's farmhouse, but as it turns out, one of his family has unexpectedly visited him."

She scribbled an account of Theophilus' appearances, then went on to describe the dangers of going into the city.

"It is remarkable how much they hate us and are willing to view everything in the worst possible light. Yet when we first arrived here I thought the Goddess had smiled upon us. Who could have predicted that when John's other holdings were confiscated this estate would be our only refuge? Realizing this, I made an offering of fruit and wine to Her the night we arrived. Need I tell you news of these so-called hellish rites has already reached Megara?"

The corner where she sat was beginning to grow dark. Writing rapidly and almost blindly, she related events up to and including the veiled threat from the City Defender.

"John again finds himself enmeshed in a dangerous situation, and in addition to the menace posed by the townspeople I am afraid there is the real risk that an imperial assassin might appear at our door. Of course, I am hoping that the emperor's whim will suddenly jump in the opposite direction and John will be recalled. Please let us know what you hear. If you have a chance to speak in John's favor, discreetly of course, I know you will do so. How ironic it is. You told us that Senator Vinius was an avid hunter. Yet now that John owns his estate it is we who are being hunted."

Cornelia sat back and looked at her letter. After a while she lifted it, shook it gently, making sure the ink was dry.

"There, Cheops. Now I've got that off my mind I should feel much better. Only I don't." She looked crossly at the silent cat. "Is that all you have to say?"

She crumpled the letter and threw it at Cheops. It hit him on his withered snout and bounced away.

He remained adamantly silent.

Chapter Eight

Peter lit the lamp and its flame cast an unsteady orange illumination around the ground floor quarters he shared with Hypatia. The foreman of the laborers had lived here, during the time when the overseer required a foreman. The only furniture was a couple of stools, the round wooden table on which the clay lamp sat, and an enormous dining couch covered in blue silk, with silver fittings and elaborately turned legs, banished from the owner's quarters by John, who found them uncomfortably crowded with luxurious furnishings.

Seeing their cramped space, Peter sighed. The room had not been designed to accommodate a couch fit for a banquet hall but he could scarcely refuse the master's generous gift, and Hypatia had been delighted with it.

"I fear the master's plans to repair one of the abandoned houses on the estate for us will come to nothing," Peter said. "It may be impossible to persuade anyone to come from town to do the job, and there are not so many workers on the farm that they could be spared for the task. Not that I should complain. The master needs to have a proper villa built. He and the mistress can't be expected to keep on living in rooms that were only meant for short stays." His expression showed outrage.

"I can't speak for the master or mistress, but we're perfectly cozy here," Hypatia replied. She was sitting on the couch with her legs drawn up.

"The place smells like the Mese on a damp day or the stables under the Hippodrome."

"That may be so, but it's a good honest smell."

Peter looked out the door across the darkening courtyard. A dim light showed through a window in the second story opposite. "I observed the master go out not long ago. He was annoyed. I could tell by the way he carried himself."

"You understand him better than I do. His expression never seems to change."

"An excellent talent to have in Justinian's court." Peter closed the door. "We don't want chickens getting in again."

Hypatia laughed. "You never thought you'd be awakened by a chicken clucking away on your chest when we lived in Constantinople!"

Peter sat down beside her. He had to shoo away two cats, one large and black, the other small and mottled brown. They retreated with ill grace. "You are supposed to be in the barn working," he scolded them. "Useless, idle things."

The cats glared malevolently at the human who had usurped their privileged position.

"If you're unhappy with our rooms, Peter, perhaps the master could direct the estate watchmen to help rebuild a house?" Hypatia suggested. "Do you think I should ask Cornelia about it?"

"You mean the mistress," Peter corrected her firmly.

"Yes, the mistress."

"Craftsmen are needed for that sort of work. The watchmen are most likely not qualified to do it. I don't even think they're qualified to watch."

"The young man in charge of them strikes me as competent."

"Competent? Perhaps, when the biggest threat is a sheep disappearing now and then and showing up again disguised with a fine sauce on a table in Megara. But for protecting us against those set on forcing us to leave?"

The black cat suddenly leapt onto the table, drawn by a moth fluttering around the lamp. Hypatia leaned over, picked the animal up, and sat it in her lap.

Peter's wrinkled face wrinkled even further with displeasure. "We shall be overrun with vermin. Those cats shouldn't be in here."

"The cat is sacred and I would never harm one, as you know well enough. I hope I have not offended the gods by ducking this pair in a bucket of water to get rid of their fleas." Hypatia stroked the cat. "Don't listen to that man," she told it and turned her attention back to Peter. "It would make me feel safer if the watchmen were properly armed with spears and swords rather than sharpened wooden staves."

Peter shook his head. "You would be surprised, Hypatia. Even as a humble cook in the military I learned how much damage such apparently puny weapons can inflict if wielded correctly. Consider the giant Cyclops Odysseus and his men escaped. And how? By plunging just such a sharpened stave into its one eye."

"At least a Cyclops is something we don't need to worry about here."

"We don't have to worry about well-armed and armored legions either. A sharp stave is perfectly sufficient to deal with the sort of villains who might seek to do us harm."

"Still—"

"Besides, the master could not obtain weapons legally. Those who are authorized to manufacture weapons are not allowed to sell them to private citizens. The master's situation is precarious enough as it is. He must be careful not to run afoul of the law. His enemies would pounce on anything like that."

"Do you suppose they are intent on having him eliminated entirely?"

"Exile is never sufficient for one's enemies. You know Justinian's whims. The exiled can return. The dead, of course, cannot."

Peter had become animated in his exasperation. The black cat squirmed, lifting its head, its attention attracted now by the shadows moving on the wall behind the couch. Hypatia scratched its scarred and tattered ears. "How would the master's enemies know what he's doing? You don't think they've sent spies here?"

"It would be a minor matter for a wealthy man to hire spies, and the emperor has almost certainly sent his own agent to

Murder in Megara 41

keep an eye on his former Lord Chamberlain. For all Justinian knows, the master might be plotting revenge, and I am certain the master could exact revenge in some form if he were not the honorable man he is."

"Illegal it may be but I would feel more comfortable if there were a few well-sharpened swords and spears close at hand. Philip told me—"

"Philip? You mean the young lout who's been hanging around the kitchen?"

"He's a pleasant enough young man."

"He's a chickpea!"

Hypatia giggled. "Oh, Peter, calling someone a chickpea!"

Peter bit back a sharp retort. He found himself not only staring at her but also seeing her. She was Hypatia, his long-time colleague, companion, wife, a collection of qualities he loved. With a sudden shock, he saw the dark eyes sparkling in the lamplight, the raven wing of hair falling across the smooth brow. He saw a woman. A young woman. Much younger than he was and moreover of a similar age as the wretched watchman.

"That rustic boy has been paying far too much attention to you, Hypatia. His task is to guard the estate, not to loiter in the kitchen gazing at you as if you were a honey cake on a platter."

"Peter! I never noticed him looking at me like that." She straightened her legs and sat bolt upright, alarming the cat, which jumped to the floor.

"Of course you didn't notice. He made sure you didn't."

She reached toward him and he felt her fingers run softly down his bristly cheek. "And even if he had designs, you don't think I would care, do you? We're married, remember."

"You told him, of course?"

Hypatia's face crimsoned and she looked at the floor. "He did not ask about our relationship and I have not felt it necessary to tell him about our private lives."

Chapter Nine

Peter wandered the grounds aimlessly, his thoughts as dim and suffocating as the humid twilight.

Hypatia had been ashamed to admit she was married to an old man; that was the truth of it. She claimed it had never occurred to her to mention her marital status to that young watchman who happened to keep visiting the kitchen. She would naturally try to spare Peter's feelings. She was not a cruel woman, just a young one.

What had possessed her to marry Peter in the first place? Had it been pity?

Was it surprising if she found Philip appealing? He bore a passing resemblance to John's friend Anatolius, who had briefly taken a romantic interest in her years before.

After a while the sound of singing drifting on the breeze drew Peter to the railed fence separating the estate from its neighboring monastery. The smell of earth blossoming as the sky darkened was joined by a trace of incense.

> "Only Begotten Son, and Word of God, Immortal
> Who didst vouchsafe for our salvation to take flesh
> of the Holy Mother of God and ever Virgin Mary,
> and didst without change become man, and wast
> crucified, Christ our God."

He immediately identified it as "Only Begotten Son," a particular favorite composed by Justinian. Peter often sang it when working in the kitchen of the master's house in Constantinople. Hearing it again in such unexpected circumstances reminded him that he should place his trust in a power beyond his own meager understanding. Perhaps after all they would find happiness in this unfamiliar place.

His gnarled hands tightened on the fence. Surely the master would lodge a complaint with the appropriate authorities about the ill treatment he and Hypatia had received in Megara? But meantime he would enjoy the peace of the deepening dusk, and join his voice to those in the monastery in praising the one who overcame death by his own death.

"…and by death didst overcome death, being One
of the Holy Trinity, and glorified together with the
Father and the Holy Ghost, save us."

A line of birds flew overhead, winging off to their roosts for the night. The hills were blending their bulk into the darkening sky. A few sleepy birds cheeped in a cluster of stunted and wind-bent pines beyond the fence. He could see lamplight springing up far across the meadow beyond. Why had he allowed himself to become so agitated over nothing, as a boy would have done?

Here he was, neglecting his responsibilities, he chided himself. Soon it would be time for the evening meal. He must return and commence cooking. There was fish from the estate's pond and a good sauce would disguise their dubious nature. What did he need? Cumin, honey, mustard, vinegar, oil, wine. Surely he could create an appropriate accompaniment from such ingredients in hand? It was fortunate he had brought his spices from Constantinople. Perhaps tomorrow a baked chicken or two? He must request the master's permission to purchase seasonings in Megara, and he would go alone this time.

By the time he turned to go back, night had fallen. A huge orange moon appeared, an evil eye staring out over the hilltops, casting its unnatural light over meadows and fields while leaving shadows impenetrable. The wide and open space of the country-side made Peter feel more exposed to danger than he had ever felt in the crush of the city where everyone knew danger lurked around every dark corner and among the glittering notables at court.

He recited a comforting verse from a psalm. "*The sun shall not smite you by day, nor the moon by night.*"

It didn't make him feel much better. Admittedly he didn't really expect the moon would smite him, but the sight of it unnerved him and made him anxious about who might be lying in wait in the shadows. He had a large armory of psalms at his command. He had studied the scriptures diligently most of his adult life, teaching himself to read while he was employed by an undemanding scholar who had allowed Peter the use of his library.

He glanced along a nearby ridge, then permitted himself a ripe oath. There, vaguely visible against the sky, Hypatia and Philip strolled close together. He couldn't make out their faces but Hypatia's profile was easily recognizable and whom else could she be meeting but Philip?

He watched them for a short time before they vanished into the shadows. He felt giddy and realized he'd been holding his breath.

Taking a shallow, painful gasp and sad of heart, he resumed walking. He did not care in what direction as long as it led away from what he had witnessed.

Peter cut across fields and meadows paying no attention to where he was going, ignoring the burrs that clumped on his tunic and the clawing brambles. Once or twice he tripped over a protruding root. Suddenly he found himself approaching the ruined temple. The sight brought him back to his senses.

"Accursed building," he muttered, glad to have something to vent his wrath upon. "An affront to heaven. It should be demolished."

Yet was it not true that the master and mistress and Hypatia all worshiped proscribed gods? Sometimes he wondered if in fact they could be the same as the one Lord he followed but just known under a different name.

He halted.

Was someone moving inside the temple?

Could it be whoever was responsible for the city's talk of unspeakable ceremonies?

Perhaps the Lord had directed his steps here for a reason?

He stepped forward, straining his eyes to distinguish details.

Surely that was the master rising from his knees?

John too had heard faint singing as he walked briskly around the estate, his usual custom when contemplating difficulties to be resolved. In this instance, he was grappling with the sudden rush of memories caused by the reappearance of Theophilus.

He would, he thought, sit in the ruined temple for a while and pray to Mithra for guidance.

Carefully skirting the trenches where excavation was under way, he passed between two standing columns.

The gibbous moon that had followed him from the house saturated the interior with an unearthly light. Stepping over a fallen column, his boot came down not on marble but something yielding. A body lay there, half in and half out of the moonlight.

He bent closer and saw the moon reflected in the staring dead eyes of his stepfather.

Chapter Ten

Torchlight did its corybantic dance around the ruins. Light and shadows gamboled on the crumpled body of Theophilus, attracting moths to flirt with a fiery fate.

A small group had gathered at the temple. Armed men, some holding torches, were stationed near the corpse. Uncaring and intent on their own business, unseen crickets trilled the same ancient chorus they had sung hundreds of years before during rites to the goddess Demeter. The murmur of hushed voices joined the crickets' song and the hiss and pop of the torches.

John stood against a column, staring in the direction of his stepfather. The flickering light continually revealed the corpse for an instant and then veiled it in shadow. It might have been a dream rather than something that added a hint of copper to the night smells of earth piled nearby. Perhaps no one else noticed the subtle odor but John was only too familiar with the smell of blood.

Glancing around, John saw all eyes were focused on the City Defender, squatting on his haunches beside the body to examine it.

Georgios stood up and looked at John. "The dark patch on his back tells its own tale," he observed. "And now you tell me yours. First, you doubtless carry a blade. Show it to me."

John didn't like the man's tone. It had been a long time since he had taken orders from anyone but the emperor. Unfortunately, he reminded himself, those days were over. He handed his dagger over for examination without comment.

Georgios gave it a perfunctory glance and smiled. "Clean. But then it would be, wouldn't it? You had plenty of time to clean it before we arrived."

There had been no reason for the City Defender to bother examining the dagger, except to make a show of ordering John around in front of the small crowd at the temple. Philip and the other watchmen were ranged behind Cornelia and Hypatia a few paces away. The blacksmith and tenant farmer, along with a couple of estate workers, stood nearby. Behind them several of Georgios' men stood ready to take appropriate action if anyone attempted to flee.

John took his blade back, careful to betray none of the anger he felt.

Georgios turned the corpse over with his boot and regarded the dead man with distaste. A pool of blood, black in the torchlight, had spread in front of the bench from where he and Cornelia often admired the sea. Had Theophilus been sitting there when the murderer crept up behind him and struck?

The City Defender rubbed his jaw thoughtfully. "I wager it's been hundreds of years since anyone performed a sacrifice in this temple. Do you suppose Demeter still protects her adherents?"

Was he speaking metaphorically or did he suspect Theophilus had been slaughtered during a pagan ritual of the kind John and his family were rumored to be carrying out?

"Not much is known about her mysteries but it is certain Demeter never demanded human sacrifices," John informed him. "Pigs, certainly."

"Oh? You are an authority on what were our local deities?"

"Any educated person would say the same. I am certainly no authority on Demeter, let alone an adherent."

Georgios stepped away from the body, sliding his boots along the marble floor with a squeaking noise to rub blood off their soles. He took counsel of the star-pocked sky and then continued. "Is it true you visit this ruin at night?"

"I do. I find it restful. Your informants will also doubtless be able to confirm the truth of my statement that I have also sat here in full view of anyone passing by during the hottest part of the day."

"Informants? I don't have that many men at my disposal, which is why I cannot guarantee your safety. Or the safety of those on your estate, as you can see." He nodded toward the corpse. "You overestimate me."

John doubted it. It would be difficult to overestimate Georgios' power in Megara. The City Defender not only had responsibility for keeping civic order, he also oversaw the city's courts. His power was backed by those who appointed him: the local bishop, the largest landholders, and the curials, the first citizens on whom the administration and finances of cities had depended before certain of Justinian's endless reforms.

"Do you know the dead man?" Georgios asked.

"Yes. He was my stepfather. I ordered him off my estate."

"It was not a happy relationship?"

"No. He was here earlier today asking for money." He glanced toward Cornelia and saw her frown. He had no intention of allowing her to lie for him and risk getting herself into difficulties.

"Going by his begging and the threadbare garments he's wearing it would appear that prosperity and Theophilus were not on speaking terms. And yet his son was a rich and powerful man," Georgios observed.

"His stepson."

"If you insist on legalisms, his stepson. What do you know of his movements of late, what he has been doing?"

"Nothing. Before this week I had not seen him since I was a young man."

"Indeed." Georgios' expression clearly showed his disbelief.

John was acutely aware that whereas the City Defender held an important post in Megara, he himself was in the unfamiliar position of being, essentially, an ordinary citizen. It was a strange sensation, as if the world had been turned inside out. Was this how those he had questioned in his own investigations felt?

Furthermore, it was obvious Georgios did not like John. He shared all the basest prejudices of his fellow townspeople. John was a stranger, a man with an unusual family, one who was out of favor with the emperor and fortunate to have retained his head. In short, he was a suspicious character.

"Didn't you inquire about your family?" Georgios pressed on. "I understand you grew up on a farm nearby."

"Why were you investigating me before any crime was committed?" John parried.

"Do you think I am accusing you of murdering your stepfather?"

"You seem inclined to detain me here with irrelevant inquiries rather than searching the area. The farm forming part of this estate passed out of my family's possession many years ago, after I had gone."

"In the course of making the purchase, you must have been curious about where your relatives were."

Why did everyone assume one had to maintain an interest in their family, no matter how little connection remained to them?

"The purchase was made by an agent, and my curiosity or lack of it is irrelevant," John snapped. "I would suggest you turn yours into ways of catching the murderer." He realized immediately he had overstepped his unaccustomed boundaries.

The City Defender didn't bother to reproach him but there was cold warning in his glare. "I doubt any criminal would linger nearby after my men and I arrived. He or them will be long gone by now." He took a torch from one of his men and held it, sizzling and spitting sparks, near Theophilus' face. "I anticipate you will not know how he received that scar either?"

Before John could answer, he felt a hand on his arm. It was Cornelia. Did she really fear he was about to elaborate on the brawls he had with his stepfather as a boy?

"Peter!" she whispered. "Peter's missing. He might be in danger. We've got to find him. We can't stand around here doing nothing."

Georgios looked up. "A member of your household? Missing? I ordered you and your servants to accompany us to this temple."

"I thought his wife would bring him with her." John turned, seeking out Hypatia.

She stood at the edge of the shifting pool of light, her face drawn and terrified in the flickering illumination. "I couldn't find him at the house, master."

Philip stepped toward Hypatia. John thought the young man was about to put his arm around her but he didn't. "Don't worry about Peter," Philip told Georgios. "He's just an old man"

"Even old men can commit murders," Georgios replied. He turned to his armed torchbearers. "Find him."

Chapter Eleven

Peter tried to scream but his throat felt paralyzed. Straining desperately he finally forced out a nearly inaudible grunt. Then another. Then a hoarse bellow broke though, brought him awake, and drove from his mind whatever it was had made him want to scream.

Or was he awake?

He was sitting up on a rudimentary bed in a cavernous room, illuminated only by an oil lamp glimmering at the far end. A strong smell of incense did not quite mask an underlying odor that reminded him of a public lavatory. In the sepulchral dimness he made out rows of beds upon which lay gray, motionless forms. Occasionally a pitiful low moan broke the silence.

Did he still dream or had he fallen into hell?

A firm hand pressed against his chest and pushed him back down. "There, there, now. Are you trying to wake the devil? Lie back. You're in no shape to be leaping around."

The hand belonged to a youngish man with a stolid, round face strangely cheerful considering the circumstances. He wore long, shapeless, unbleached robes. "My name is Stephen," he said. "The same name as our monastery, so if I get lost they know where to send me. And you?"

"Peter," Peter replied, having to think about it.

"You're in the hospice of Saint Stephen's monastery. Not that you are in need of such care but there was a spare bed. Don't worry about all the blood on your tunic. It seems an excessive amount considering your scrapes and scratches are slight."

Looking down, Peter saw dried patches of blood on his clothing and abrasions on exposed skin. His injuries might have been minor but they were numerous. He ached everywhere and his head throbbed painfully.

Stephen smiled benignly. "I shall see you are escorted home shortly and this time you will be on the road rather than blunder about in the dark. We don't want you falling down another hole."

"I fell into a hole?" Peter groped back into the oblivion prior to his panicked awakening. He remembered walking, approaching the temple. After that, nothing. Had his waking scream carried over from the startled cry he gave as he fell? There were excavations beside the temple.

"A pit, in fact. There are plenty of them around Megara, most very old. Every so often legends resurface and people go about looking for the treasure supposedly buried when Corinth was overrun and destroyed a century and a half ago. According to some of the tales, the church spirited its treasury out of the city, along with valuable relics, so naturally people will get it into their heads to search in our vicinity. We fill them up when we find them. Recently the story's been revived. One of our goats fell into a fresh pit last month not a stone's throw from the chapel."

"I must have been very careless," Peter said, futilely trying to recall how he put himself into such a predicament. "My eyesight isn't what it used to be, especially in the dark."

"Don't blame yourself, Peter. The older pits are overgrown with brush and weeds. They're hard to see even during the day. You shouldn't wander around at night without a light."

"I will have to inform the master. He won't want to have traps like that on his land."

"You are from the estate? A nest of godless pagans, I hear. I shall be able to correct that impression now, given you are a good Christian."

Peter, puzzled, asked him how he knew.

"You were muttering prayers before you woke up. If you were beseeching the Lord to rescue you from whatever brought on that hideous shriek you let out…well…I should not like to meet whatever it was and especially after sunset."

"I can't remember what made me scream or anything else before that…" As he spoke, it began to come back to him. As he neared the temple, he'd seen John there. Something—what it was he didn't know—told him to keep this information to himself. "How did you find me?"

"I heard a cry and found you curled up like a baby at the bottom of the pit." Stephen smiled. He looked so much like one of the rustics Peter had haggled with in the markets of Constantinople he half expected him to begin to extol the virtues of his fish or radishes. "I thought you were dead of a broken neck at first. I returned to the monastery for help and we brought you back. And here you are."

"Did I wander onto the monastery grounds?"

"No. I had gone out to get a closer look at the temple. I must admit it was curiosity. There was a commotion over there and I could make out a crowd with torches from my window. Was it a celebration of some kind?"

Peter tried to force his thoughts forward, past the instant when he'd spotted John in the temple. But the bridge between then and now was missing, washed away by…what? John had been alone, hadn't he? There were no torches, were there? "I have no notion what you saw, Stephen. It must have been while I was unconscious. The master never said anything about a celebration." He paused. "Do you mean pagan rites?"

"I can't say. That's why I was curious. I heard no singing. Pagans in the old days would sing more lustily than we monks, so I understand, not to mention other lusty matters."

"My master was not doing anything unlawful, of that I can assure you."

Stephen looked disappointed. "You saw nothing at the temple, then? Saw no one on your way there?"

"No."

Stephen smiled. "Then my curiosity will have to go unsatisfied. You are a good and loyal servant, Peter. I should have been attending to my own business rather than trying to get a peek at what might have been blasphemous doings. We must never give in to our foolish weaknesses. I shall need to do penance for it and for thinking ill of your master. Now I shall fetch you a poppy potion for your pain."

"Please don't trouble yourself. My wife is knowledgeable about those matters."

The thought of Hypatia brought back to Peter the sight of her walking along the twilit ridge next to Philip. How he wished his fall had erased that from his memory. But it was best he know, wasn't it? He needed to acknowledge his own surrender to foolish weakness. "May I see the abbot before I leave?"

"Certainly. I shall take your request to him."

It did not occur to Peter until he was shown into the abbot's study that it was the middle of the night and he would be interrupting his sleep. He apologized profusely. When the abbot assured him that he had been awake anyway, waiting to hear Peter was comfortable, he apologized further.

The abbot hovered solicitously while Peter lowered himself with care onto a bench in front of a table buried beneath codices. The codices, some bound in leather and others between boards, were piled so high and haphazardly it seemed a minor miracle they didn't all slip off and slide down to the floor.

"Evidence of my scholarly endeavors," the abbot explained. "There is so much of interest in the world and our lives are so brief. Are you able to read?"

"Yes. I taught myself long ago."

The abbot nodded his approval as he sat down on the opposite side of the table. "It is a fine thing to be able to read." To Peter, peering at him through twin pillars of codices, he resembled his rescuer Stephen if the younger monk had been left outside to weather for thirty or forty years. His round, cheerful face was reddened and lined. Deep furrows in his high forehead and dark creases radiating from the edges of his pale, watery eyes told of countless late night hours spent pondering the written word.

"I am very grateful to Stephen," Peter said. "If not for him, I don't know what would have become of me."

"A fine young man. He is one of those who attend the ailing and elderly in our hospice and a favorite with our residents. Those who are lost on the dark roads the elderly often wander down smile when he appears, even if they can no longer speak or remember their own names. He is a blessing to all. I would not be surprised if in due course he succeeded me as abbot."

"I wish to ask a favor on his behalf," Peter said. "Stephen said he should not have been indulging his curiosity when he found me. I hope you will not be too harsh with him."

To Peter's surprise the abbot chuckled. "I will refrain from exacting punishment altogether. His curiosity about such matters might be partly my fault because I too have an interest in the ancient religions." He waved a hand at the tottering stacks between them. "It is remarkable how many and various are the delusions we humans have believed at one time or other."

Delusion? Was the abbot reading Peter's mind? Peter stared at the other, anguish suddenly etched on his face. "I am afraid."

"Afraid?"

"I have deluded myself. Because of this, I have committed a terrible sin." Peter drew a trembling hand over his face. The physical aches from the crown of his head to the soles of his feet were nothing compared to the pain he felt in his heart, or was it in his soul?

"If it would help you to tell me more?" The abbot's voice was kindly.

Peter took his courage in his hands. "I married a young woman, an Egyptian. We have both served the same master for years. She is barely half my age, and at the time I was ill. Perhaps she felt sorry for me, but I have come to realize it was not fair to her. I succumbed to pride and covetousness and lust. How can I complain now she prefers someone younger? How can I rectify my error?" To Peter's horror tears began rolling down his cheeks.

"Remember, Peter, a husband and wife become one flesh. The marriage union is sacred."

"But I have noticed she talks to a young watchman on my master's estate a great deal. Do you think she is miserable, waiting for me, an old man, to die?"

"Young persons talk to each other but it means nothing. Try to conquer your jealousy, Peter. As for being old, you are as vigorous as a spring lamb compared to the sad state of some of our hospice residents. My advice is to talk to your wife quietly about your concerns and pray for the health of your marriage."

Chapter Twelve

The City Defender had departed, four of his men carrying the body of Theophilus in a blanket. Cornelia sat in the bedroom, staring at Cheops as John came in, a cylindrical wicker work basket in his hand. He sat down beside her. "I hid it in the barn after sending word to Megara to notify the City Defender of Theophilus' death."

"Why? Is it important? It's just a shabby old basket." Cornelia's response betrayed both exhaustion and exasperation.

"It could be very important. There's nothing unusual about the basket but when I found it next to Theophilus it was decorated with these." Reaching into the neck of his tunic, he pulled out several strips of dark blue cloth.

Cornelia looked at them and then at John.

"They were tied to the basket," he explained. "Strictly speaking they should be purple ribbons but I suppose these were as close as could be managed at short notice."

"Scraps of blue cloth? Baskets? Do you mean we have to worry about someone with deranged humors lurking in the bushes and popping out now and then to leave gifts for us?"

John gave a thin smile. "This is hardly a gift, Cornelia. It's a sacred basket, a cista. It resembles those used during the rites of Demeter."

"You mean the City Defender was correct and Theophilus was murdered during a pagan ritual?"

"That's what the basket would doubtless suggest to many."

Cornelia's jaw tightened in anger. "Or would have suggested, if the City Defender had found it with the dead man. I see why you removed it."

"Leaving the basket with the body was an inspired act of malevolence. So I brought it back and hid it in plain sight, knowing the house and barn would be searched. As indeed they were. Without the strips of cloth it appears to be nothing more than another old basket."

"Was there anything inside?"

John opened the lid and showed her the empty interior. "Not when I found it. During an actual ritual it would have contained a serpent."

"I hope it didn't contain a snake tonight. I would not like to think a poisonous snake had taken up residence in the ruins."

"It would not necessarily be poisonous."

"But who brought the basket to the temple?"

John stared into the basket as if the answer might be written on the bottom. "Theophilus or his murderer or someone wishing to perform a ritual or wanting to make it appear someone else had been performing one, or—"

"Or it might have been left there by accident by one of the men shoring up the temple foundations. There's shade inside, a good place to have a bite to eat while taking a break from digging. Perhaps you were too long at court, John. Everything appears to be a plot of some kind."

John snapped the lid shut. "A workman would hardly have decorated his lunch basket in that fashion. The only difference between court and countryside is that those with evil intent would not be dressed in silk garments, though their blades would be as sharp."

"You're right, John. I'm too tired to think clearly. Nevertheless, baskets are generally used to carry things, not to throw suspicion on people. Isn't it possible that whoever brought it to the temple carried something in it?"

John nodded. "We should consider the simplest possibility first. If something was in the basket it might have been extremely valuable, worth killing for, yet small enough to fit in a basket. And if it was in a basket, why not take it away in it? Theophilus could have been involved and his partner or partners decided to dispose of him rather than risk him telling what he knew. We know he needed money, the City Defender would pay him for information…it fits together."

"Oh, John, the plots you weave!" Cornelia took the basket from him, laid it on the floor, and slid over beside him. "And what about you?"

"What do you mean? You know I'm accustomed to this sort of situation."

"Your stepfather was just murdered."

John's expression hardened. "You are well aware of my feelings toward Theophilus."

"Still, you grew up—"

"Besides, I hadn't seen the man for years and certainly never expected him to come back like a shade to haunt me. He died long ago as far as I'm concerned."

"With the rest of your past."

"Exactly."

"Like me, John. You never bothered to seek me out either."

"How, Cornelia? How could anyone have found a woman who traveled all over the empire with an obscure troupe of performers?"

"You were Lord Chamberlain. You could have hired agents. How many troupes recreate the bull leaping of ancient Crete? If someone had asked innkeepers at Antioch if bull leapers, complete with a bull, had stayed with them do you imagine they would have asked which one?"

"As far as I knew you found someone else. I had vanished and never returned. Why wouldn't you? The young mercenary who had been hired to guard the troupe, who had an affair with a pretty performer, had suddenly decided to move on, as young men of that kind always do. You had no reason to know I'd fallen into the hands of the Persians. And after that…after the way I was treated, and sold as a slave, I wasn't fit for you anyway."

Tears were overflowing the dark smudges beneath her eyes and running down her cheeks. "Don't ever say you are not fit for me, John!"

"Ah…now…please, Britomartis," he muttered, invoking his old pet name for her, alluding to the Cretan Lady of the Nets because she had snared him at first sight, a name they both joked only John would have thought to use.

Cornelia pushed him away. "No! Don't you Britomartis me!"

She wiped her eyes. "Here I am weeping over your lost past. We must think about Peter."

"We'll take up the search again at first light. I'm sure if Georgios' men had located him they would have paraded him in here. Hypatia said he'd got into a dark humor and went out to calm down. He'll be disappointed that he missed all the excitement."

"Yes, I suppose you're right." She put an arm around him. "Now you can Britomartis me."

◇◇◇

The roosters crowed before Hypatia realized that morning was finally arriving. She had begun to think it would never come. The window of the bedroom remained dark, opening as it did on the still-shadowed courtyard. It was a relief to abandon trying to sleep and get up. Peter had alarmed her the night before by bolting, obviously agitated and upset. She went after him but he was nowhere to be found. After returning to their quarters she lay awake all night waiting for his return.

She went into the other room, smoothing down the wrinkles in her light sleeping tunica. She had done so much tossing and turning it would have been more restful if she had simply stayed up all night. She half expected to see Peter asleep on the couch, having crept in and not wishing to awaken her, but it was occupied only by the two cats who opened their eyes reluctantly and gave her resentful looks.

Where was Peter?

Had he seen her walking with Philip?

She bit her lip.

Had he seen anything further?

Philip had led her to a cliff projecting into the sea, giving her a stunning view of the monstrous moon trailing its long silver tail across the glassy water. The handsome young watchman had told her that it was the favorite spot for disappointed lovers to cast themselves into the sea. He had been joking, she thought.

Her imagination ran wild. She saw Peter, in despair, approaching the edge of the cliff and throwing himself over, or perhaps taking a track down to the shore and walking into the water. Or coming to the edge of the estate and carrying on, walking until he was ambushed by persons seeking to rob him. Or perhaps meeting someone from Megara who recognized him as one of the loathed newcomers, out on a lonely road, unarmed, in the dead of night.

What had Peter seen?

She must have been talking to herself because a voice from the doorway answered her.

"What did I see? What are you talking about? Is that any way to greet your husband?"

Peter stood there, one hand on its frame to steady himself. By the faint predawn grayness that had begun to seep into the courtyard she saw his clothes were torn, his face haggard. He looked older.

"Oh, Peter," she cried. "Thank the Goddess!"

"Thank the Lord," he corrected her as she clung to him.

Chapter Thirteen

The sun peeked into the room in shy fashion as John and Cornelia ate a frugal meal of boiled eggs accompanied by olives and stale bread, served by an apologetic and hollow-eyed Hypatia. John had ordered Peter to rest for a few hours before taking up culinary chores again, stifling the loyal servant's protests about laziness and not carrying out his duties with a threat to increase the time he was not permitted to work.

"I'm surprised the sun dares to look in on us," Cornelia remarked. "Who knows what dreadful event it will see happening next?" She pushed her plate away without touching her bread. "When do you expect the City Defender to speak with you again?"

"When he's ready, which will no doubt be after constructing a theory, no matter how ramshackle, concerning why I murdered Theophilus and who my accomplices might be."

"You have decided the intent is to blame you?"

"We cannot know what was intended by Theophilus' murderer or the person who left that basket beside his body, or whether it was the same person in each case. However, I am expecting Georgios to prosecute me for the murder. Towns have long memories. I wouldn't be surprised if somebody remembered a rumor about how Theophilus got that scar." John dunked his bread in his wine cup and took a bite. "At any rate I found the body, which was on my property, and I have a family connection to the victim. There are three good reasons to suspect me."

"Not to mention the City Defender will become a hero in Megara for prosecuting you."

"Perhaps he has designs on the provincial governorship."

"An ambitious bumpkin. He'd wouldn't last an hour at Justinian's court," Cornelia said scornfully.

John swallowed his wine-softened bread. "Oh, I think he would do very well in the capital. It's his bad fortune he was born in the provinces. A dangerous man."

"I hope you are wrong, John. But of course you rarely are when judging men." She stared down at the table top and her face grew thoughtful. She might have been reading auguries from the pattern of scattered bread crumbs. "You'll begin investigating the matter immediately?"

John was gazing outside. A light fog had begun to dissipate. Another torrid day was in the offing.

"I shall pay for Theophilus' funeral if no one else comes forward, which seems likely. Even he deserves decent rites. Beyond that, the matter is out of my hands. I am not Lord Chamberlain now, merely an ordinary citizen. It is the job of City Defender to uphold the laws in Megara."

"But John…" She paused, uncertain how to continue.

"And beyond that, solving this murder will almost certainly mean raking through my family's history, I would rather not. I am tired, Cornelia, tired of digging through people's secret lives, turning over the boulders of the past to see what they conceal. I did it when it was my duty, but it is not my duty now."

"What about your duty to your family? We are all in danger of being caught in the nets the City Defender casts."

"I do not see that. If necessary I will engage Anatolius to defend me, but there is absolutely nothing of legal significance linking me to the murder, let alone anyone else here. How could there be? His plan is to use the threat of prosecution to drive us away from Megara, that's all. Remember I said I expected him to try to prosecute me, not that I expected he had any chance of success."

"You also said he was a dangerous man."

"I am familiar in dealing with dangerous men!"

Cornelia stared at him, speechless. Then she shook her head from side to side and gave a thin laugh. "Oh, John, a heartbeat ago you were explaining to me why you were a suspect. Now you are telling me it's not even necessary to investigate. And there's something else I've been worrying about. How do you know you weren't the intended victim?" Her voice rose.

John stood. "Always losing your temper or asking unanswerable questions, Cornelia." He put his hand on her shoulder and bent to kiss her furrowed brow. "Or both. Of course I had thought of that possibility."

"Goddess! You appear remarkably unconcerned," she snapped back.

"I didn't want you to worry. We'll talk about it later today. Now I have retired from my official duties—"

"An involuntary retirement!"

"Indeed. But an estate owner must direct his men as to the tasks to be undertaken and the sun tells me I am already late in attending to that. You wanted me to be a farmer. That's what I am now. You should be pleased."

As he turned his back to leave Cornelia picked up her uneaten bread. Rather than throwing it at him she dunked it in her wine and forced a mouthful down.

◇◇◇

The day became as hot as the morning sun had promised. Cornelia uncrated a set of silver dishes and pondered whether she and John should begin using the triclinium for their meals. Situated on the ground floor, it was more convenient to the kitchen. Hypatia would not have to carry plates of food up the stairs.

She went to look over the triclinium where the crudely rendered waterfall in one corner caught her attention. It's as if we were logs in a river, helplessly carried toward destruction, and about to go over a raging torrent like that, she thought. Helpless and nobody willing to throw a rope to rescue us. Nor wanting to, which was even worse.

Then she began to notice the satyrs hiding in the painted bushes, and the peculiar, childish drawings of stranger beings apparently added to the wall murals more recently. They made her uneasy, even in the daylight. Was there a story behind them?

She went across the courtyard and to keep busy began to check the amphorae of oil stored for market. Most were empty. The bundle of vegetation Hypatia had tied together was still hanging into the amphora in which the dead mouse had been found. What was it Hypatia had said she had used, coriander?

She began to consider what needed to be purchased in the market for the week, although she wasn't certain how the trip into Megara could be made safely. Corinth was less than a day's journey. Would it be better to take a wagon there for supplies, a larger city where no one would pay any attention to a few strange faces? Or perhaps Athens, just a bit farther?

Perspiration ran down her sides, tickling her ribs. Suddenly she decided she needed to bathe. It wasn't just her sodden clothes or the gritty dust from the courtyard that had stuck to her. It was everything that had happened recently. The hatred of the city. Murder. The City Defender barging into their home, poking into every corner.

The bath was on the ground floor. In contrast to the triclinium its mosaics featured a city scene which gave the user the impression of bathing in a public fountain in a forum. Perhaps the artisans who had decorated this country house had indulged their senses of humor at the expense, in both senses of the word, of the owner.

The hypocaust was not working, but on a day like this tepid water would be a relief. She left her clothes in the cramped vestibule and went down the steps into the pool. It was not large, but larger than the one in John's city house. The dome overhead was blue but sooty from lamps that burned in wall niches during the evenings. She couldn't tell whether the vague white shapes flying in the mosaic overhead were intended to represent clouds or angels.

Angels, she eventually decided, given a domed church dominated one side of an open square, just as the Great Church loomed over the vast plaza of the Augustaion near the imperial palace in Constantinople. There was even a stylite on a column, getting a clear view down into the bath, along with numerous classical Greek statues, marble sculptures rendered in miniature with tesserae.

Cornelia sluiced herself down and pushed dripping hair away from her face. As she stretched out her arms, letting the air play luxuriously over her wet body, she noticed several carefully detailed pedestrians facing in her direction.

"Go ahead, don't bother moving. Stand there and stare if you must. I don't care. On a day like this I'd happily bathe in the Hippodrome on race day if I could feel cool!"

She reached up and toward the dome and writhed sensuously, a move from long ago days when she'd danced after leaping from bulls for a living. "There, are you happy or would you like more?"

"More, definitely," came a voice from the doorway.

"John! How long have you been standing there?"

"Hardly an instant!" He marched naked into the room and down into the water. "Before you say anything, Cornelia, yes, I will investigate this wretched matter. Now let's say nothing more about it and just sit together for a while and enjoy the scenery!"

Chapter Fourteen

The cooling effect of the tepid bath didn't last as long as it took John to interview Peter. By the time he left the room where Peter remained in bed, although now propped up on pillows, he felt as sticky and uncomfortable as he had before.

The old servant seemed confused. His memories of the previous night were at some points fragmentary and at others nonexistent. He paused often, fumbled for words. Except for the accident and the likelihood he was still suffering from the shock of it, John would have suspected he was being evasive.

"You don't need to be concerned, master. The Lord was watching over me. I have tried hard to remember everything and I finally recalled that while I lay in the bottom of the pit I dreamed that an angel in robes emblazoned with golden crosses stood watch over me." A look of bewilderment crossed his face. "Before that I could only remember the nightmares that came afterward. I must have been safely at the monastery by then, nearly awake and feeling my bruises."

Hypatia had stood in the doorway looking on with disapproval, her arms folded. "Perhaps his memories will come back when he has recovered, master," she offered when John had given up his questioning.

There didn't seem to be anything to be learned that hadn't been divulged earlier when Peter arrived home. Peter had left the house in a dark humor. Hypatia followed but failed to find him. Peter fell into a pit and was rescued by a monk from Saint

Stephen's Monastery who had ventured onto the estate to see what the commotion at the temple meant. Peter had remained at the monastery for hours, explaining why neither the City Defender's men nor the workers sent out by John had located him.

"You haven't recalled anything you didn't tell me this morning, Hypatia? Nothing has come back to you? Perhaps some detail you forgot due to your concerns for Peter?"

"No, master."

"You are sure you saw no one else on the estate while you were searching for Peter? You didn't hear anyone?"

"No. Nothing."

John heard a hesitancy in her voice. "This isn't just about Theophilus. Whoever murdered him probably meant, at the very least, to drive us out of Megara. For all we know Peter was also attacked. We're assuming he fell into the pit by accident but he can't actually recall how he got there so we cannot be certain."

Hypatia glanced over her shoulder into the room where Peter was lying and lowered her voice. "I talked to Philip, master. You know the watchmen were out and about as usual. I asked him if he had seen Peter, but he hadn't. I'm afraid Peter would misinterpret matters if he knew about my talking to Philip."

"Where did you and Philip have this talk?"

"He was patrolling the ridge overlooking the sea, not far from the temple."

"He hadn't noticed anyone?"

She shook her head.

"I will have to question him. He might have seen something after you parted."

Hypatia glanced nervously back into the bedroom again and John's gaze followed hers. Peter lay with his eyes closed, looking old and frail.

"If Peter remembers anything else, let me know. He may be more inclined to speak to you. And be careful and aware of your surroundings, Hypatia. Pretend you're back at the palace."

"You think Peter's in danger?" Her dark eyes widened as she

grasped John's meaning. "If someone attacked Peter or pushed him into that pit, because he saw something…"

"We need to be alert to every possibility."

He went back out into the oven of the courtyard. Why had she been so reluctant to mention speaking with Philip? Why would it upset Peter? Did she have something to feel guilty about? He had to remind himself that he was investigating a murder, not his servants' domestic affairs.

Philip, son of John's tenant farmer Lucian and head of the estate watchmen, was sitting half-asleep on a bench outside his father's dwelling when John arrived. The foliage of a fig tree planted by the door provided welcome shade, and bees buzzing around a row of hives nearby added a somnolent note to the day.

Perhaps it was the particular angle of the sun casting dappled shadows across the bench through the leaves of the fig tree that made John remember his youth, when on such a day he would be studying, seated at a bench under a tree at Plato's Academy, and much further back, when his mother would be singing in a sunny kitchen as she performed whatever mysterious and necessary domestic rites mothers carried out in kitchens. He forcibly pushed his memories back into the past and hailed Philip as he approached.

The young man rubbed his eyes and stood. "Sir?"

Not for the first time Philip's dark-haired handsome looks reminded John of his friend Anatolius back in Constantinople. Or rather, the younger version of his now gray-haired friend. John winced inwardly. How cluttered with the past one's mind became. Whichever direction one turned, there was the past, always getting in the way. He was almost pleased when a light breeze sprang up, carrying the unappealing stench of pigs, a smell he recalled well enough but for which he harbored no nostalgia.

Philip wrinkled his nose. "My father has had great success with swine, sir. What can I do for you?"

"You were on duty overnight, Philip?"

A nod.

"Did you see anything of the dead man?"

"No, sir. If I had I should have informed the City Defender."

"Hypatia says you weren't far away when she spoke to you."

"She mentioned our meeting? Quite by chance, it was. She asked if I had seen the elderly servant she works with. She was out searching for him. It was unwise of her and I told her so. You can't see the temple from that spot. You know the land there, all low hills and shallow depressions."

"The moon was bright last night."

"You can only see the temple from farther along the ridge in the direction of the monastery. I turned back before that point because the grounds curve away from the sea there. I wasn't patrolling the far end. I'll question the watchman who takes that section."

"You didn't hear anything?"

"Only the monks singing."

The young man's father emerged from the house, squinting against the sunlight. Lucian was one of the fattest men John had ever seen and at Justinian's court, thronged with the obscenely wealthy and well fed, he had seen some very obese men indeed. The farmer wobbled a few steps forward, then stopped and inhaled the odoriferous breeze. "Ah. You know what that is, sir? That's the smell of good money."

Lucian's voice boomed out, deep and resonant, as if his massive, bulging figure was as hollow as an untenanted tomb inside. "Don't be hard on my boy," he continued. "It's too bad intruders got onto the estate but the property lines are long and the watchmen few."

Philip shot a look of consternation at Lucian. "Father, please!"

"There's some truth in what he says," John replied. He didn't add that he had attempted to engage more watchmen but found no one willing to work for him.

Lucian broke in before John could say more. "You'll be asking me if I saw anyone wandering about last night. Not that they'd try to get to the temple from this end of the estate. More likely to come up the path from the shore. I can't tell you, since I was abed, like all laboring men should be at that time of night."

John ignored the remark. Lucian seemed altogether too jovial. With some that was their humors, with others their mask. "You've been a tenant here for years. Do you know anything about the dead man?"

Lucian scrunched up his face, the movement highlighting multiple jowls and chins. His eyes were large and brown. In a different sort of man they might have been described as sensitive. Was a handsome man like his son buried under the years of accumulated flesh? "Theophilus left the area some time before I got here, sir. All I know I heard in Megara. His farm was at the other end of the estate and he never farmed it properly. Sold it to Senator Vinius. The senator had owned it for a while before I started renting this property."

Surely Lucian was aware of the gossip and knew that Theophilus was John's stepfather? Was he pretending not to know or did he simply think it better not to mention it? "Do people say what he has been doing since then?"

"He hired himself out as a laborer. Imagine that! But he hasn't been in Megara for a long time. Moved, he did, sir. To Corinth, or was it Athens? Begging in the street for all anyone knows. What did he do with all the money he got for that farm? Must have squandered it. What I wouldn't give for a windfall like that. But here I am, working myself to the bone."

"Your industriousness is admirable, Lucian. However, when it extends to putting estate land to your own personal use it is a different matter."

The accusation clearly took Lucian off guard. "What? What do you mean, sir? I farm my own parcel, nothing more."

"Not according to what I have discerned after talking to workers and the manner of cultivation—"

"Untrue," Lucian interrupted. "I deny any wrongdoing."

"Father!" snapped Philip, who immediately turned to John. "I assure you, sir, if what you say is true it was a mistake. The fences are in bad repair and this past winter we had to burn many of them for fuel."

John pointed out that landmarks such as a particular tree would serve just as well to show where Lucian's land ended. "See that the fences are erected in the correct place as soon as possible," he ordered Lucian.

"Certainly, certainly," Lucian muttered. "Now, if I may excuse myself sir, there are matters to be attended to. A farmer's labors never cease."

◇◇◇

After waddling into the house Lucian stood at an angle to the window, unobtrusively watching John confer with Philip. As soon as John had departed a tall man with a long face crept out of a back room, his soft boots making little sound.

Diocles, the former overseer, clucked in a scolding fashion. "I heard that conversation, Lucian. Didn't I tell you to leave those fences alone?"

Lucian gave a massive shrug. "Fences are easily rebuilt. Philip, attend to it." He addressed his son who'd just stepped inside. "You don't have to be too accurate about where you place them either."

"You don't want the new owner angry with you, Father."

Lucian didn't bother to answer. Instead he rumbled at Diocles. "You can't stay here much longer. If the eunuch sees you it will cause problems for me."

"I'd like to hear you call him eunuch to his face," the other sneered.

"It's not wise to be disrespectful to your landlord and some things are better left unsaid," Philip pointed out.

"You are only polite because you're after that dark-skinned servant of his." Lucian smirked. "You've been given a job, go and do it." Turning back to Diocles, he continued. "I want you to leave, my friend."

"Impossible. I need to stay on the estate, as you well know, at least until—"

"Forget that. It isn't worth the risk."

"Why did that fool Vinius have to die?"

"We all have to die sometime. You should have thought of

what might happen if we were burdened with an owner who wasn't absent all the time."

"Easy enough to say now, Lucian. But who could have predicted anyone from Constantinople would come to live in this place?"

"Not me. I'm a farmer, not a prophet. But I can definitely smell trouble on the way if you don't get off the estate."

"After all I've done for you—"

"It doesn't look like you're going to be able to do anything more for me, or anybody else. And your presence here puts us all in danger."

"Where is your gratitude? You can't even put a roof over my head for a few days?"

"I have put a roof over your head for a while. Now go lodge with someone else you imagine owes you something."

Diocles' heated tone turned to ice. "Is it wise for you to turn me out, considering what I know?"

Lucian shuffled forward until his enormous bulk was leaning menacingly near to the former overseer. "You're not going to hang yourself to hang me. I am telling you to vacate this place immediately after dark."

Chapter Fifteen

John traversed almost the entire length of the estate on his way to interview the blacksmith Petrus. For the most part he kept to the ridge along the sea. As he passed within sight of what was known locally as the Rock of Deliverance, he suppressed a shudder. Here, it was said, those disappointed by life came to find deliverance from their woes in the sea.

He had heard the rumors about his father—his real father. He had been a child when his father had abruptly, shockingly, inexplicably simply ceased to be where he had always been. His mother told him that John—for he had been named after his father—had died. Only later, when he was old enough to go off alone with his friends out of his mother's sight and hearing, had he heard the rumors. That his father, beset by financial difficulties, had escaped by way of the rock.

The boy who told him had merely been repeating what he'd heard his parents say. Neither he nor John were sure what "financial difficulties" were, except that from the tones with which older people said the words they guessed they must be very terrible indeed. John had imagined his father pursued up the rock by hideous dragon-like creatures. He had had many nightmares about it.

Later, when he learned more about people's ways, he decided the story was probably nothing but malicious gossip.

He increased his pace and cut inland to visit the temple. There was no breath of wind and no sounds save for the occasional cry of a gull and the crunch of John's boots in the grass. The drowsy peace of a day of honest work nearly completed seemed to be settling over the parched landscape. Theophilus' murder seemed far away, a half-remembered dream.

John shook his shoulders in irritation. Not a dream, he told himself, a nightmare, and here he was mooning around as if he were a lovestruck youth attempting to write a poem to his beloved and had all the time in the world to wait for inspiration.

He stepped into the temple. He dared not kneel but stood facing east. "Lord Mithra, Lord of Light," he prayed, "This was once a holy place. I have no other, despite its desecration by the body of Theophilus, in which to petition Thee that I be guided to the truth and so continue to serve Thee, slayer of the great bull."

Afterward he inspected the ruins but could see nothing of interest aside from a small pink flower emerging from a crack in the marble floor. There were only the excavations and piles of dirt around the sides and back of the ruins. The dirt might have revealed footprints before it had been trampled over by the crowd that had gathered during the night. Now it was too late.

He continued on his journey and crossing a rise arrived at Petrus' house. The blacksmith was unloading a wagon in the packed earth yard by his forge.

Petrus came toward John, slapping grime off his hands on the long leather apron that seemed attached to him as a second skin. "I've just come from your house, sir. I'd have given you a ride if I'd seen you along the road."

"I walked along the ridge."

"It offers a fine view of the sea but very hot on a day like today. Will you honor me by sharing a jug of wine? My throat feels as if I dined on rust this morning."

John readily agreed and soon the two men were sitting on a green-stained marble bench under a large pine, surrounded by the fragrance of the fallen pine needles that cushioned their feet. It was near sunset. The shadow of the pine stretched away, impossibly elongated, across the dirt yard, over the wagon, over wagon wheels lying against a stack of metal rods, losing itself in a mass of dead weeds beyond.

"No, sir, I saw nothing," Petrus said in response to John's questions. "As you see, my house is shielded by the rise there, and I certainly heard nothing suspicious."

It was true. Though nearby, the temple could not be seen. Neither could the monastery, which was even closer. The land had the peculiar characteristic that although mostly fields and meadows interspersed with small orchards and vineyards it did not offer many unobstructed vistas due to its low hills and depressions. It would be surprisingly easy to creep up on someone who felt safe because of the apparent openness of his surroundings.

"You live alone?"

"I do, sir. There was a girl, but she preferred to marry a rich man and so…but I hear she has grown shrill and is never satisfied with what he buys her. Perhaps I had a fortunate escape after all. A man who lives alone may boil his eggs as he wishes, as they say." He spread big, calloused hands and smiled.

"It appears so, Petrus. What do you know about Theophilus?"

Petrus' good-natured face clouded. "Too much, sir, and that's a fact. I made a gate for him, a large gate. After it was installed, he refused to pay for it. Naturally I took my case to law. Bribery must have been involved since I lost. After that I refused to do any further work for him." He paused and gave a wide smile. "I did however insure that Megara knew he couldn't be trusted to pay his debts. It was the least I could do to protect others, but not, as I am sure you will agree, a reason to stab him in the back, even though that was what he had more or less done to me."

"Indeed." John did not add that in his opinion there were a number of valid reasons to put a blade into his stepfather even if he couldn't condone such an act. It was not surprising his mother had allowed him to be sent off to Plato's Academy. He might have been executed for murder if he had remained at home.

"This gate was made some time ago when Theophilus still lived near you?"

"That's right, sir. Before he sold the farm."

"Did you see him after he went away?"

Petrus' expression turned as black as his apron. "Once. At the monastery. I was returning some cooking utensils I had repaired and Theophilus was there. He told me he had been doing odd jobs for the abbot. I asked him if he was being paid to carry them out and reminded him of his debt and he just laughed. Well, you know what they say, sir. Small debts make debtors, large ones make enemies."

"I understand how you must have felt," John told him. "Let me ask about another matter. The work being done at the temple. How did it come about?"

"Oh that, sir? It was begun by order of the previous owner. The foundations need shoring up before what remains of the building collapses, so I've been told."

"It seems odd to spend money on such a task, considering how the rest of the estate has been neglected."

"I gather the ruin is of interest as a monument to former beliefs. Apparently the former owner was interested in antiquities and after all, who can fathom the reasons for the fancies of rich men? They swim in a different sea from the poor, as they say."

Senator Vinius interested in antiquities? So far as John knew, the late senator hadn't taken an interest in anything older than race horses and nubile prostitutes. Then again, perhaps the gossips underestimated the range of his tastes.

John finished his wine, stood, and placed the cup on the bench.

Petrus rose also, somewhat unsteadily since he had drunk most of the contents of the jug. "Dusk is creeping in. May I respectfully suggest, sir, given recent events it may be folly on your part to be wandering around in the dark?"

"You are of the opinion I am not safe here?"

"You may not be, sir. Theophilus wasn't."

Chapter Sixteen

John sat in the temple, contemplating the broad silver finger the moon had laid across the sea.

Strange to contemplate the earthly road that had led him from Megara as far as Bretania and Egypt, to Persia and Constantinople, and then back again to his starting point.

Unfortunately, the silver road did not point to any solution to his difficulty in grasping the thread that would ultimately lead to useful information. He sensed those on the estate he had interviewed were concealing knowledge. But how could he be surprised? They would be anxious about being punished for their blatant robbery of the absent former owner more than assisting him with anything they might know of Theophilus, even though to do so might serve to soften whatever justice was to be meted out. Meantime he was little further along in his investigation.

He saw very little likelihood of gaining any help from anyone in Megara, even assuming they had knowledge of an event that had happened away from the city.

He listened to the ratcheting of insects, the occasional distant barking of a dog, and tried to get his thoughts to march in order. It had been less difficult in Constantinople, where at this time of night he would be sitting in his study, sharing his cogitations with the girl in the wall mosaic and drinking what his friends termed his "foul Egyptian wine."

He thought back to his conversation with Cornelia before she

fell asleep and, restless, he had come to the temple to attempt
to think of a plan of campaign.

"I am so sorry we came here of all places. If I had known—"
she had said wistfully.

"It was inevitable," he had replied. "After ordering the books
for all my estates examined, this was the one place Justinian
would not expect to be able to sell for a high price. And given it
was Theophilus who sold the family farm, he must have inherited it from my mother. So with both of them dead, that closes
another avenue to possible enlightenment to me."

There was certainly light, and to spare, out here. The cold
clear moonlight washed a landscape sculpted of marble. Trees
and bushes might have been monuments to the dying year.

His thoughts wandered back to his mother. Was there anyone
left on her side of the family whom he could consult?

It was unlikely, what with the passage of time, and given
she was her parents' only child. She had belonged to the curial
class, one formed from respectable, well-to-do townspeople.
Not that it had been as comfortable as it seemed, for over the
years the class accumulated too many responsibilities for civic
works, administration, and tax collection, though admittedly,
Justinian had sought to lift the burden from them with officials
such as the City Defender.

John's tutor, Antigenes, had once informed his students that,
in the old days, if a person was of this class, they had a choice of
fattening their finances in various ways—not spoken about too
loudly—or trying to carry out their duties honestly, resulting
in financial ruin.

John's grandfather had been of the latter sort.

Cornelia had asked him why, in that case, anyone in that
position would act in an honest fashion.

"Integrity. Pride," John had answered. "The position ran in
families for generations. It was a great Roman tradition. My
mother used to tell me how my grandfather wore a formal toga
when performing his civic duties. Unfortunately, pride and
integrity won't pay for the necessities of life. My father might

only have owned a small farm but his income was better than that of my mother's family. She had insisted I had tutors, saying my father would have approved. I was hardly more than an infant when he died."

And then she had remarried and Theophilus had taken his father's place and John's world changed into one much darker. For his stepfather mistreated everyone. In John's opinion someone was bound to kill Theophilus in due course. Had not he himself threatened to carry out the act often enough?

Was there anyone in Megara who remembered hearing of those threats? If so, it was certain the City Defender would know all about them by now.

But if not, who remained in the city who would recall those long ago days and perhaps shed light on at least the beginnings of a road leading to the culprit?

Chapter Seventeen

John was returning to Megara.

He had dressed in a plain blue garment whose only decoration was a thin gold stripe at the hem, one chosen to indicate the more formal nature of the calls he intended to make when he arrived at his destination.

Provided, that was, he could locate Leonidas and Alexis, two friends from his schooldays.

Mithra had granted his earlier prayer for guidance.

As John sat contemplating the sea the night before, he had suddenly recalled them as possible sources of information about what had happened to his family after he left the area.

A thin smile quirked his lips as he remembered Antigenes, the severe old stoic who conducted classes the three had attended and was wont to wax particularly sarcastic in several languages at their tortoise-like progress in their studies.

Alexis was the son of a church official and by far the most blasphemous boy of John's acquaintance, which was to say very blasphemous indeed. Leonidas' father worked in the offices of the tax collector. Thinking on it as he approached Megara it occurred to John that he and his two friends could be described as representing the base supporting local society: religion, administration, and agriculture.

Compared with the capital, Megara was small, though still large enough that John did not to expect to accidentally run into two men he had not seen in almost forty years, particularly

Antigenes, who had been old when he taught the boys. However, since John knew the location of his house and had no notion where Leonidas and Alexis might have gone, he decided to begin his search in the narrow street leading from the thoroughfare called Straight, not far from the town walls.

Were Antigenes still alive he would no doubt fail to bat an eyelid when John told him he had risen to the rank of Lord Chamberlain, but rather content himself with observing in lugubrious fashion that he was not at all surprised that John held the position no longer, given the wretched state of his Latin.

Whether or not Antigenes was still residing in Megara berating his flesh-and-blood inferiors or was hectoring the shades in Hades, the house where his classes had assembled was gone, leaving a vacant site filled with charred timbers and blackened stones overgrown by weeds and vines.

John stood and stared at the gap where the house had been, trying to reconcile his lively memories with the empty desolation that remained.

He recalled a verse Antigenes was fond of quoting to the effect a man's days were as grass and he flourishes like a flower, but the wind passes over him, and he is gone and his place no longer knows him.

Those old Israelites were the first stoics, the teacher had invariably assured his pupils, none of whom had any real inkling of what the composer of the psalm was writing about, and who would have been surprised to realize then that someday the ancient words would make altogether too much sense to them.

So, John thought, it seems I must continue searching those places the wind has passed over and seek the past that is gone.

The next place to look, from a logical point of view, would be the house, situated not far away, where Alexis had lived with his parents. He was unlikely to have remained there but his parents might be alive, or perhaps other relatives now residing there would know where Alexis had gone. Since his father had been a church administrator, John could inquire about the family at the church but he preferred to avoid officialdom if at all possible.

Unlike their old tutor's home, Alexis' brick house still stood along the narrow dirt street running parallel to the city wall. During John's boyhood, large gardens reaching to the wall behind two- and three-story houses attested to the prosperity of the owners. John saw the change as soon as he came to the head of the street. Many of the houses were shells, invaded by tangles of what had been ornamental trees, now unpruned and rampant. Most of the rest of the buildings were in disrepair. A few skinny-ribbed dogs slunk in the shadows and such pedestrians as were in evidence matched the dogs.

Justinian had expended huge sums in rebuilding the center of the city, but despite a grand new theater, forums, monuments, and administrative complexes, Megara, like many provincial towns, remained underpopulated and had begun decaying around its edges.

A sickly sweet perfume emanated from the open door of Alexis' old home. John entered. A fountain featuring a chubby cupid still stood in the atrium, its presence more appropriate now that the house was, obviously, a brothel. A girl clothed in what appeared to be a scarlet shadow leapt from one the couches arranged against the walls and trotted coltishly over to him, reaching him at the same time as a stout middle-aged woman in thick makeup who emerged from a nearby room.

"I am so pleased to be visited by a gentleman of such refinement," the latter smiled, giving a bow. "I can tell by your manner that you are not the sort of ruffian with whom we are normally burdened, sir. What is your desire?"

"I wished to see the fountain again," John said with perfect truth. "A friend and I once tried to raise frogs in it."

The madam's visage continued to smile indulgently, as if to say we see numerous men with deranged humors here, and as far as we are concerned their money is as good as the next man's. "A fine aristocrat such as yourself may desire something out of the ordinary. As it happens, little Theodora here is newly arrived with us. A virgin I have been saving especially for just such a one as you, excellency."

"Hmmmmm," said Theodora, looking John up and down, which for her, being very short, was a long way up. "Mmmmm. I imagine you would be different than one of them smelly old dock workers."

"Very much different," John agreed. "However, having seen the old fountain I will be off. First, however," he addressed the madam, "could you tell me who owned this house before you?"

She frowned and gave him a suspicious look. "Are you a tax collector?"

"No. I am simply looking for an old acquaintance."

"So you say. All the former owners I know about ran the same kind of establishment as I do."

"You don't want me then?" Theodora put in.

"Apparently not," sniffed her disappointed employer. "You are very much different from a dock worker, you claim. You flatter yourself, excellency."

"I am just speaking the truth," John told her before exiting hastily.

◇◇◇

The observer waited in the dark doorway of a half-collapsed house until the tall, lean man in the dark tunic emerged from the brothel. The former Lord Chamberlain looked up and down the street before walking off briskly. The observer waited a short time, then slipped out of his hiding place and followed, keeping close to the house fronts and occasionally sliding into doorways, alert to every movement of the man he was following.

John was approached twice, before he reached the end of the street. A prostitute he sent away with nothing more than a withering glare, but dropped a coin into the dirty hand of a grubby beggar. The coin flashed in the sunlight.

When the observer reached the beggar the man rose hopefully from his nest of rags, hand outstretched. The observer showed him the point of his blade. That also caught the sunlight.

John turned down a wider, colonnaded thoroughfare. Here it was easier to follow him since there were more passersby coming and going from the various emporiums. The observer closed the distance between himself and his quarry, not wanting to lose him in the crowd.

John stopped abruptly to look over a silversmith's display. The observer found himself beside a table piled with cloth. He picked up a bundle of bright green linen and watched John examine bowls and spoons.

Surely the fool hadn't come into Megara to buy such items?

"Ah, sir, a fine choice for your good lady." The beaming merchant almost obscured his view of the silversmith's display. "This just arrived. These bright colors are what all the ladies at the emperor's court are wearing this year. They look like flocks of pretty birds, sir, in their cheerful plumage. Pretty birds in the jungle, as some would say of the imperial court. Why, here in Megara—"

"Yes, yes. I'm just looking."

A big cart pulled by two oxen lumbered down the street. As it passed the silversmith's premises John turned to cross to the matching colonnade on the opposite side. As he did so he vanished behind the cart.

The observer threw down the linen. By the time he'd trotted to where he could see around the creeping cart, his quarry had vanished.

John moved quickly through an unobtrusive archway beneath the colonnade, hoping it didn't lead to a private residence. Fortuna was with him. He found himself in a courtyard surrounded by workshops. He cut down an alley beside a building occupied by dyers, then turned off into what was little more than a cleft in the wall behind a bakery. He could feel the heat of the ovens radiating through the masonry at his shoulder.

During his years in the capital John had developed an ability to feel a hostile gaze on his back. He could not say how it warned him and thought perhaps his eyes and ears were taking in information that did not register in his thoughts except as a sensation of danger.

Cornelia would like the silver earrings he had just purchased.

His plan was to mingle with the crowd in front of the semi-ruined temple that housed the unfinished statue of Zeus, enter the building, slip out of the back, and from there proceed to the house where Leonidas once lived. He was careful not to appear in a hurry, to pause and gawk as an ordinary traveler might at the towering columns that remained standing.

He had one boot on the lowest step to the temple entrance when he sensed someone nearby.

He whirled, hand going to the blade in his belt.

A gap-toothed man smiled up at him.

It was Matthew, the self-styled guide. "I am so glad you have returned, sir. My lecture was sadly interrupted. Shall I resume?"

Chapter Eighteen

The modest dwelling where Leonidas once lived with his parents was still standing. John glanced in both directions before approaching, making certain his stalker had not picked up his trail. John had had to be brusque with Matthew, for fear the man he had just shaken off in the alleys and byways would come upon him out in the open in front of the building housing the statue of Zeus. The last thing John wanted to do was to bring old friends and their families to the attention of whoever was following him.

John had some difficulty picking the house out in a row of homes of identical design but there it was, looking much as ever, the faded stucco seemingly in the same state of near, but not quite, disrepair. The staircase leading from the street to two floors of what he knew was rental housing was in similar condition.

He went up three steps to the tiny, columned porch fronting the entrance to the private residence on the ground floor. Yes, still there in a shadowed corner he could see his own initials, Leonidas', and those of a couple of other friends, traced surreptitiously in the wet concrete when Leonidas' father had had the porch replaced.

Emperors, generals, high officials, philosophers, and even charioteers were immortalized in stone, marble, and bronze in Constantinople. This was the only monument in the empire for John, former Lord Chamberlain.

Leonidas' father opened the door.

He gazed at John with the same air of gentle bemusement he seemed to carry through life. He was the sort of man who would not attract attention on the street. If asked for a description the person questioned would have a hard time thinking of any feature that might separate him from anyone else.

"John!" the man exclaimed, smiling broadly.

And then John realized he could not possibly be seeing Leonidas' father, unchanged by the years. This was his old friend Leonidas himself.

"Please come in. Helen and I lived elsewhere when we first married, but both my parents died years ago and so, as you see, we moved back here."

John studied his friend. Leonidas looked as if he had been middle-aged for a long time and would remain middle-aged for quite a few years yet. His hair had not grayed much but was not so dark as to make him look any younger than he was. His face displayed wrinkles, but no more than might be expected with the passing of the years.

"Here is Helen now," Leonidas said. He introduced a plump, matronly woman whose smiling face would not have launched a fishing boat.

"I'm so glad you came to visit, John," Leonidas said. "I heard you had returned—who hasn't? But I thought it best not to intrude, knowing how…well, how you are about such matters."

"I appreciate your consideration, Leonidas."

The entrance opened onto the large familiar front room from which other doors led to bedrooms and a kitchen. There was still the faint odor of the strong fish sauce Leonidas' father had favored. Had Leonidas adopted his elder's taste as well as his looks, or had the aroma of so much cooking of fish over the years saturated the walls with an olfactory memory?

Leonidas invited John to sit down.

The dining table still sat by the row of windows lining the wall facing the street. Sunlight sparkled in through many small panes, illuminating the abstractly patterned floor tiles and the colorful but loosely rendered mythological scenes on the walls.

The beaming sun, the beaming faces of the couple, gave the impression of a happy home.

With a slight smile John noticed the partridge, still occupying its wicker cage on a table in a corner, just as he remembered. But surely not the same partridge?

"That is Julius Caesar," Leonidas told him. "Unlike his name-sake, he can only dream of crossing the Rubicon, confined as he is."

And never imagine a fatal dagger thrust through his feathers, John thought.

When Helen had gone for wine John said, "I am sorry to hear about your parents, Leonidas."

"It was the Lord's will that they depart early. And you are no less an orphan than I am, my friend. I couldn't help noticing in the tax records years ago that Theophilus had sold the farm. Ah, I said to myself, so John's mother is gone now too."

"Do you know the circumstances?" John asked, reluctant, not wanting to turn over the stones concealing the past but knowing it was what had to be done.

"No, John. I'm sorry. After you left the academy, I visited the farm more than once asking for news, but you didn't return and it finally became obvious you were never going to come back. Then, too, I disliked being anywhere near Theophilus. He made me feel unwelcome. I was afraid he was going to suddenly grab me and fling me out the door."

"And my mother?" John's gaze met Leonidas'. They both knew what he meant. How many bruises did she have? How often were her eyes blackened?

"She was well, John. Truly."

Perhaps she had given up the fight, John thought, or they had stopped quarreling over him once he had gone. Or was Leonidas trying to spare John's feeling? "There's something you aren't telling me?"

Leonidas looked sheepish. "Your mother was well when you first left but in more recent years...age wears us all down eventu-ally. I met her in the marketplace from time to time and some years ago she suddenly couldn't remember who I was. I heard that the City Defender's men sometimes found her wandering around lost in parts of the city she shouldn't have ventured into. Finally, several years ago she stopped coming into town and a year or so later word got back to the city that she had died. Given her condition no one was surprised. Probably it was a blessing. This was right before Theophilus sold the farm."

"I see. Thank you for telling me." John had realized she was dead, but the manner of her passing distressed him. "What about Theophilus? I understand he fell on hard times after he sold the place."

"I couldn't say. I am sorry I can't tell you more." Leonidas' face darkened, as much as possible given its plain, good-natured features. "I suppose I should commiserate with you over the death of your stepfather...." Leonidas took one of the cups Helen provided and poured wine. "I also know that however you felt about him, you would never have taken his life."

John took a sip of wine without tasting it. "You have heard the rumors."

"All nonsense."

John took another sip. Not Falernian, but not what might be sold in a tavern either. "I went to the house where Alexis lived, but the family had gone."

"You haven't visited him yet? He went into the church. He's the abbot at Saint Stephen's Monastery, next to your estate. The local bishop is of advanced age and it is said Alexis could well be considered as a replacement. Our son, Stephen, decided to enter the church. He is presently a monk there."

John reflected that the church was more and more becoming a favored career path. He asked Leonidas how his own fortunes had fared.

"Very well, John. I followed my father and work on tax collection records. Of course, compared to what you've accomplished..."

"You mean managing to be exiled with the emperor liable any day to change his mind about the wisdom of leaving my head attached to my shoulders?"

"There it is, you see. I wouldn't want to be in your shoes, John. I am perfectly happy with the life I have. I've never wished for what some would call a big life. A big life often means big tribulations."

"You always spoke of seeing the world. Were you ever able to travel?"

Leonidas shrugged and blushed slightly. "Well, I have seen Athens!"

"We're going to visit the Holy Land someday," Helen put in.

"Oh, yes," Leonidas' eyes lit up. "I study every travel account I can find. As soon as there's time and money, we'll go. Well, as soon as there's time. I suppose I've spent as much on studying as several trips would have cost."

"He knows Strabo by heart," Helen said. "He can tell you how long it should take to ride between every way station from here to Jerusalem, along five different routes."

"Six now, and I'm starting to plan a seventh—" He broke off. "But I will not bore you, my friend. You have seen the world. Rather than prattling on about my plans I should be asking you about the adventures you've had."

"My travels have not always been pleasant."

"I suppose not. Of course, everyone in Megara knows of you. When a native of a place such as this rises to the post of Lord Chamberlain, news soon reaches us."

"From the attitudes I've encountered so far, I would rather they didn't know who I was or what post I held."

Leonidas waved a hand in dismissive fashion. "We don't all share the same attitude. There are troublemakers everywhere. Diocles, for instance. The rascal's been spreading rumors since he left your employment. There is great deal of enmity toward you in Megara. I happened to be in the marketplace the other day when your servants were attacked. I had been doing my best to defend your reputation. Little good it did. Are they all right?"

"Yes. Fortunately."

"Leonidas," said Helen. "Show your old friend your work."

Leonidas reddened again. "Helen, I'm sure he doesn't—"

"Of course I should like to see it!"

"I'll light the lamp." Helen hurried through the doorway in the wall opposite the row of windows. By the time John and Leonidas had stepped into the tiny windowless room it was illuminated brightly.

"You remember my bedroom?" Leonidas asked.

"How would I forget a room painted with scenes from the Odyssey?" The Cyclops, the cannibalistic Laestrygonians, Aeolus and his winds, shades from the underworld, but not the sirens or Circe or Calypso. It was a room for a young boy.

"It was our son's too. But now it is mine again."

Tables of all kinds and shapes and every number and arrangement of legs stood against the walls. For an embarrassed instant John was afraid Leonidas was going to tell him he collected tables. Then he noticed displayed on a single-legged stand a model of the pyramids, and next to it, on a marble slab supported by four lion's legs, the Parthenon.

"You see this?" Leonidas directed John's attention to a miniature re-creation of a high wall featuring a wide gate. "This is Troy, or the walls, at least. More accurately, improved walls. For several years now I have been pondering how the city might have been better defended and making adjustments to my model as they come to me. What I wanted to show you first, though, was my Constantinople."

Helen moved away from the largest table, allowing John the view gulls enjoy looking down on the Great Palace and its tiered gardens, the Great Church, part of the Mese.

"It's nothing but clay and paint, a little marble, plenty of wood, brick. Just bits of everything." Leonidas' voice rose with excitement.

"It is remarkable," John said and meant it. "And amazingly accurate so far as I can tell. Though I have never flown over the capital to be able to look down on it. Where did you find your descriptions?"

"I'm always on the lookout for any kind of travel writing or history or treatise on architecture. And I've arranged interviews with visitors from the capital and people who have journeyed there. I hope that you will be able to assist me. I would like to try my hand at the Great Palace."

"I can describe the grounds and buildings to you in detail, when there's time."

Helen smiled with evident pride. "Any emperor can expand the empire but how many men could shrink it to this size?"

Seeing the couple standing there looking down on the tiny city, John recalled the statue of Zeus he still had to inspect, and couldn't help comparing Leonidas and Helen to Zeus and Hera gazing down from Olympus.

"Who could want anything more?" Leonidas observed, displaying the uncanny ability he'd always had of seeming to read John's thoughts. "From our little home, Helen and I can see to the ends of the world. And I actually know the emperor's Lord Chamberlain and a man who will, one day soon I wager, be raised to bishop. I have been blessed."

Chapter Nineteen

Alexis led John into the monastery library. John could hardly recognize him. The unruly hair of the impulsive young prankster John remembered had receded, revealing the broad forehead of one who thinks deeply. The perpetually flushed cheeks had grown hollow, the full lips, spouting every kind of juvenile outrage, were narrowed. What struck John most were the eyes, once gleaming with mischief, now vague and staring as if focused on some distant vision. The face might have been formed by years of living on prayer under a desert sun, but so far as John was aware, Alexis had never left the comforts of Megara.

"And so you have returned after all these years," Alexis said. "When we were boys, who would have thought we would take such different journeys?"

They sat at a long table piled with codices and many scrolls, most of obvious antiquity. There was as much papyrus as parchment. The sun, near setting, had tinted the walls of the whitewashed room gold, now gradually turning to orange.

"Some of our holdings have taken equally long journeys, and I think you will find looking at a few of great interest." Alexis turned to address the young monk who had entered bearing a polished wood box. "There you are, Stephen. Yes, that's the box I want. Some of the greatest rarities I keep under lock and key," he explained to John. "And this is Leonidas' son. Stephen, our visitor is an old friend of your father's and has just come from his house."

"I am honored to meet you."

At Alexis' instruction, Stephen began to light lamps in the wall niches.

Alexis pulled a ragged sheet of parchment from the box, holding it to catch the last light from the windows.

"Yes, this is the document I mentioned. A few lines on the worship of Demeter in this area, written by an anonymous monk some centuries ago. There is nothing left but this badly decayed piece of parchment. Nevertheless, it is fascinating if fragmentary. Perhaps you could read it aloud to refresh my memory?"

John took the brittle sheet and began to read. "The goddess' daughter stolen by...pigs driven into a chasm...remains later retrieved for certain rites...initiation...torchlit procession... sacred basket an important ritualistic artifact...little is known of mysteries of the higher grades..."

Fragmentary was a charitable description, John thought.

"There is great antiquarian interest in these old religions," Alexis tucked the sheet gently back into the box. "Though spending so much time poring over ancient texts has made my eyes dimmer than they should be at my age. Stephen, you may return this to my study now."

The younger monk retrieved the box with a deferential nod to John.

"What is the situation with the hospice?" Alexis asked Stephen. "Are you able to accept Crassus' father yet?"

"We are still short of spaces. You know how it is. I would not wish to overcrowd the charges we already have."

"Certainly not. But Crassus has been a generous benefactor. Couldn't we use one of the temporary beds we keep for our own brothers when they fall ill?"

"I suppose so, but we've already turned most of them over to hospice residents." Stephen replied. "We have one or two poor souls who seem to be failing. Perhaps the Lord in his wisdom and mercy will make room for Crassus' father soon."

After the young man left Alexis said, "An exemplary young man. When I learned that the son of our old friend Leonidas had decided to devote his life to the Lord, naturally I invited him to join us at Saint Stephen's. And I have not regretted it. I don't know what I would do without him. All the unfortunates he cares for, the sick and elderly, arrive and depart faster than I can keep track. I depend on him to do so."

John couldn't help wondering if he detected a glimmer of young Alexis, always ready to desert his responsibilities for some mischief. "I am sorry if my servant further strained your resources. I hope you will accept a small payment."

"Thank you, John, but I would not expect to be compensated for kindness. To tell the truth, the hospice has enlarged our treasury considerably. Those who enter into our care often turn their worldly possessions over to us and families give us generous donations. It would be better if they showed their gratitude by doing the work of the Lord, but they mean well. We simply need to build an addition. But let us not become bogged down in business. We were speaking about old religions? You inquired about the temple on your estate. I'm happy to see you share some of my interest in such antiquities."

John murmured his assent, hoping the abbot would not inquire too closely about his personal religious beliefs.

"I showed you that fragment because it is rare, as originating locally, but there is a certain amount of information regarding Demeter worship, generally. But nothing too detailed or reliable since it was a secret cult."

"I understand," John said truthfully, since his own religion, Mithraism, kept its rites secret from all but initiates.

"She is an agricultural goddess. In this area, in particular, she was known as the giver of sheep and worshiped as the one who inspired the raising of sheep."

"I can appreciate the importance of that. I have never seen so many sheep as hereabouts."

"It is also said our thriving pig-raising industry resulted originally from the use of sacrificial swine in her worship."

John observed that the goddess had certainly left her impression on Megara.

Alexis nodded enthusiastically. "Yes, yes. Very much so. You'll doubtless remember the rock known as Recall where the goddess is said to have sat, calling her daughter to come back from the underworld?"

"Near the marketplace, yes. The one Leonidas fell off." John replied. "Though in those days you were more curious about, shall we say, more earthy rites?"

Alexis laughed quietly. "But of course. Were we then not boys as yet uninitiated into the mysteries of women?"

"Given this long-held interest, I confess to some surprise you entered the church."

"You're not the only one, John. My library is famous—or should I say notorious?—and a number of local residents have made it plain they consider my studies to be not quite proper. My reply is always to say it is wise know thy enemy."

"I found that to be true in Constantinople, although there it is hard to know who your enemy might be."

"In my line of endeavor I have no such problems. But as to this pagan enemy I have made it my business to know: Demeter. Your surmise on the significance of the sacred basket found by Theophilus' body would seem to be correct."

Shadows had begun to advance across the high-ceilinged room, fingering their blind way along the floor, gathering in corners as the light began to soften and turn gray.

"Peter said he was told that the pit he fell into may have been dug by treasure hunters. It occurred to me that I might have dug the pit myself when I was a boy. Has that old legend come back to life again?"

"Yes, it seems to have caught people's imaginations lately."

"It certainly caught our imaginations, but we were only children. And what is your opinion now? Have your studies revealed anything?"

"A foolish legend. You know the story. In fact, Alaric and the Goths did loot Corinth and burn it down so there would have been reason for someone to want to smuggle valuables away. But there is no evidence it happened."

"But if there was such an attempt, what would have been hidden?"

"The church treasury, or priceless icons, or perhaps a hoard of Corinthian bronze which would be worth more than the other two combined, given the very process by which it was made has been lost. What few references I've run across are nothing but rumors. The authors obviously didn't know anything more than we did when we searched."

John smiled. "I do remember that time in the woods when we were digging under the ledge and Leonidas broke through into a kind of hole. We were excited."

"And even more excited when the fox burst out! And nothing has changed. No one knows where the treasure is, most likely because there never was one. From time to time a hopeful hunter asks permission to dig on the monastery grounds. Naturally I refuse. Sometimes they return and dig after dark anyway. I also take the opportunity to explain that the wish to locate it is caused by the desire to obtain riches without work. However, it does not seem to stop people from digging here and there. If only they put as much energy into their spiritual lives, they would be much happier, if less wealthy!"

Alexis made a sweeping gesture indicating the codices and scrolls in their wall niches and on tables and shelves. "Ignore all these pagan gods and goddesses. The most evil of all idols, and the most worshiped, is wealth. But, then, you aren't here to listen to me preach, John. Truthfully, this monastery would benefit from any windfall. For one thing we could enlarge the hospice and for another—but no, I must not continue. I am falling into a different sort of pit, if you'll pardon my pun!"

"I should not keep you away from your duties." John stood.

"We'll have ample opportunity to renew our acquaintance. Being nearby, the monastery does quite a bit of business with the estate. We used to rely on it for much of our olive oil, but the groves have been neglected. Stephen generally dealt with your overseer, but perhaps we could deal personally?"

"Certainly. However, before leaving I must ask about the monk who rescued Peter. I would like to question him, in case he observed anything in the vicinity of the temple that night."

"As it happens it was Stephen who found your servant."

Stephen was gathering herbs. Their delicate scents filled the twilight in the inner courtyard.

"I should not have ventured out without permission," he told John. "Abbot Alexis reprimanded me, with justification. I couldn't contain my curiosity. I have prayed for the strength to control my impulses in the future."

"In this instance, it is fortunate for Peter that you failed to do so," John said. "I must thank you for bringing him back here and caring for him."

"Anyone would have done the same, sir."

The young man shared the bland family features. The older Leonidas had reminded John of Leonidas' father, the son reminded him of the boy who had been John's friend. The overlapping of past and present was unnerving. The similarities were not entirely physical either, for while Stephen's father devoted much of his time to recreating far corners of the world which remained invisible to him from Megara, Stephen had sworn allegiance to something that was invisible to everyone.

"We have often seen lights at the temple during the night these past few months," Stephen continued. "But that night the place was ablaze. I could see the sky lit up over the hill, as if there were a great fire."

"The City Defender's men were out in force. What time did you go to investigate?"

"After evening devotions. I was curious to see what was going on."

"What did you suppose might be going on?"

Stephen snapped twigs off a low bush and transferred them to his basket, enveloping both John and himself in a cloud of fragrance, which, John thought, Hypatia would be able to identify. Or his mother, in the old days, for that matter.

"I don't know. There's been talk of rituals. Not that I believe the stories about you and your family, sir. You can't know everything that goes on everywhere on your land at every hour."

"It seems not. How did you find Peter?"

"I heard him cry out."

"He had just fallen into the pit then?"

"I would think so, but he couldn't remember how he'd got into the pit, let alone when. He could have been crying out in pain."

"You went straight from the monastery in the direction of the temple?"

"That's right, sir. It wasn't as if I wanted to be roaming around. I didn't want to be caught outside the monastery so I took the quickest path."

As the two spoke, Stephen moved from one planting to the next, selecting herbs. For potions used in the hospice, he had explained when Alexis escorted John to the courtyard and left him there.

"Did you see or hear anything before finding Peter?"

"I heard nothing. I noticed a figure up on the ridge, I think. But we've become used to seeing your watchmen patrolling along your border. The whole estate was generally unguarded before you arrived."

"You're certain it was one of my men?"

"Who else would it be?"

"Was that all you saw?"

Finished with his gathering, Stephen made his way back to the covered walkway around the courtyard where torches burned at intervals, spreading a weak glow along the periphery of the garden. "I'm not sure. What I mean is, I may have caught a glimpse of another person. Nothing more than a shadow, and possibly literally a shadow. For an instant I thought I saw someone moving just beyond the temple but whoever it was vanished before I could be certain. All these hills and hollows make it hard to see."

Stephen used a torch to light a lantern he removed from a niche and when the flame came to life John was surprised to see that Stephen carried a clay replica of a church, reminiscent of the miniature Great Church Leonidas had constructed. The perforations in the lantern sent bright crosses of light around the dark corridor they entered. They passed a door. From within John heard faint sounds, rustlings and groaning, suggesting the winter wind in the dry branches of ancient trees. Human noises from the hospice.

Alexis rose from a bench in the shadows. He had been waiting.

"I hope Stephen has been able to answer your questions, John. Now let me show you out."

Chapter Twenty

"You can't go into town with an injured ankle, Peter."

Hypatia knelt by the side of their bed, gently prodding the purpling, bloated mass of flesh where an ankle should have been.

"It doesn't hurt," Peter insisted. He grimaced as her fingers examined the injury. "Not much. Nothing I can't stand. A walk to the marketplace is nothing like a forced march through the Isaurian mountains."

Hypatia stood. "You're not in the military now. There's no need for you to go."

"I must have landed on that foot when I fell into the pit," Peter said. "I wish I could remember. I'll be better once I start moving around if you'd give me a hand to get up. "

Hypatia sighed inwardly. She was rarely aware of Peter's age. With harsh morning light highlighting his cuts and bruises, the time-weathered face, the last vestiges of gray hair, his thin limbs, she saw, for an instant, an old man. "No, Peter. Lie back down and rest. I heard the master and mistress speaking at breakfast. He's going into Megara and I'm certain he'll allow me to accompany him."

"I suppose that would be all right if he doesn't feel inconvenienced," Peter allowed himself to fall back. "It is my duty—"

"Your duty is to recover from your accident." Hypatia bent and kissed his forehead before leaving the room.

Crossing the courtyard she realized she felt a maternal solicitude toward her elderly husband. Was that appropriate? They had only been married a few months. Should she feel differently toward Peter now they were wed than she had beforehand? They had grown closer during all the time they had worked together in the Lord Chamberlain's household until finally it had seemed only natural that they should marry. But was that a good reason to marry?

The master and mistress weren't married in the legal sense but they might as well have been. Theirs was not what anyone would call a traditional marriage. John was not yet old, but in a sense he was. He and Cornelia had had a child together before his terrible mutilation. That was long ago, however. Did Cornelia feel her marriage to John was what it should be? Did she ever see him as…what he was? But no, Hypatia told herself, she shouldn't even be having such thoughts.

What most distressed her about Peter's age was how little time they might have together. She tried to keep it out of her mind.

She took a basket from the alcove off the kitchen. Lying in its bottom was the paring knife with the cracked handle she'd been using to cut herbs during her forays into the meadows. Considering how she and Peter had been attacked it might not be a bad idea to take it into Megara with her or to keep it with her in case Theophilus' murderer was still slinking around the estate. She tucked it away in her tunic, out of sight.

In the kitchen, Cornelia was still lingering at the table, contemplating a plate holding a few crumbs and olive pits. When Hypatia inquired about John, she said he was already on his way to Megara.

"I told Peter I'd go with him," Hypatia said. "Do you think I could run and catch up?"

"Why bother?" came the reply in a masculine voice. "I'll be glad to accompany you. And my companion here will gladly come along for safety." It was Philip, standing in the doorway, hefting his sharpened stake.

"Shouldn't you and your friend be keeping an eye on the property rather than…than the pots on the brazier?" Hypatia had almost blurted out "keeping an eye on me."

"If the mistress doesn't mind…" said Philip.

"I don't mind," Cornelia replied. "It would be an excellent arrangement. If you can catch up to the master you can provide protection to him as well."

"There, Hypatia, you've had your orders. Let's not delay."

Philip told himself that Hypatia wasn't as cross as she pretended. He showed her a shortcut through the fields, all the while admiring her out of the corner of his eye. A bronze-skinned, black-haired beauty. Nothing like the farmers' daughters he saw outside Megara.

They did not see John. When they reached the track leading to Megara he wasn't in sight.

"The master always walks at a fast pace," Hypatia said. "We won't catch up."

"Why should we try? I'm here to look after you if necessary."

"You aren't watching the estate while you're watching me."

Did she emphasize the word "watching" or was that his imagination? Surely an attractive woman would not object to being watched politely?

"You must have some time off from your work," Philip said. "There's more to see in Megara than the marketplace. It may not be Constantinople but I could show you some sights."

"It's not a good idea for any of us from the estate to be spending time in town, the way everyone feels. If you're seen with me too often, Philip, they'll think you're in league with me."

"Don't worry. No one in Megara is going to turn against me. I've lived here my whole life."

Walking casually close to her, he managed from time to time to brush his hip against hers as if by accident.

"Why aren't you married at your age?" Hypatia asked.

"I've been waiting for you," he grinned and watched for her reaction. Consternation, on the outside, but masking what? Did he see a flush of pleasure creep into her cheeks?

"You've lived with your father all your life?" She was trying to change the subject, he thought.

"On our farm, yes."

"Just you and your father?"

Philip paused. Why would she be wondering whether he lived alone? He had to restrain his eager imagination.

"It's just my father and I. Except when Diocles was staying there. An unpleasant man, not suited to be overseer, in my opinion. But he's gone now. If you would like to visit sometime, I could show you our house. I am sure it is much grander than a servant's room. My father is out often, tending to his pigs."

She glared at him and fell silent. Now she was obviously blushing.

It's true, Philip told himself. She's definitely attracted to me.

To an observer they might have been a married couple walking together. The dark-haired, sunburnt man protectively hovered near the dark-haired, tawny-skinned woman. Occasionally he would touch her arm, as if ready to steady her. When she sorted through the melons on sale, lifting them to her face to inhale their aroma, then passing them over for his opinion, their fingers brushed.

Did they see the sellers looking at them with hostile eyes, or notice their curtness? Did they feel the subtle pressure of a multitude of stares directed at their backs?

The man kept glancing around, as if alert for danger. One hand moved nervously, causing the wickedly pointed end of the stake he carried to waggle back and forth.

The observer looked back across the square, past the stylite column, at the entrance to Halmus' mansion, but no one had emerged yet.

Chapter Twenty-one

Halmus' servant told John that his master was currently resting from his devotions and free to discuss earthly matters. He showed John into the atrium. Atop the stylite column, half-naked and draped in chains, Halmus had looked the part of an ascetic, but in his atrium, dressed in fine garments, he resembled any other successful businessman, solid, well fed, and one who would not take orders from anyone.

Or no mortal at least.

"Yes, I have dealt with Diocles. I am glad you have removed him. He was a villain but the former owner of the estate wished me to do business through the man. I would not willingly have chosen to have anything to do with him. You will not be overseeing the estate yourself?"

"My son-in-law will be overseer. He has been delayed but he's a competent and honest man. He has had charge of a large estate not far from Constantinople."

"Very good. Except of course…"

"As you say. There is a great deal of animosity here toward myself and my family."

"There is no animosity toward you in this house."

Was that true, John wondered? Who then were the evil ones releasing demons and conducting wicked rites, against whom Halmus had been fulminating from his column? He was starting to suspect the merchant was transformed into a different person, having climbed back down to the ground, when Halmus disabused him of the notion by launching into an account of his travels in the Holy Land.

"We are a godly household. I have visited the summit of Mount Sinai, sat on the very rock upon which Moses smashed the tablets, and seen the spot where the golden idol stood."

As Halmus spoke he embarked on a peregrination of his home, which led them along corridors decorated with gaudy mosaics and through a huge kitchen into the garden behind the house. It couldn't have been more different than the immaculately groomed grounds of the Great Palace. This was more of an untamed jungle, confined between walls like a wild beast.

Halmus spread his arms, gesturing toward tangled brush and drooping tree limbs. "I think of this as my wilderness, a place to which I can retreat from the affairs of the world and commune with the Lord. My first intent was to re-create the rugged, rocky deserts of the Holy Land but in such a confined space the effect would not have been the same. I would have found myself sitting on a patch of bare ground, surrounded by walls, almost a prison. With this vegetation on all sides I can't see the walls. I can imagine I am in the middle of a vast forest, far from humanity—a hermit, if you will."

John nodded politely. He had attempted to discreetly establish Halmus' business relationship with the estate but Halmus was not forthcoming. Perhaps he didn't want to tell John anything of his business, or possibly he was one of those men who left most their affairs to underlings. No doubt a churchman or another devout Christian would be impressed by the man's pilgrimages.

"Careful," Halmus cautioned as they pushed through a thick planting of rhododendrons lining the steep banks of a small stream.

The flashing trickle, appearing from and vanishing back into the overhanging vegetation, was just narrow enough to step across.

"But perhaps I shouldn't be talking about religious matters," he went on. "Please do not take offense. In business matters I only judge people by their wealth, but I confess I do wonder about this rumor you worship Demeter."

So that was what Halmus had been trying to establish. "I can assure you, I do not worship Demeter."

"I am glad to hear it. Not that I would allow it to interfere with business. We must all render unto Caesar what is Caesar's. Not only does the emperor demand it, but Jesus commanded us to do so. And in order to render what is Caesar's we must first obtain what is Caesar's, is that not so?"

John agreed.

"Have you met Abbot Alexis? I believe his monastery's land borders your estate. He is a good friend of mine. I will give you an introduction to him. You may want to attend services there."

"I've known Alexis since boyhood."

"Is that so? Excellent. A most competent man. He has greatly expanded Saint Stephen's holdings. I will not be alone in recommending him to replace our current bishop when the time comes. After all, the church must make its way in this world, if it is to do the Lord's work. A good bishop must first be a good businessman."

There appeared in front of them a dome-shaped hill largely overgrown with moss and weeds. It loomed large in the enclosed garden, vanishing back into the overhanging vegetation. As they approached he noticed the hill itself was constructed of concrete, left unfinished and lumpy to simulate rock.

"Here is my hermit's dwelling." Halmus pushed back an animal skin hanging down inside the entrance, allowing them to enter a rough walled cubicle, its back also hung with an animal skin, a cramped space furnished only with the stub of a candle sitting on a flat rock against the wall. It could almost have been the beginnings of a miniature mithraeum had it been below ground, John thought.

"I will be staying here tonight," Halmus explained. "An angel appeared to me this morning as I preached and instructed me to pray here from nightfall until sunrise. Evil is loose in Megara and I must pray for our deliverance."

John said nothing. The businessman spoke of angelic visitation as if it were the price of olive oil. There was something odd about Halmus' retreat. Before John had a chance to latch onto the thought, Halmus reached down and picked up a small stick laid beside the candle, extending the former in John's direction. "A relic from the Holy Land. Please be careful how you handle it."

John grasped the stick and gave an inquiring look.

"You have in your hand a small part of the bush that burned with holy fire. Can you feel some lingering warmth? Can you hear a faint vibration after all these centuries of the thunderous voice of the Lord speaking to Moses?

"After descending Mount Sinai, where I visited the cave in which Moses stayed for forty days and nights, a cave not unlike this one I may add, I was asked whether I wanted to see the burning bush which still lived," Halmus continued. "I was eager to do so, so after cautioning me that the journey would be arduous, my guide and I set out across the desert. This was near the head of the valley that runs in front of the holy mountain and which is easily crossed in two hours. But on account of the miraculous presence of the bush, the geography of the place is like nothing else on earth.

"We walked all morning and on into the afternoon and although we never turned, as far as I could tell, the mountain lay sometimes before us, and other times behind us, and at others was invisible. So, too, the position of the sun in the sky moved around the zenith mysteriously, and also I sensed I was walking downhill or up an incline when my eyes told me the barren ground remained level.

"Finally, late in the afternoon, we came to an utterly flat and bare expanse upon which grew not a single blade of grass. The surface beneath my feet was gray and hard. It might have been solid rock. And in the midst of this deathly landscape grew the bush from which the Lord spoke in the fire.

"After falling on our knees to pray we turned our backs and left. In a few steps we were at the edge of the valley and looking back could see no sign of the bush. But it had shed a few twigs for pilgrims such as I, and the one you are holding proved that we had been there."

Chapter Twenty-two

"You did not tell me the truth, Hypatia." Peter said when she arrived back from the market with a full basket. His harsh greeting startled her.

She put her basket on the table and set down the small bunch of yellow wildflowers she carried.

"Did your young man pick those for you?" Peter asked.

"What do you mean?"

"I saw you coming back with Philip. You told me you were going to go into town with the master."

"He'd already gone. The mistress agreed Philip could accompany me. Ask her if you don't believe me!"

"It isn't fitting for us to question the mistress or the master."

"Then you'll have to take my word for it. Isn't your wife's word good enough for you?"

"I used to think I could trust you."

Hypatia could not remember seeing Peter so furious with her. "I don't like the way you are looking at me, Peter. I've done nothing to deserve it."

Peter looked pointedly at the flowers on the table. "That young man has been following you around like a cat after you've given it a bowl of milk, expecting more."

"Oh, Peter! I certainly haven't given Philip...anything!"

"Why should you be angry? I'm the one who has something to be angry about. Do you think I'm too old to be jealous? Is that it?"

"But you have nothing to be jealous about!"

"That's the first thing everyone says."

"If you need to be angry about something, then be angry about this. Philip told me that odious overseer Diocles didn't leave the estate as soon as the master ordered. He stayed with Philip's father for a while. Supposedly he's gone now, but how can we be sure? The master should know, don't you think?"

Peter fell silent. He looked as if he wanted to keep arguing. "Yes, you're right. I had better tell him."

After he limped out Hypatia tossed the flowers into the brazier, went into their bedroom, roughly pushed the cats off the bed, sat down, put her head in her hands, and cried.

She wasn't even certain what she was crying about.

Perhaps everyone and everything.

On returning from Megara John searched the house and outbuildings until he found Cornelia in a gloomy, musty room attached to the barn. Covered ceramic jars, some pierced with numerous holes, filled shelves.

Cornelia leaned her broom in a corner, picked up a jar, and handed it to John. "Look at that!"

He brushed cobwebs away and looked inside. Delicate bones lay amid bits of walnut shells. "Someone forgot he was fattening dormice, or decided not to bother any longer."

"Snails too. I'm sure we can guess who's responsible."

"Or irresponsible."

"The overseer, of course. Too busy swindling the owner to care." She picked up the broom and resumed cleaning.

"You should leave that for Hypatia or the farm workers."

"I can't sit around doing nothing, John. Besides, I enjoy exploring the place. You never know what you'll find. And what did you find in Megara?"

He described his visit to her, sneezing more than once as dust whirled through the air. As he talked he watched her reaching, bending, stretching, admiring her lithe form and the unconscious grace with which she moved, even when performing a mundane and dirty task.

When he had finished telling her about his visit, her face was bemused. "I'm surprised Halmus can conduct any business at all, between going on pilgrimages and preaching and having visions."

Before John could reply he heard shuffling footsteps and turning, saw Peter enter.

"Master, I am sorry to bother you but I have just heard something I think you should know. The former overseer was staying with the tenant farmer, Lucian."

Cornelia banged the broom angrily against the floor. "Wretched man! He ought to be staying in a jar, starving like these poor dormice."

"Where did you find this out, Peter?"

"Hypatia just told me. She got it from that young watchman who keeps bothering her."

"Thank you. I will look into Diocles' whereabouts."

Peter hesitated in the doorway. "Master…about that story the merchant told you…I overheard…I didn't mean to eavesdrop but I didn't want to interrupt you when you were talking to the mistress." He looked at his feet nervously. "Well, to be honest, you know how I love to hear pilgrim tales."

"I do, Peter. Halmus' tale was certainly colorful. You have something to say about it?"

"He was lying to you, master."

Cornelia gave a faint snort of derision. "Of course he was lying, he's from Megara."

"What do you mean, Peter?"

"His description of the burning bush was not correct. I know because I've seen it with my own eyes when I traveled through that country during my days in the military. It isn't in the desert. Not at all, master. At the head of the valley, at the base of the mountains, the monks have built a church surrounded by cells in a beautiful garden. There is plenty of water, enough for a thriving orchard."

"I see. Perhaps Halmus has difficulty recalling events?"

"It may be so, but it seems to me a person never forgets where he saw that bush."

Cornelia waited until Peter was out of earshot before saying, "You know how these Christian pilgrims like to exaggerate."

"Perhaps he had a vision, or thought he did," John mused. "I'm not certain his humors aren't deranged, or perhaps wants people to think they are. There would be advantages."

Cornelia set aside her broom. "What about Diocles? You're going to make certain he's gone, aren't you? The man might be dangerous."

"Indeed. For now, if he's still here, I like knowing where he is without him realizing."

Chapter Twenty-three

John ran a finger along a row of numbers in the codex lying open on the triclinium table, shaking his head now and again and frowning. He had returned to the overseer's books. The mundane task made less of a change from listening to Halmus' heavenly visions than he would have guessed. Diocles' figures appeared to be little more than visions themselves. After less than an hour, John's fingertip was black with ink from tracing the malfeasance of the so-called overseer.

Whereas one might expect entries that supported each other in the manner of the blocks forming the walls of a city, with each expenditure entered against income and the resulting sum transferred onward, they revealed nothing approaching such an ordered arrangement.

It was obvious Senator Vinius had never sent an agent to check the accounts. John continued reading. He came to an entry recording the purchase of a herd of goats a few months before. There were no subsequent references relating to the sale of the herd, yet John had seen no goats on the estate.

He was about to make a note of the discrepancy when he found, farther down, an entry for a large sum spent on "remedies for sick goats" and then another for "disposal of goat carcasses."

It seemed amazing an entire herd of goats would die within such a short time and given John was already suspicious of what he could only call Diocles' unusual accounting methods, it seemed highly unlikely. It was not to be wondered the former overseer dressed well. When it came to the estate's books, the overseer could produce goats out of thin air, send them straight back, and make money off the herd in the process.

What was Diocles doing now, John wondered, apart from spreading malicious rumors about the new owner of the estate? In addition to worrying about whoever killed Theophilus, should he also be worried about any vindictive actions the former overseer might take? Was Diocles capable of violence as well as fraud?

He was contemplating the question when Peter limped into the room accompanied by a dusty rustic and announced: "A messenger seeking to speak to you, master."

"Are you the person in charge, sir?" his visitor inquired.

When John confirmed that he was, the messenger handed over a writing tablet, bowed, and was escorted out.

John watched Peter's obviously painful exit. The servant shouldn't be up and about, but it was useless to tell him so.

He cut the thin cord tying the tablet's two beechwood frames together and opened them. The wax surface within bore a confirmation relating to the purchase of a large flock of sheep. More of Diocles' imaginary livestock? Unlike goats, there certainly were plenty of sheep on the estate.

John consulted the codex in front of him. He wasn't surprised to find no mention of any such transaction on the date given in the tablet, nor for a week before or after.

Was this some peculiarity of business in Megara? Or business as conducted by Diocles?

The message must have been intended for the overseer. The messenger hadn't asked for John or the owner of the estate but for whoever was in charge, which for years had been Diocles. No doubt the rustic bearer of the tablet was unfamiliar with Diocles and had naturally assumed John's answer meant he was the estate overseer.

What could the purpose be? Diocles didn't need such a message delivered to him to falsify the accounts. Unless he was being instructed to make a false entry?

No doubt Diocles would have understood what it meant.

Was it in code perhaps?

Having just spent time talking with people who seemed to be concealing information and now being immersed in Diocles' duplicitous accounts, the idea of artful concealment was not far from his thoughts.

John muttered an oath and picked up the tablet again. He pondered what the reference to sheep could possibly mean. The world was full of things the gentle-faced animals could represent.

As he reread the message he noticed a mark on the wooden frame around the wax. A deep gouge marred one of the raised borders of the right hand leaf. Similar marks on the outer leaves were to be expected, but an inner location seemed peculiar given that, when closed, the two inner surfaces lay together, protecting both frame and wax.

During his years of imperial service John had learned of many ingenious methods for secret communications.

He gently scraped the wax from its shallow rectangular tray.

"Mithra!" he muttered.

Carved into the wood under the wax was a short message. Evidently written in great haste, as witnessed by the uneven depth of its lines, one of which ended with a deep scratch stretching to the gouge which had alerted him to investigate further.

The secret message was as cryptic as the original in that it appeared to be too innocent to require concealment:

"Per July agreement. Delivered to Nisaea iron in agreed quantity."

Chapter Twenty-four

Like all the ports John had ever passed through, Nisaea was a scene of controlled chaos. By the time he arrived, the evening sun cast long ropes of shadow across the crowded docks where lines of workers moved unceasingly between moored ships, piles of merchandise, warehouses, and waiting wagons. The last time John had seen this raucous ant heap was when he and his family landed after their journey into exile. It was with mixed feelings he paused and watched several men running around and between some large crates stacked at the edge of the nearest dock, leaving a lurid trail of loud oaths hovering in the humid air that smelled of spices, fish, and the droppings of cart animals.

Now and then one of the men would leap upward and grab at something hidden from John's view by the crates and then there would be another outburst of inventive swearing echoing across the water.

It might have been some arcane ritual performed when landing cargo.

However, he had not walked from his estate to the port to ponder local customs. What he sought was information on who had shipped a consignment of iron. Certainly it was an unremarkable, everyday kind of arrangement, but what raised his suspicions was why such a transaction should be recorded in a secret fashion when inscribing it on the wax surface of the tablet would have served as well.

It did not seem normal business practice and was therefore worth investigating.

He skirted a large fish tank sunk into the dock into which a pair of fishermen were transferring their catch from a boat that had seen better days, while a third man haggled about the price for a small octopus with a party who engaged in emphatic denigration of its value. Making his way to the harbormaster's hut, John found a visitor arguing with the official in residence.

"It wasn't my fault they got away," the visitor shouted at the furious harbormaster as John entered the cramped untidy space buzzing with flies. "It was an accident. Accidents happen."

"You mean one of your men let them loose deliberately to cause trouble, so your crew better catch them. The well-fed fool in Megara expecting them is not going to be very happy to hear his three monkeys have escaped and will probably never be seen again. Go and help the search and hurry up. His servant will be here in an hour or so to pick the demons up."

"I'll borrow a fishing net, that should help trap 'em. If not, you could always say they died during the voyage."

"Possibly. I should have to levy a small charge to pay for that service. Now get on with it."

As the other left, the official turned to John. "What do you want?"

His tone of voice made it plain his temper was short and his sunburnt face wore an angry expression emphasized by a deeply creased frown bridging dark eyebrows.

"I wish to inquire about a shipment of iron for my estate."

"Your estate?" The harbormaster looked him up and down and sniffed, as if to say servants are all the same, talking about their estate as if they owned it. "You wish to know about an iron shipment? I know nothing about such a cargo and—"

A hoarse burst of swearing entered by the open door as a man in a ragged tunic raced past waving his arms and screaming abuse at an unseen colleague who, it seemed, had allowed the hairy little bastards to escape.

"It seems rather lively this evening," John observed with a thin smile.

The harbormaster glared at him. "As I was saying, I don't know anything about a shipment of iron. Have you any proof it even belongs to your estate? Valuable goods, iron. I can't authorize its release to any vagabond who arrives claiming ownership."

John, silently noting the harbormaster had just tacitly admitted he did in fact know of the shipment despite his initial denial, produced the tablet with the message burnt into it.

"Ah," the harbormaster said after a brief glance. "Yes. Yes, this proves you are entitled to information. I am instructed to release it only to a person carrying this message. We do have your shipment, sir, and I shall see it arrives at the estate as soon as possible. It will involve a small charge for delivery, the usual arrangement to release goods landed here if they are transported on to their destination." He paused. "You are not the usual courier."

"I have not been in the area very long. Do you recall when the last shipment occurred?"

The harbormaster shrugged. "No. And the businessman involved does not send documentation. I admit it is somewhat unusual but shipping iron isn't illegal and, after all, we must be flexible in dealing with the contingencies of marine business. I don't have time to ask questions, considering the volume of goods landed here daily."

John handed him a couple of coins. "The charge you mentioned and a little extra for the information."

The harbormaster grinned. "I see you are an honest businessman, sir."

"Then you will understand that, being honest, I need to know who the usual courier is, in case there is some irregularity."

"You are most conscientious, sir. I really don't know anything further I can tell you other than the man has a scar on his face and not many teeth and the ones he has are all on one side of his mouth." He rubbed his chin and screwed up his face as if thinking hard. "I wish I could remember where the shipment originated. It's on the tip of my tongue."

"Sometimes it helps to think of something else. Like this." John dropped another coin into the man's hand.

"You're right, sir. Why, it just occurred to me when I was admiring Justinian's profile. The vessels carrying these shipments sail from Corinth. As you are new to the area, I should warn you about Corinth. A notoriously sinful city since ancient times, where honest men are cheated and murdered and public women flaunt themselves."

"In some ways, then, it resembles Constantinople," John observed as he turned to leave, stepping to one side to avoid a stout, perspiring man who rushed in as an agitated monkey leapt through the open window and scuttled into a corner.

Chapter Twenty-five

Another evening, another port, this time Lechaion, the western port of Corinth. John had spent much of the day traveling. Who could the courier with the scar and singular arrangement of teeth have been except his stepfather? So John had come here, to the city where the mysterious shipment of iron had originated, to look for Theophilus' past.

Rows of masts pointed accusing fingers at the darkening sky, and intoxicated men were already staggering in and out of the taverns lining squalid alleys radiating away from the water. The dying sun gave its blush to white marble-faced civic buildings. A large basilica stood within sight of the inner harbor, a mass of busy streets stretching away around it. Herds of cows voiced loud bovine complaints as they were driven into pens in a nearby market.

It was to an alley off a wide thoroughfare leading from the marketplace that John went in search of lodgings. By the time dusk had settled in and torches flared he had moved into a small room at the top of a house that leaned wearily on its two neighbors, inclining precipitously with them toward the rubbish-strewn ground to such a degree that going up the stairs meant a giddy, near crawling ascent to avoid tumbling down backward.

The stairway was greasy, dimly lit, and malodorous, but had the advantage of creaking loudly when pressure was placed on its steps, giving tenants ample warning of visitors who, by the appearance of the area, might not be welcome.

John took the room on a daily basis, being careful to pay in coins of the smallest value, and with one hand on the blade tucked in his belt as the landlord's agent counted them.

"What's the best tavern in these parts?" he asked the agent, a wizened little man with a distinct stoop and gray hair.

"Depends what you seek." The reply was accompanied by a leer. "If it's a woman looking for a friend, you can do no better than sample the delights of the tavern run by my son. Step outside and I'll point it out to you."

The tavern to which the old man referred was a large establishment across the street and appeared well patronized. John noticed a huddled shape lying against the wall.

Following his glance, his informant chuckled. "That's Maritza. A harpy with red hair and a scorpion's tongue," he said. "She must have had good fortune and met a generous stranger tonight. Since her man went away she's had to fend for herself. Easy enough if you're a woman, but her ways are so well known in this quarter she hasn't been able to find anyone to take his place yet."

The old man grew confidential. "Let me put it this way. I would not want to have her walking behind me in daylight, let alone in the middle of the night. She slashed the face of a girl who made a too-loud comment about aging whores in that very tavern. She keeps returning and my son is anxious about more outbursts from her in case the authorities get involved. Fortunately no one saw or knew anything about the first incident, if you follow me. Now, it happens my son has a couple of girls in residence who are as gentle as lambs and most willing to please. And when I say willing to please…"

John endured a lurid description of the delights available for a few coins in the upper room of the tavern in hopes of gleaning useful information. With none forthcoming, he finally escaped from the garrulous agent and made his way across the street. As he approached the tavern, two men were thrown out. Struggling futilely, shouting oaths and insults, they resembled a couple of seagulls with broken wings doing their best to take flight but not quite succeeding. By the time the revelers had picked themselves up from the dirt and reeled away together singing loudly, the woman had gone.

The tavern stank worse than the street. John went to the counter where the smell of fresher wine in vats sunk into its marble top and partially obscured the stench of stale wine, spilled or expelled onto the floor in various ways.

John clicked a coin loudly on the counter until the owner appeared, glowered at him, and ladled out a drink. He wasn't a big man, but he looked as tough as a charioteer, with a face resembling stained leather.

"The next time you see Theophilus tell him a friend of his is looking for him."

The owner handed John a brimming cup. His face had suddenly become expressionless.

"I was certain the bastard said this is where he came to sell our takings," John said, loud enough for everyone in the room to hear. "He told me the owner's father had it all arranged with the authorities, to make it safe for business."

"You don't know what you're talking about."

"Of course I do. Out the window, across the roof, through the alley, straight in here, open your sack, and by the time the night watch arrives you'll be strolling out with coins in hand and your merchandise off to good homes. Those were Theophilus' words, and if he doesn't know thievery, who does?"

"I don't want trouble," the owner said.

Two huge men whom John had taken for patrons had suddenly got up from the table where they were sitting. No doubt they had been the means by which the two revelers had been put, almost literally, to flight.

"I'm certain your father doesn't want trouble, either."

"My father knows it is wise to be silent. He didn't tell you anything. Keep him out of this."

"Perhaps he knows what I need to know. Perhaps he's easier to talk to."

The owner's expression changed just enough to betray anxiety "Look, I never heard of this Theophilus. What does he look like?"

John described his stepfather, again loudly, stressing the scar on his cheek and lack of teeth. He half turned to face the room and saw he had everyone's attention. "It's worth a lot to me to find him," he concluded.

"He hasn't been in here. Perhaps he drinks in another tavern nearby. More likely he was lying to you."

John laughed. "You think I hadn't considered that? The man's a better liar than he is a thief. Has anyone else been in here, talking about iron shipments?"

"Iron shipments? No." The man's obvious bemusement satisfied John that he was telling the truth. John took his cup and sat at a table as far away from the looming thugs as he could get. He sipped his drink slowly, hoping for someone to sidle up to him and whisper he had information on Theophilus, or a man with a scar, or some questionable dealings in iron, but no one did. After a time he surreptitiously emptied most of his wine onto the floor and left. He had a number of other taverns yet to visit.

Chapter Twenty-six

Hypatia was talking with Philip yet again.

From her bedroom window Cornelia could see them standing where the dirt track behind the house passed through a sagging gate in a ruined fence. Hypatia's basket was full of the herbs she had gathered. Perhaps she was talking to Philip about the herb bed she intended to start, a larger version of the one she had cultivated in the inner garden of John's house in Constantinople, rather than meeting Philip by arrangement.

At least that was what Cornelia hoped.

Philip was supposed to be patrolling the boundaries of the estate and yet he invariably appeared to meet Hypatia whenever she went out.

Hypatia turned away and continued down the path. Philip followed, gesturing, saying something Cornelia couldn't hear.

Cornelia pulled herself away from the window, feeling guilty and chagrined at feeling guilty. She certainly had the right to know how her servants were behaving, particularly when it might lead to disruptions in the household. Nevertheless, what she could only admit was spying made her uncomfortable.

She caught the mummified cat staring at her.

"No, Cheops," she muttered. "No matter how isolated we are here I refuse to start talking to you."

She went downstairs to the kitchen still contemplating the problem. She could, and probably should, order Hypatia not to spend time with Philip, or ask John to change the young man's duties. It wouldn't do to have their only two servants quarreling.

Traveling around the empire as a performer in a troupe had not prepared Cornelia to serve as mistress of a wealthy household, and neither had her years sharing John's spartan life in the capital where his only servants had been, just as here, Peter and Hypatia.

They were more like family than servants.

Hypatia came in and set her basket down. It looked heavy. She'd dug up herbs by the roots for planting. Her cheeks were red from the exertion of carrying the basket, or from anger or some other strong emotion.

"Are you and Peter…?" Cornelia paused, groping for words that would not seem offensive.

"He's only a little bruised and scratched and my bump is getting smaller." Hypatia gingerly touched her head.

"I didn't mean that. I meant are you…well, it's been hard for all of us coming here. A big change. And you and Peter have already had a big change in your lives."

Hypatia bent and settled some plants threatening to fall out of the basket more securely. The mixed scents of the herbs and fresh earth filled the air. "We're happy, mistress."

"Sit down, Hypatia. I want to talk with you."

"Certainly I have time to talk to you, Peter. I hope our conversation the other night was helpful." Abbot Alexis pushed a stack of codices out of the way and regarded Peter, seated on the opposite side of the table in the monastery study. "You remain fretful about this marriage of yours to a younger woman. Is that so?"

Peter nodded

"Are you familiar with the teachings of the apostle Paul?"

"Yes. In fact I have a special fondness for him." Peter reached into the neck of his tunic and fished out a small, crude coin attached to a string. "I have taken to wearing this lucky coin around my neck. We need protection here. The coin is from Derbe. I found it along the way when I was serving in the military. I know that it sounds blasphemous to say it is a good luck charm, but Paul preached in Derbe and sometimes I think perhaps it fell from Paul's own purse, or he may have sat to rest near where it was dropped, and that something of his spirit remains in it. But that isn't what I came to talk about."

Peter chided himself silently, exasperated. Why had he babbled about his coin? Was he too nervous and upset to control his tongue? Or was that another ability one gradually lost with old age?

Thankfully the abbot did not appear offended. In fact he smiled. "An portable icon one might say. There is nothing blasphemous about icons. We know that although the saints are everywhere they are most strongly where their icons are displayed."

Peter turned the worn coin over thoughtfully before tucking it back into place. "My belief is not wrong then?"

"Not at all. Who knows what, exactly, the truth is? So long as we are making an honest effort to find it, where is the harm? The pagans I studied had their own icons, which they called idols. Yes, they were wrong. But they were trying to find the truth. Just as you are."

Peter wasn't certain it was necessarily a good thing to be compared to ancient pagans.

"You must be aware that Paul recommended marriage to those with less fortitude than himself," the abbot said. "Better to marry than to burn."

Peter felt his face getting hot. "Yes, but, that wasn't...well..." What could he say? At his age he didn't burn. There might still be a warm coal buried under the ashes in the brazier.

"You don't need to be embarrassed, Peter." The abbot went on to talk at length, citing scripture and the teachings of the church fathers.

By the time Peter left the study he was relieved to escape the torrent of learning. He had felt a need for spiritual assistance but had come away mostly with a feeling of mortification at his own weakness. What went on between Hypatia and him was no one's business but theirs. Not even a clergyman's. What had he been thinking coming here?

"Peter. Back to visit us."

For an instant he didn't recognize the young monk who spoke, then he realized it was his rescuer. "Stephen. Yes, I was speaking with your abbot."

"Or rather he was speaking."

"True enough. How did you know?"

"I've seen enough visitors emerge from that study looking as if they've been beaten about the ears. He's a fine man, is our abbot, but his scholarship is boundless."

They went into the sunshine, Stephen leading Peter to the monastery herb garden, the sort of garden Hypatia talked about planting, Peter remembered with a pang. Their voices, which had sounded so loud in the narrow, dim hallway, were suddenly quieter in the open landscape, under the high dome of the sky. Bees hummed, gulls cried, occasionally there came the sharp clang of a hammer from the direction of the blacksmith's forge.

"I brought you here because I would like to talk to you in private, Peter. Has any progress been made in finding that poor soul's murderer?"

Peter told him there had not been, so far as he knew.

"What does your master say? Does he suspect anyone?"

"The master would not confide such matters to me, Stephen."

"He's been investigating, hasn't he? I've heard he had a great reputation for solving crimes for the emperor."

Peter agreed, without offering more information on that matter.

While they walked through the garden, Stephen inspected the plantings, each variety confined to its own square plot. "We use a lot of these in the hospice. Abbot Alexis encourages our efforts and they provide much comfort to all. He is so caught up in his studies I sometimes doubt if he'd recognize any of our residents if he met one in the halls. Not that they should be wandering away from the hospice, though it has happened now and then."

He paused and pointed out an aromatic shrub bearing light purple flowers. "Dew of the sea. A beautiful name for a beautiful herb. Strengthens the failing memory, you know. Yes," he continued, "I once discovered an old fellow drawing with a pilfered kalamos on a page torn from one the abbot's valuable old codices. He must have found his way into the study and stolen it along with the kalamos. A messy palimpsest that made!"

Peter murmured it was a shame anyone would steal from an abbot, not certain what Stephen was trying to tell him.

"My point," Stephen said as if he had asked that very question, "is that Abbot Alexis is not perhaps the best person from whom to seek advice on worldly matters. Not that he isn't a fine man, but oftentimes his thoughts fly nearer to the angels than to us earthly beings."

"You know I've been seeking advice?"

"Don't be embarrassed, Peter. I may be much younger than you but like the abbot I am a man of God and am here to serve all in such ways as can be done."

"And what would you advise?" Peter asked reluctantly, since it had become obvious he was going to be given advice whether he wanted it or not. It occurred to him Stephen's personal solution to worldly entanglements may have been to avoid them by entering holy orders.

"You know what the scriptures say, Peter. The wife is bound to obey her husband. It is up to you to instruct her, and it is up to her to follow your instructions."

Peter murmured a reluctant assent. He was not comfortable giving orders, especially to Hypatia.

"And just as importantly," Stephen continued. "You must pray to the Lord together."

◇◇◇

"You may go now, Hypatia." Cornelia finally said.

The conversation had been brief and awkward. Cornelia had done her best to indicate her concern to Hypatia, stressing that her private life was considered such but that a certain standard of behavior was expected.

"Thank you for speaking with me, mistress," Hypatia told her. "I will take your advice and pray to my goddess."

Chapter Twenty-seven

Both Bacchus and Fortuna frowned on John.

Posing as a petty thief and talking loudly about his grudge against a man who dealt in iron shipments, he stopped at every tavern he could locate. But a sip of wine in this tavern, two sips in another, made him sleepy before he chanced upon anyone with anything useful to pass on. No farther forward, he carefully groped his way up the creaking staircase at his lodgings as dawn ushered in another day for the swarming residents of Lechaion.

It was afternoon before he rose, prepared to resume his search. Given it seemed likely those who might have information for sale would not emerge from their dark corners and squalid rooms until the day was further advanced, John spent a few hours sitting on the steps of a church watching passersby and catching fragments of conversation as the crowd ebbed to and fro along the dusty thoroughfare.

Occasionally he heard enough to distinguish the topic under discussion. By and large they represented the cosmopolitan nature of the port. There was a heavily bearded, wide-shouldered man with a rolling gait suggesting his profession was that of a sailor, whose shorter, blond companion recommended a certain house on the other side of the sacred building as one where a lonely stranger could find all the comforts of home.

A man with a broad Germanic accent strolled by, singing a war-like song, beating time with a large fist, pausing to glare at a woman who accosted him. However, John noted, they went off together after a short conversation.

Two wine merchants stood at the foot of the steps bewailing their losses, with dark references to a certain captain whose transport fees were ruining their business and furthermore was not reliable in his promises, no doubt because, as one remarked to the other, it's empty barrels that sound the loudest.

A pale, stooped fellow carrying two tablets hurried by, perhaps a clerk in one of the warehouses around the harbor. Occasionally a priest left or entered the building behind John, sparing no glance for the nondescriptly dressed lounger on their steps. A man breathing wine fumes advised John to trust no one but his own person and his horse if he had one, and if he had one he was a rich man indeed, before sprawling in the shadow of the building and falling asleep in the dirt.

The streets and forums of a great city presented an epic richer than Homer could, for anyone who cared to sit quietly and keep his ears open. Not surprisingly, however, on this day, in this part of Greece, Theophilus did not appear in the story.

The inebriate snored and shifted fitfully, as the descending sun gradually pulled the shadow away from him. John got to his feet, walked to the docks, and purchased a meal of hot peas. After that he began his quest again, seeking out taverns and inns he had not visited the night before.

"Looking for that swine Theophilus, if that's his real name," he would announce in a loud voice on entering each establishment. "Owes me money. Ran off without paying. Him and his so-called iron shipments! Silk in them crates, I'll be bound. Anyone know him? There's a coin or two in the telling."

In one place a little man who looked and smelled as if he'd just crawled out of a hole in the scabrous wall sidled up to John. "Theophilus? I seen the man. Scar on his cheek, like you said."

John turned a hopeful look toward the fellow. "Heavy, black beard?"

"That's him!"

"Theophilus doesn't have a beard."

The man's whiskery face twitched. "The light was bad."

John reached for his blade. "Stop wasting my time."

The man vanished as quickly as a rat caught in the sudden light of a lamp.

The scene recurred with variations more than once.

And so the afternoon wore away. Shortly after sunset, John decided to return to his room for a short rest. The landlord's agent dozed at his post, hardly stirring as John passed. The lamp at the bottom of the stairs had sputtered out and John started up gingerly, clutching the wobbly handrail as his heels threatened to slide backward on the weirdly tilted steps.

He wasn't prepared for the figure that came flying out of the dimness, shrieking and clawing at his garment. Knocked backward, he managed to twist around so he slammed into the wall rather than falling down the stairs.

The hands stopped clawing and clung instead. A miasma of cheap wine and cheaper perfume enveloped him. "Demons take these stairs!" the woman said in a hoarse voice. "I lost my balance, sir!"

John grasped a pair of bony shoulders and pushed her gently away. In the glimmer of illumination from the corridor above he made out an elderly face framed in red hair. The same woman he'd briefly seen lying in the street when he'd first arrived.

"Your name is Maritza?"

What he could see of her face in the shadows registered surprise. "You are a sharp one, aren't you? I heard you were looking for that bastard Theophilus. I have information for a price. He has a scar here—" She indicated its location.

"A black beard too?"

Maritza gave a cawing laugh. "Beard? I doubt that miserable worm is man enough to grow a beard."

"Do you know where Theophilus lived?"

"Do I know where he lived? With me, sir. I'm his wife."

The residence she claimed to have shared with John's stepfather was a room in a tenement situated behind a looming building whose strong odor penetrated every corner and identified its trade as that of a tannery.

"We were married last year, or was it the year before?" she said, lighting a lamp set on the floor beside a rusted brazier. "I forget. Of course, he will deny it. In any event, what do you know about the swine?"

"I thought you were going to give me information, not the other way round?"

"Well, my personal charms are somewhat faded and I had to say something to get you here, didn't I? He's deserted me and I want to find him. He took some jewelry of mine."

John wondered if she were more interested in finding the man or her jewelry. "I see. But he hasn't deserted you, he—"

A flush of anger darkened her pallid face. "What do you mean? Do you know something I don't? Gone off with another woman is it, gave her my jewelry?"

"He has not deserted you or anyone else. He's dead."

"So you say."

"I do say. Believe me, Theophilus is dead. I saw his body myself."

She went silent. The set of her mouth made it obvious she was more angry that the man she claimed was her husband had managed to escape her wrath. "Didn't happen to have my jewelry on him when you found him, did he?"

John shook his head.

"You weren't really looking for him then?"

"Only for anything I can find out about him."

"Well, this is where he lived. That must be worth something."

John gazed pointedly around the room. Two chairs, a bed, a couple of battered chests, a table cluttered with bottles and jars of cosmetics. Whatever schemes Theophilus had taken part in couldn't have been very profitable. Unless he'd spent all his money on jewelry. "In the circumstances, I'd be happy to buy anything he left behind."

Maritza let loose a polyglot torrent of curses she must have learned from sailors. John recognized several that had traveled from Egypt where he had spent considerable time during his

youthful career as a mercenary. "Bastard keeps on cheating me
after he's dead. He left very little behind. There's a couple of
odds and ends, but I'm keeping them to pay for what he stole
off me. Oh, and a bit of parchment. He was always reading it
and swore it would make his fortune but I can't read so it's no
good to me." She stopped. Her eyes narrowed with suspicion.
"Could it be that what you're really after?"

John half closed his own eyes. The smell from the tannery
was making them water. "No. But it might be helpful to me,
worth money to you. Let me see it."

She rummaged in a chest and finally produced a grubby
sheet of parchment. Reluctantly she placed it in John's hand
and waited anxiously, as if she expected him to bolt off with it.

John carried it nearer to the lamp and read:

> *"My father on his deathbed told me in his youth he saw
> Corinth looted and razed at Alaric's command, and
> described deeds that should have been cloaked in merci-
> ful darkness seen on every street by the glare of burning
> buildings, and how he aided certain priests to flee from
> the bloody chaos, thereby learning they intended to place
> gold and silver sacred vessels, and such diverse holinesses
> as they had been able to rescue, into the care of she who
> wails her daughter, the unwilling bride, and thereafter
> make pact the burial place would remain secret until
> they could restore such glorious tributes to the church,
> and though he became separated from them by the grace
> of heaven he escaped capture, yet none with whom he
> fled returned, he believing they were caught and put to
> the sword or sold as slaves along with such inhabitants
> of Corinth as were not slaughtered, and although he
> had dug here and there in many places over the years
> after his return the sacred treasures remain hidden to
> this day, and he told me..."*

It appeared to be nothing more than a page from a history,
or considering the rather poor quality of the penmanship a copy

of such a page. Holding it closer to the light, he could discern traces of the erased writing over which the account of the sacking of Corinth had been penned.

"I thought it was nothing but nonsense, that the fool was fooling himself," Maritza said. "But perhaps I was wrong. If you are willing to buy, it is valuable."

John couldn't make out the words beneath the historical account but he could easily read the greed written on Maritza's face.

He showed her a handful of coins, of a denomination she rarely glimpsed. "This scrap is worth something to me, along with everything you know about what Theophilus was doing before he left."

Chapter Twenty-eight

Everything Maritza knew about Theophilus' activities before his disappearance turned out to amount to nothing. Or so she insisted. Even the emperor himself, pleading from a gold nomisma, could not jar any memories loose.

"'Man's work' is all he ever told me. We kept our noses out of each other's business."

"You must have known he was a thief," John insisted.

"I do now," was her sharp reply.

John had put the gold coin back in his pouch and left, telling her the emperor would be happy to see her again if she suddenly recalled anything. He wasn't surprised Theophilus had kept her in the dark about his schemes. Her sort might easily have betrayed him to the authorities for less than John had paid her already.

Walking back to his lodgings he tried not to think about his mother being married to a man who would marry the woman he had just interviewed.

Although Maritza had told him very little, he hoped the scrap of parchment would have something to say to him—or rather the faint writing he could see beneath the historical note would. The message about the iron shipment had been hidden under words engraved in the tablet's wax. Perhaps Theophilus had regularly employed such concealment.

John passed through light spilling from the door of a tavern. He had decided against further investigations tonight. Word about the man looking for Theophilus had obviously spread, as evidenced by Maritza's approaching him.

This time John approached the dim stairway at his lodgings with caution. He didn't want to fall prey to a real attack. As always the steps creaked loudly enough to drown out any sound made by someone lying in wait in the shadows above. He arrived at the upper hallway unscathed and pushed open the warped door to his room, which, as with most of the doors in the place, hung partly ajar in its crooked frame.

The man seated on John's bed gestured for him to come in with a wave of the long-bladed knife in his hand. "Please shut the door quietly behind you. We don't want to disturb the other guests, do we?"

"You're the fellow on the church steps who told me to trust no one except myself and my horse," John said.

"I'm glad you remembered me. I forgot to add one should also trust a man with a drawn blade."

"You were not so intoxicated or sleepy as you appeared, it seems."

"No one pays much attention to public drunkards."

The man was right, John thought ruefully. Now he noticed that aside from apparently being nothing more than a pathetic fellow reeling about in a haze of wine fumes, the speaker was a big, solidly built man in early middle age, with close cropped hair and enough scars showing on his face and the backs of his hands to indicate an intimate knowledge of the weapon he displayed.

"I've been keeping an eye on you," the man went on. "You claim to know Theophilus, which I wouldn't have believed except that I saw you leaving Maritza's room."

But he had not, seemingly, seen her going into John's lodgings or John and her leaving.

"Do you know where the bastard is?"

"You don't think I believe your story, do you? You're no petty thief. I don't know what you are, or who you are, but a simple thief? No."

"Why don't you try asking who I am?"

"Because you won't tell me the truth, any more than I would tell who I am."

John was still standing in front of the closed door. Could he yank it open and escape downstairs before the man with the knife could leap off the bed? Could he get his own weapon out in time to defend himself?

The long blade waggled at him. "Away from the door, friend. Have a seat."

John lowered himself onto the indicated stool.

The blade pointed at him from the bed, not much more than an arms-breadth away. "Good. Now we are face to face. Let's just call ourselves businessmen."

"And our business is…what?"

"According to you, it is iron."

"That's right. Theophilus hasn't paid me for the assistance I gave him with his last shipment." John repeated what he had been proclaiming in various taverns. "But then you said you didn't believe I was a petty thief, so why would you believe I am telling the truth?"

"I don't believe you're a petty thief, but I might entertain the idea that you are involved in the iron trade, and as far as the matter of Theophilus cheating you—well, I would take that as a given. Which shipment was it?"

John related the details so far as he knew them, watching the other's face. "Theophilus cheated you too, didn't he? Being cheated is the price of working with him!"

The blade plunged into John's bedding and ripped across it. Cloth tore with a high thin noise. "Wait until I find the swine! I've been waiting for him to get back for over a week. If he's taken flight with my share I'll be joining you in your search with the intention of slipping sharp metal, and not necessarily iron, between his ribs."

"I could use a man who enjoys using a knife," John said. "As for this iron…I'm not so much interested in the money as the principle. We businessmen need to maintain certain standards. What I want is to see the bastard brought to justice. If you can take care of that, you can have whatever money you can carve out of him, and I'll throw in something for good measure."

"You'll admit to being more than a thief? But what of it? You don't know where the swine went to any more than I do."

"I have contacts in many fields of commerce, only I'm not sure who to ask. These are busy men, you understand. They don't like being disturbed over nothing. So one of the things I want to know is what else was Theophilus involved in, besides this iron business?"

The man on the bed studied his knife and smiled faintly, as if he were imagining what it would look like in Theophilus' throat. "Oh, he was a very busy man. Anything you could smuggle, he smuggled. Iron, silks, counterfeit coins, forged religious relics."

"And you assisted him?"

"I'm not saying any more."

"Good, because I don't work with men with loose lips. I will make further inquiries. Come back in a few days."

When the stranger had gone, John sat on the edge of the bed and ran his finger along the rent in the fabric. Mithra! He'd just more or less arranged to have his own stepfather killed as far as his visitor was concerned.

Did it matter that his stepfather was already dead?

Chapter Twenty-nine

The flames of hell snaked up Peter's legs, reached his arms, and ran along the flesh, gobbling it as if it were parchment.

"Fire, Peter! Wake up!"

He became aware his arm was being shaken. By Hypatia.

He managed to get his eyes open and lifted himself up on one elbow in time to see her jump out of bed, drag on her tunic, and run into the courtyard.

Dazed and grumbling, he followed as fast as he could. He was too old for such terrible awakenings.

As he emerged, blinking, into what should have been darkness, he saw a red glow dancing across the buildings surrounding the courtyard. A dozen or more unfamiliar men shouted oaths and abuse at Hypatia, waving swords and spears, and promising a swift end to anyone who interfered with them. Several carried torches. They had set fire to straw piled against the workers' quarters. Laborers began to emerge, half-asleep, confused and terrified. Some were driven back and knocked down by the arsonists.

It would only take a rising wind to set the entire collection of buildings ablaze.

Hypatia, fists clenched, looked ready to dash straight at the vandals. Peter rushed to restrain her. "Stay away from them! You're not even armed!" The thought of Hypatia's danger brought another fear into Peter's mind. "The mistress? Have you seen her? What can she do with the master away?"

A man whose features were thrown into relief by the fire's flickering shadows grinned demonically as he approached. "Don't worry, old man. No doubt her pagan god will take care of her. If not, all it will take is another sacrifice in that ruined temple. Now…" his ugly gaze wandered over Hypatia. "Since the owner's wife is hiding, this one will have to do. Grab her!"

Several followers started forward.

Peter pushed Hypatia behind him. "Run!"

Too late. Hypatia was struggling in the grasp of the ring-leader. Desperately but ineffectually Peter tried to pull her back to his side.

"I've got the woman!" the ruffian shouted and dragged her toward the gateway. Then hesitated. A look of confusion crossed his face. Then he bellowed in pain.

As if by sorcery an arrow had appeared in his shoulder.

He looked around the courtyard furiously, cursing.

Another arrow hissed past. The man knocked Peter down and ordered the others to retreat.

Peter staggered to his feet, heart pounding. He had no idea where the arrows had come from. Nor did he care. They might as well have been thrown down from heaven itself. All Peter could think of was Hypatia's safety.

He stumbled out of the gate into the darkness.

Just in time to see Philip arriving at a run and Hypatia standing alone, steadying herself against the outside wall.

"Sent my men after the villains," he shouted. "As soon as they saw us coming they split up. I'm going after the ringleader."

Peter watched him race off. He felt Hypatia's hand on his arm and an overwhelming sense of shame. What use had he been to her when she needed help?

"I'm going to help him."

"Oh, Peter! Don't be foolish!"

He pulled away from her grasp and forced himself to run on legs that felt as unsteady as a ninety-year-old's, or for that matter a two-year-old's. As soon as he was out of Hypatia's sight he slowed, gasping, his chest feeling as if it was on fire.

Glancing back over the nearest hill he could see only a sullen glow in the sky. Without interference, the estate laborers would be able to douse the flames with water from the fishpond.

Dizziness made him bend over, hands on knees. His mouth was so dry he could barely swallow and every breath hurt. He'd shown Hypatia he was eager to assist her young admirer. Perhaps now he should just sit down and rest.

But no. He had a task and he would do it. The former military man asserted himself and he straightened up and marched on across the dark, uneven ground, scuffling and stumbling. The leg he had injured falling into the pit protested at inclines too slight for him to make out.

As he hobbled past the temple, he spotted movement. Ignoring the jagged pains in his leg, he got down on hands and knees to crawl closer without exposing his silhouette against the sky. The master would be proud of him recalling that maneuver from his military days.

If only the master hadn't been gone tonight.

Straining his eyes, he had to get very close to the ruined building before he recognized the leader of the arsonists, standing at the corner of the temple, scanning the landscape. How had he eluded Philip? Or—the idea struck him like a blade to the back—perhaps he hadn't. Perhaps Philip had caught up to him and…

Better not to think about that. Peter clung to the ground, the smell of earth filling his nostrils. He felt himself trembling uncontrollably.

He had expected to catch up to Philip after Philip had caught up to the leader of the mob. At least Peter would be able to say he'd been on hand for the capture, which shouldn't have given Philip much difficulty, considering the arrow in his opponent's shoulder. Running the man down, by himself, unarmed as he was, hadn't been in his plans at all.

What he needed to do was slip away and notify whomever he could find. He began to turn, keeping low. His calf cramped. The pain was so sudden and excruciating he cried out involuntarily.

Peter tried to rise but before he could get back on his feet a face loomed over him, a grinning moon, and a sword appeared, poised for a killing blow.

However, it did not descend in a powerful arc. Instead it dropped sideways harmlessly, as its owner crumpled to the ground, revealing behind him a figure holding a jagged rock.

"Bastard," remarked Peter's savior in a casual manner, tossing down the stone, one side of which was dark with blood. "You're lucky the arrow got him in his sword arm or he'd probably have split your skull before I cracked his."

Chapter Thirty

"I should have gone after Peter, mistress." Hypatia paced across the kitchen and peered out the doorway yet again. The estate workers continued to haul buckets of water from the fishpond to pour on smoldering straw. Not much damage had been done. The house and surrounding buildings were safe. Was Peter? "He made me so angry, running off like a stupid boy, and I was so upset already. I didn't know what to do."

"What could you have done for him? Unarmed? As like as not you'd have run into one of the arsonists." Cornelia came to stand beside her and survey the damage. There was little to see since the flames had died down. The courtyard had fallen back into night. Plumes of pale smoke billowed up into the darker sky. "Don't worry. I'm sure Philip caught up with the ringleader. The fellow wasn't in any shape to put up much of a fight. Sit down for a while."

Reluctantly Hypatia seated herself beside the table on which a hunting bow and a handful of arrows lay. "I know hunting is popular with the aristocrats at the emperor's court but I didn't realize you had taken part, mistress," she observed.

"Oh, I didn't learn to use a bow in the imperial parks. The troupe I traveled with had an archer, a Persian by birth, whose specialty was a display of marksmanship. Called himself Xerxes. I learned enough of the art to play Artemis from time to time, when I wasn't leaping from bulls."

Hypatia had never been sure whether the mistress intended to be taken seriously when she spoke of her days as a performer. Was it a jest, or had she really entertained crowds in dusty city squares with reenactments of the lost art of Cretan bull leaping? Well, the late empress had worked as a circus performer in her youth, and her performances had been of a much lower sort. "The arsonists must have thought they were under siege when arrows started raining down from who knows where."

"The second-floor windows offer a perfect shot at anyone in the courtyard. And I've never forgotten my skill."

"I'm grateful you remembered."

"Barely remembered. Xerxes would have been greatly displeased with me. I meant to put the arrow in that rogue's ear."

There was a commotion in the courtyard. Philip came in, closely followed by Peter and a stranger in a dirt-encrusted tunic.

Hypatia started toward Peter. Philip stepped in front of her, grasping her shoulders. "Thank heavens you're safe," he whispered, then in a louder tone, addressed Cornelia. "Mistress, we captured the ringleader and brought him back. I've ordered him bound. The City Defender will have a nice neat package waiting when he gets here. My men will be back soon with the rest, I'm certain."

Hypatia removed Philip's hands from her shoulders, shrugged out of his grasp, and went and put her arms around Peter. "Don't run off like that again, Peter. I was afraid for your safety."

"You shouldn't have been. You keep forgetting I have military experience. I caught up with the villain. Julius here gave me some help. I insisted he have a cup of wine and something to eat."

"It's fortunate I found you when I did," Philip said.

"Yes," Peter shot back. "Our prisoner was getting heavy to carry."

The dirty stranger, Julius, stood silent, looking uneasy.

Cornelia frowned at the man. "Aren't you one of the men kept as slaves? I've seen you working in the fields."

"Yes, mistress. I have been staying nearby since the master freed us. Not to sound ungrateful, but it is one thing to tell a man that he free and another to make that freedom legal."

"Indeed. The documents are being drawn up in Megara and the master will sign them as soon as he returns. Not that we really expected any of you to come back for them." She looked him up and down. "But why are you covered in dirt? Did you also fight?"

"No, mistress."

Philip broke in. "And why were you on the estate in the middle of the night in the first place?"

Hypatia flared up. "Philip! What sort of question is that, considering what he's just done for us?"

"Why are you so quick to trust him, when you know the whole city's against you?" Philip snapped back. "He was obviously up to no good and now he's trying to protect himself."

"I'm sorry, Julius," said Cornelia, "but Philip is right. No matter how helpful you've been I really must ask you to explain why you were on the estate, and covered with dirt no less, at this time of night."

"And the answer had better be convincing," Philip added, "because the City Defender will be here very soon and he can take you back to Megara along with the other wrongdoers."

Julius shifted his feet, started to brush dried earth from his clothes, and stopped when he realized all he was doing was making the kitchen floor dirty. "Mistress, freedom is more valuable than wealth, so I will answer truthfully. I returned to the temple, secretly, to look for the valuables buried there. The overseer Diocles ordered us to dig there day after day. He claimed it was to prepare for reconstruction work, but we all knew better. Everyone's been talking about the treasure from Corinth, and he kept warning us to dig carefully, in case we happened on anything of historical value."

Cornelia shook her head. "Is there anyone in Megara who isn't busy hating us or searching for riches? Goddess help us!"

Hypatia knew the mistress was not addressing Demeter. Whether the goddess could make this city full of Christians stop hating them, she couldn't say. But at least Peter was safe and the arsonists would be brought to justice.

Chapter Thirty-one

"It was because of the demons, sir! Released swarms of demons, they did, what with all their digging round that pagan temple! Should have been destroyed a long time ago, if you ask me."

The City Defender glared at the captured arsonist, a man named James. "Demons, is it? Explain yourself."

"Sir, I am a law-abiding seller of fish. Well-known for the excellence of my wares, landed fresh each day. Don't sell anything over a day old. Work hard, pay my taxes, attend church faithfully, and—"

"Yes, yes, a pillar of the community. But what has this to do with your criminal behavior last night?"

John, newly returned from Lechaion, was present as injured party as the City Defender conducted an arraignment interview. The arsonist was a rough-looking man, his upper arm and shoulder wrapped in bandages. The door of the whitewashed room stood open, allowing the mixed odors of the city to enter on the rectangle of strong sunlight lying across a mosaic floor depicting a pastoral scene.

But not enough sunlight to dispel the darkness of Megaran justice unfolding before him, John thought.

"And then there was those unspeakable rites they was doing in that ruin," the seller of fish continued. "Orgies, sir. Blood. Torture. Bound to free demons. And as we all know, they can take over a man, hook their sharpened claws into our souls, cause us to do terrible things we would not dream of, could not dream of, as sober and responsible citizens."

The man appeared ready to burst into tears at the thought of what acts he might be capable of doing while in his possessed state.

"And so those others with you, companions you say you cannot identify, were all possessed by demons, leading to the crimes committed last night?"

The accused man nodded violently. "And my wife is worried about what I might do next. What if I get up at night and murder everyone in their beds? What if I start selling fish I know to be unfit to eat? What if I suddenly attack Halmus, who has done so much for Megara?"

The City Defender raised his hand for silence. "So your defense boils down to the fact you and your fellow conspirators were possessed by demons forcing you to set fire to this man's property and assault his servant?"

The fish seller nodded.

"I see," the City Defender went on. "I have heard this defense before and there is much in what you say. Given your sterling character, I find it to be acceptable. I am accepting it on condition you consult your church on appropriate ways to free yourself of the demon possessing you. In addition I order you to make a large donation to the church. No compensation is due to the owner of the property under the circumstances. If he can collect it from demons, he is free to do so. You may go."

The seller of fish bowed, mumbled his gratitude, and scuttled away.

John hid his consternation.

"Now," said the City Defender, "about the charges levied against you."

"Charges against me? For raising demons?"

"For illegal weapons. Specifically a bow and arrows. As you are aware, private individuals are forbidden from making or purchasing weapons, including bows and arrows."

"They are also banned from purchasing spears and swords, yet the arsonists had both."

"This is the first I have heard about it. Do you have proof? You could see James was wounded. Do you have an explanation?"

"Yes. You may examine the bow if you wish. You will see it was not privately manufactured but rather bears the imperial seal from the armory at the Great Palace. Nor was it purchased illegally. Justinian authorized Senator Vinius to hunt with it in the parks beyond the city walls. It is a common aristocratic pastime. The senator must have brought the bow to Megara in case he wanted to hunt here. We found it in his residence."

The City Defender seemed to consider this. "I see. I will allow it to pass. I have noted that your watchmen have been equipped quite legally."

"Thank you." John's tone was acerbic. "Before I leave, Georgios, I wish to consult you on the matter of my property."

The City Defender frowned. "There will be no compensation, if that is what you wish to argue about. A seller of fish has fewer financial resources than a man who owns an estate, and in this instance he was obviously not responsible for his behavior."

"The man who owns an estate, in this instance, is twice injured. Once by those who sought to burn his house down and then again by the man who purports to administer justice. But in fact the matter on which I wished to talk to you relates to records applying to my property. I wish to consult them."

Georgios shrugged. "It is not possible, I am afraid. Many of our land records were destroyed some years back in a fire. Ironic, is it not? However, in that particular case the fire followed an earthquake."

"An earthquake, as I recall, not long after Justinian ordered more thorough audits of such records, not to mention the resulting fire offered a convenient way to dispose of incriminating documentation," John pointed out.

"But why wait for a fire or earthquake? It would be simple enough to extract documents from the archives or replace them with forgeries. We have had some difficulties over land holdings since that fire, but, after all, earthquakes respect nobody, not even emperors. Who knows what evidence of malfeasance might have been destroyed?"

Chapter Thirty-two

Helen's face clouded briefly as she opened the door to John. Then she smiled and welcomed him. "You may have a difficult time getting Leonidas' attention. When he's engrossed in one of his models well…"

Her husband sat hunched over the table. A miniature tower, a cylindrical construction circled by a rising stairway, stood partly finished, surrounded by thin curls of wood. "Can you guess what this is meant to be?" He pointed a small, thin-bladed knife at the model.

John examined the construction briefly. "A very fair rendering of the Tower of Babel?"

Leonidas smiled broadly, obviously pleased. "That's right. I've begun working on a series of important buildings from the scriptures. Many interesting structures, to say the least. Solomon's palace will present a real challenge. It'll take a vast amount of gilding for a start. And here is the wine."

Helen set cups and a wine jug on the table. "Other men boast of their large houses and vast estates. But none have anything like the vast holdings of my husband here, even if they are just small re-creations. Still, so long as he is happy why complain?" She gave Leonidas a fond smile, patted him on his shoulder, and disappeared into the kitchen.

"Of course you will stay for a meal?" Leonidas said, putting down his knife and pouring wine. "I heard about the fire. Helen tells me the wag-tongues in the marketplace have it only one of the culprits was caught."

John confirmed the truth of the rumor, adding he had just come from seeing the seller of fish released and that no compensation had been ordered by the City Defender.

Leonidas swore and gulped down a mouthful of wine. "May those demons bite his backside and that of the seller of fish also! I wish I could do more than just offer sympathy, John. If there is anything I could do…?"

"I think you can assist me. I spoke to the City Defender concerning the land records for my estate and learned they had been lost in a fire sometime since. You work in the tax office and so would know, is it true records were destroyed by fire after an earthquake?"

"You must think Megara is a city swarming with arsonists, but in fact it is true many records did vanish at that time. I suspect officials, who better remain nameless, used the disaster as a pretext to destroy documents they would prefer not to exist, although I have also heard others claim citizens actually set the records office on fire to escape unpaid taxes."

John pointed out that the administration in Constantinople kept records for tax collection, but he could hardly travel there to consult them personally, and as for any remaining in Megara, it seemed to him if he requested from the City Defender particular records he did not wish John to have, they would doubtless be among those said to have been destroyed. "But what if someone else, someone whose work involved taxes, so had every right to scrutinize the records, were to quietly consult them?"

"You are asking me to copy anything I can find relating to your estate? But why, John? Is there some question of ownership?"

"No. At least I don't think so. However, I am beginning to fear the authorities will use any excuse to get rid of me, and what easier way than administratively, by confiscating the estate for non payment of taxes?"

"Yes, you're right. There are endless ways tax assessments and payments can be found to be in error. Occasionally the mistakes are actually honest ones. Certainly, I'll look into this."

John could see his old friend's gaze return to the tower and left shortly thereafter with a plea of business needing attention.

Leonidas picked up his knife and gently poked at his creation. "The problem with this is that I can't be certain where to stop," he told himself. "It never reached heaven, but how close did it come, and how high is heaven? I'm assuming for this little tower heaven is the ceiling. Still, one prefers to see a clear end to a thing."

It was a sentiment with which John would have agreed.

After John left, Helen came to the table where Leonidas was working. Instead of taking away the cups and jug she sat down next to him and put a hand on his wrist, stopping the motion of the knife with which he was paring a section of stairway.

"Is it wise, do you think, to be searching through tax records?"

"Why wouldn't I do John a favor? He's an old friend."

"Which is bad enough as it is."

Leonidas set the knife down. "What do you mean?"

"You know what I mean, Leonidas. It isn't good to have a friend everyone hates."

"He's not hated by me. Or you. Is he?"

"Oh, Leonidas. You're a good man. Too good. What if it's discovered you've been snooping through city records on John's behalf? People may think you're involved."

"Involved with what?"

Helen gave him a cross look. "With whatever they're involved with out on that estate."

"But they aren't involved with anything."

"Does it matter whether they are or not? It's what people will think, what the City Defender thinks. We have a nice life here. A little home that suits us. Our son has taken up an admirable calling. We're comfortable. We're happy. Why risk ruining everything?"

Leonidas shut his eyes as if that might make the discussion go away. "If I supposed there was any real risk—"

"Of course there's a risk." Helen's voice grew sharp. "John isn't the boy you knew. He's a former Lord Chamberlain to the emperor. Men of his sort are like the wind from the north, they bring storms with them."

"It seems to me trouble was already waiting here in Megara for him."

"He chose to be ambitious. He wanted wealth and power. He decided to take the risks. We didn't travel that path, Leonidas. We've been content with our quiet life."

Leonidas squeezed her hand, bent, and kissed her forehead lightly. "Please don't worry. I won't do anything to draw attention to myself. No harm will come to us, I promise."

Peter completed chopping vegetables for the evening meal and left Hypatia in the kitchen hanging up bundles of herbs to dry. She was safe for the time being. Safe from arsonists and kidnappers and stone-throwing mobs. And safe from temptation. Perhaps.

He had thought the two of them could be happy with a simple life. But he had served the master long enough to have learned that the master's life, and the lives of those around him, would never be simple.

As Peter entered the rooms he and Hypatia shared with two felines he would prefer to be elsewhere, he saw the large black cat sitting on a stool watching disdainfully as its smaller, mottled brown companion, batted something around the floor.

"No! No!" Peter shouted. "Wretched creatures!" First they brought fleas in, now it was larger vermin. He looked around for the broom to sweep it out.

The small cat knocked its prey against a table leg, leapt back, hissing, then crouched and crawled forward warily.

Not seeing the broom he sought, Peter used his foot to move the cat aside, gently for Hypatia's sake, and leaned over, putting a hand on the table to steady himself. "What did you drag in, you nasty beast?"

It was the size and color of a large rat. Peter had to crouch down almost to the floor before he brought the thing into focus.

There were too many legs for a rat. And rats didn't have long tails with stingers at the end.

It was the biggest scorpion he'd ever seen.

He tried to jump up and out of the way, but lost his balance. Twisting, grabbing at the table, he realized he was about to come right down on the poisonous horror.

His knee hit the curled tail.

It disintegrated under his weight, bits of mud skittering across the floor, sending both cats to flight.

It was only one of Hypatia's protective charms. It had been some time since she'd made any. Peter had nearly forgotten about them.

He hobbled into the bedroom and sat on the edge of the bed, noting another clay scorpion on the chest against the wall, directly below the simple wooden cross he had hung there.

The monk Stephen had suggested he and Hypatia pray together. That would be difficult. Long ago, Peter had tried to convince Hypatia she should convert to Christianity, to give up worshiping her Egyptian deities. He knew it was better not to attempt it again.

And what difference did it make what a person chose to call the God of All? Or whether, like the master and mistress and Hypatia, they called Him by different names? It was simply what a person was born into, like the language they spoke, and who would condemn anyone for having been born speaking Coptic rather than Greek?

Peter did not pride himself on being a theologian, but it struck him as simple enough. He read the scriptures and he could think and ponder such matters. He didn't need anyone to explain such matters to him.

So whatever their problems, they would not pray together. Hypatia prayed to the gods of Egypt and constructed charms of clay. Peter prayed to the Lord and read verses from the psalms.

Peter's prayers had one advantage. The cats couldn't stalk them and frighten him half to death by doing so.

Chapter Thirty-three

John shrugged as he listened to the oaths Cornelia lavished on the heads of the City Defender and seller of fish.

They were an unwelcome contrast to the peaceful olive grove he had purposely sought out after his frustrating trip into Megara. He had never quite become used to the remarkable repertoire of curses Cornelia had learned during her years on the road.

"So it was all our own fault," she concluded. "We forced those poor souls to attempt to burn down our home. I'm surprised Georgios didn't fine us for releasing demons. And I thought Constantinople was corrupt."

"Nowhere is free from corruption, no matter how small. In the meanest village you'll find men every bit as corrupt as any at the emperor's court, only fewer of them, with less wealth and power within their greedy reach."

"And not dressed in silks," Cornelia said.

John gave her a questioning look, then recalled he had said something similar to her before and probably more than once. "A sign of age. I'm repeating myself."

"Perhaps it bears repeating. What kind of place have we come to?"

John had recounted his experiences at Corinth's port during their walk to the grove. They took a long, circuitous stroll, purposefully avoiding the ruined temple. Their destination grew on the part of the estate that had once been his family's farm.

The grove looked much as he remembered it, scattered clusters of gnarled trees. It was obvious they had not received much care.

John scowled in disapproval. "Harvest time is fast approaching and look at them! My father—my real father—kept these trees well pruned,"

He made his way across the small grove. There were larger olive groves elsewhere on the land he now owned, planted on a scale to serve an estate rather than a farming family. He stopped at an enormously wide-boled tree, a gnarled patriarch with branches twisting out above chest level.

"You see how there's a natural nest up there? My father used to lift me up and I'd sit and watch during the harvest. It was a memorable day when I was able to climb up myself."

Cornelia ran a hand along the bark. "Going by its size, it must be very old."

"My friends and I convinced each other it was thousands of years old. There were broken branches at the top and Alexis claimed they'd been clipped off by Noah's ark sailing over it."

"But a grain of truth perhaps? After all, olive trees can live for centuries."

"Several in the grove at Plato's Academy were ancient too. Plato taught in their shade."

Cornelia was silent but John could read her puzzled expression.

In truth he had been drawn here by the memory of the grove, which had surfaced suddenly for no apparent reason on his way back from the city. Had his unaccustomed feeling of helplessness during the City Defender's ridiculous hearing reminded him of being a toddler, lifted up into the tree by strong hands? Later in his childhood, when he could reach the nest himself, it had been a secret place where he came to think and observe the world. He had not thought of the secret places of his boyhood for many years.

He had an urge to climb back into his old perch. He resisted. What a sight that would make!

"You were telling me you asked Leonidas to look into the tax records," Cornelia prompted.

"Yes. I'm going to visit him tomorrow evening to see what he discovers, if anything."

"Surely Anatolius investigated very carefully? I would have thought we could be certain there are no outstanding amounts to be paid."

"I agree, but in addition I was hoping there might be something to assist me in finding my way out of the labyrinth we have been thrust into."

"When you arrived back from Lechaion you told me you thought you'd located a thread there, before I persuaded you it wasn't the time to discuss murder."

"That's right. And you were right. It was much too late to speak of murder."

John felt he had lost an entire day. His further inquiries following his interview with Maritza and the informer with the knife had yielded no new possibilities for investigation. He had not reached home until well after dark, only to be greeted with the story of the attack on the house and the news that the City Defender had delayed the arsonist's arraignment until that morning, to give John the chance to attend as the owner of the damaged property.

John pointed out that Georgios had made certain the travesty of a hearing was technically fair. "Unfortunately," he continued, "the thread I found in Lechaion involved my stepfather's doings, so I disliked touching it. I haven't had an opportunity to examine the mysterious scrap of parchment yet. It's going to take some care and good light."

"It's that difficult to make out?"

"Not the writing on top, but what's underneath. Theophilus or someone associated with him hid that message about the iron shipment under the writing on the wax. The same general method may have been used."

"What are the words you can read about?"

"That legend I related to you. The usual nonsense. Alexis, who studies that sort of thing, told me he had never seen any reliable accounts."

Cornelia looked thoughtful. "Are you sure it's nonsense? Julius, one of the slaves you freed, told me that Diocles had the slaves digging around the temple."

"Preparing to repair the foundation."

"Julius claimed that was a pretext. The slaves knew very well Diocles was hoping they would find valuables."

"This fantasy is spreading through Megara like a plague. Everyone's infected." John let his gaze climb up through the branches of the olive tree. "And yet...the priests passed what they rescued into the care of she who wails her daughter, the unwilling bride."

Cornelia gave him a questioning look.

"It's part of what is visible on Theophilus' document," John explained. "'She who wails her daughter' would be Demeter, whose daughter Persephone was kidnapped by Hades."

"So Theophilus must have thought the treasure was buried at the temple of Demeter on the estate?"

"He might have, but Demeter was popular in this area. There must be hundreds of ancient shrines and places associated with her around here. I believe it explains how he happened to be at the temple when he was killed."

"Do you suppose Theophilus told Diocles about the possibility of the cache being buried at our temple?"

"I wouldn't be surprised. Theophilus was involved in all manner of activities."

"You think it likely Theophilus was killed in connection with the illicit business dealings you learned about while you were away?"

"It's a risk criminals always take." He saw the doubt in her face. "I'm certain I wasn't the target, Cornelia. I know you're worried about that."

"He was killed at the temple on your estate. Why here? Why not in Lechaion?"

"His murderer may well live locally. It seems likely Theophilus had dealings in Megara. Until we arrived, the ruined temple would have made a good meeting place, isolated as it is, and considering how little attention Diocles paid to what was happening on the estate. A meeting might have been scheduled weeks ago, with no time to notify anyone else concerned of our suddenly taking up residence. Fellow criminals don't necessarily want to tell each other where they live."

Cornelia still looked displeased. "I can tell you've been thinking about the situation at length, but I still can't help wondering if the murderer was trying to harm you. Even if he didn't mistake Theophilus for you, he may have killed him on your land to cast suspicion on you, which, I may add, he's clearly accomplished."

"Suspicion is one thing, but—"

"Suspicion may be all that's necessary, given the quality of justice you've just witnessed in Megara, John!"

She was right, which was one reason John disliked the feeling of having lost a day. He needed to locate the culprit while he still had a chance. "Theophilus was involved in smuggling. It's not like simple robbery. Quite a number of people have to cooperate and those deals often fall apart for one reason or another. I have to make inquiries locally."

"You mentioned counterfeiting. There's a blacksmith on the estate not far from where we are, nor the temple ruins for that matter."

John had hoped she wouldn't have realized Petrus, living so close by, was a natural suspect. "Let's not leap to conclusions. There are other blacksmiths in Megara and an endless variety of goods to smuggle. Another possibility is the man responsible might not be from the area. He might live in Lechaion too, but arranged to kill Theophilus away from the scene of their work together, so as to attract less attention there."

"Illegal activities, murderers on the loose, townspeople possessed by demons! Not the quiet country life we envisioned, is it?"

"Cornelia…"

She held her arms out. "Don't say anything John. Help me up into this tree so I can see the view of the world you had as a boy."

Chapter Thirty-four

Rumors went around the marketplace, a slight breeze turning up the undersides of leaves before the storm broke.

"The new estate owner is visiting Megara again!"

"It's rumored he's been making human sacrifices!"

"The City Defender suspects him of murder!"

"Why is he allowed to go free?"

Word of his arrival preceded him. Ears trained to hear picked up half-whispered conversations. Practiced eyes found the tall, slender figure as he skirted the marketplace.

He went down several side streets. The observer was nothing more than another evening shadow.

This time the quarry did not cut down an alley.

The observer saw John go up the stairs to the door of a modest dwelling in a three-story building faced in stucco.

Leonidas opened the door. "John, I wanted to tell you before you came in, my wife, well, she—"

"She does not wish you to be associated with a dangerous pariah like myself."

Leonidas looked embarrassed. "I know she's being foolish."

"Not at all. It is dangerous. She is wise to be cautious."

"I'm sorry, John. I am happy to help an old friend, but women worry and she is my wife. You understand...."

"I shall make this visit as brief as possible."

They went inside. Helena could be heard in the kitchen. She did not bring wine. John observed the Tower of Babel had risen two or three stories since his last visit.

Leonidas brought him several sheets covered with numbers and notations. "I've copied the tax records for you. I apologize for the writing. I'm no scribe! But as you'll see, everything is in order."

"Thank you, Leonidas. No question of missing entries or alterations then?"

"No, at least not this morning. While I was consulting the documents, I learned your estate was owned for a long time by an absentee senatorial family. It seems this family has, over many years, bought up adjacent land whenever it became available. It has never been productive and I have no notion why they would wish to own it."

"Yes, it belonged to Senator Vinius. He lived in Constantinople."

"I imagine, given the over-crowding in the capital, owning a large area of open land might be attractive. Perhaps he'd planned to retire here?"

"Or he was just given bad advice when seeking to buy land."

John could sense his friend's unease, so much different than his first visit when it had seemed it might be easy to slip back into their old camaraderie.

As John turned to leave, Helena emerged from the kitchen. Leonidas raised a warning hand but she ignored him.

"John," she said, "my husband and I have disagreed about this but my feeling is it's only right you should know what happened with your mother. Since Leonidas is reluctant to tell you, I shall."

"I was just going," John told her. "I won't bother you again until the trouble has passed."

"Oh, that's a fine thing to hear! You're more interested in your tax records than your mother!"

Leonidas was appalled. "Helen, please…"

"A man ought to know about his family," she said. "Even if he doesn't want to know. If a man wants to avoid his past he shouldn't come around disturbing friends from his past."

"She's right," John said, mostly to soothe Leonidas and partly because he could see no graceful way to escape whatever revelations Helen intended to impart.

Leonidas cast an apologetic glance at John, a silent plea asking what he could do in the face of her determination to speak.

"Anyway, everyone in Megara knows about her. Why shouldn't her son?" Helen continued.

"If that's true I'd find out soon enough," John said, resigned to hearing what would probably turn out to be a farrago of rumors. "What is it everybody knows about my mother?"

"Well, late in life, Sophia became extremely religious. If it had just been increased church attendance no one would have taken any notice, but it got to the point where she would wander around the city and preach on the street. She held religious discussions with Halmus, shouting up to him when he was perched on his column. Much of what she spoke about was repentance and the life to come."

John bit back a denial. He remembered his mother as quiet and self-effacing. A down-to-earth woman and certainly not a brazen religious zealot. Seeking out public attention would have been the last thing she would have done. But then, what did he know about her later life?

Helen seemed to sense what John was thinking. "We were all shocked, John. It wasn't like her at all. Eventually it became obvious she was…unwell. Age affects some people like that. Of course, it was dangerous for an older woman to walk the streets alone at night, and more than once your stepfather had to come into Megara to take her home. After a while she no longer appeared in town and eventually she died."

"I see."

"Do you? Do you imagine people here had forgotten the poor woman had a son? Why is her son not helping, they asked."

"Helen," snapped Leonidas. "Sophia had a husband to help her."

"We all know what sort of help he was," she shot back. "According to what we heard, Theophilus began to wager large sums, got deeply into debt, and sold the farm. Of course, he had inherited it as Sophia's husband. Then he vanished, leaving his creditors empty-handed. Those tax records won't have anything to say about that."

"No, they wouldn't," John agreed. "But knowing that may shed some light on Theophilus' death." He hoped his comment would make Leonidas feel better about his wife's outburst.

Helen had run out of disclosures. Did she regret having forced the information on him? "I am sorry, John. It is hard to lose a parent."

Leonidas showed him to the door. "It was all a long time ago. I'm happy you were able to buy your childhood home back, John. It must have meant a lot to you to be in a position to be able to do so."

Chapter Thirty-five

Leaving Leonidas' house, John wondered if his friend recognized the irony of that parting comment. John had been in a position to buy his childhood home, but he had returned only because he had been removed from his position at Justinian's court.

It had not been a pleasant homecoming so far.

As if John wanted to reflect on his financial good fortune, Halmus stood atop his pillar, silhouetted against a red sky fading to gray, fulminating against the love of money.

"Love of money is a peril to your immortal soul!" he boomed, sounding louder in the twilight than under the glare of the midday sun. "Instead of leading godly lives, such love leads sinners to covet and steal their neighbor's goods, wagering in the hopes of increasing their hoarded sums, the bribing of officials to pretend not to see when discovered committing crimes, the worm of avarice gnawing at their vitals, never letting a man rest, always seeking more, and yet no matter how much he has it is never enough."

John wondered if the rich man atop his column was as blind to the irony of his words as Leonidas had probably been. When Halmus clambered down to return to his mansion, a veritable banquet would doubtless be laid out for him and he would spend the night in comfort and warmth, unlike street beggars who would be grateful for a corner out of the night wind and a crust or two from his table. The elaborately worked iron gate in the base of the column that gave access to the stairs inside must have cost Halmus enough to feed and clothe every beggar in Megara.

Hadn't the blacksmith Petrus said something about not being paid for a gate he had been commissioned to make for Halmus? No, John remembered. That had been for Theophilus. Still, it was possible Petrus had made the gate for the column. Diocles had told John that Petrus did regular work for Halmus.

It had occurred to John that the blacksmith could have been assisting Theophilus in the illicit activities John had learned about in Lechaion. And Petrus conducted business with both Halmus and Theophilus. So what about Halmus? Might he have also been involved with Theophilus?

The thought of those who lived in constant deprivation rather than just during convenient hours brought to mind Halmus' artificial cave, where, as on the pillar, he played at poverty. Or so he claimed. If Peter's memory was reliable, Halmus had lied about his pilgrimage to see a sacred bush. Could anything else he said about his religion, or his business dealings for that matter, be trusted?

There had been something wrong about that hermit's cell. At the time, John had been distracted by Halmus showing him a supposedly sacred twig, and the thought had gone out of his mind before he'd completed it.

Now, reminded, he followed it through to its end.

Halmus railed on about rich men and camels and needles, reminding John of an extremely wealthy and loudly self-professed Christian merchant in the capital who had constructed the main doorway to his mansion in the form of a gigantic needle's eye, through which two imperial coaches could have passed side by side.

John walked past the tall brick wall of Halmus' garden. When he turned the corner and went around to the back of the property, the stylite's voice became only slightly muted. Darkness had fallen in the canyon of the street but the last red glare of sunset illuminated the tops of the buildings across the way.

The walls were too high to scale, and even if it were possible to reach the top, the intruder would be clearly visible to the guards who must be on duty.

However, John remembered a stream ran through the caged wilderness behind the mansion. He guessed it would emerge back here. In fact it did, and continued along the back of Halmus' wall and the backs of the buildings farther on, no doubt offering a natural storm water system. Here, though, due to the dry weather its channel was mostly dry, exposing a rusted grating set in the wall above a deep bed where a mere trickle of water emerged from the garden. The grating would have barred entrance to the garden but the lack of water exposed a gap between the bottom of the grating and the uneven streambed wide enough for a slim man to squeeze under.

Or so it appeared.

John paused, listening. He could still hear Halmus preaching. The street was deserted.

He slid down the steep bank to the stream, through broken pottery and shards of glass. The dark shapes of rats darted out of his way. Then he stood amidst rocks, mud-encrusted rubbish, and the smell of mold and decay.

Down here the space beneath the grating didn't look as wide as it appeared from the street. Beyond he could see only darkness where the stream approached the wall.

He yanked at the bars. Flakes of rust came off, staining his hands orange, but the grating felt solid.

After a few more futile attempts to pry a bar loose, he bent down, carefully cleared away several jagged pieces of shattered ceramic, then lay down, grabbed the grating, and pulled himself forward.

He got his head underneath and rolled onto his back to find clearance for his shoulder. Pushing his boots against rocks greasy with the rotted remains of water plants, he forced himself further into the darkness.

And could get no further.

His heart pounded. Pushing his head into the darkness was too much like submerging it in deep water. He tried to reach down, feeling for whatever was impeding him, but caught in an awkward position, could not raise himself. He felt he couldn't breathe, as if the blackness was filling his mouth and nostrils.

He knew this was nonsense. He pushed harder with his feet, his soles failing to find purchase on slippery stones. Finally he gained leverage. A high-pitched ripping noise filled the narrow space as his tunic tore where it had snagged on a sharp piece of the grating.

Then he had slipped all the way under. He tried to sit up but there was barely room for him to roll over. Doing so, he scraped his shoulder against what felt like rough concrete above him. He may as well have been in a tomb.

He paused to allow his eyes to adjust but still could not make out even a glimmer of light ahead. It would be dark in the garden by now, but not, he supposed, this dark. The channel was not much wider than his shoulders. Was there room to turn around if it were necessary? If not, would he be able to get back under the grating feet first?

He began to pull himself forward. His fingers touched water and he yanked his hand back.

Calming himself, he put his hand back out. Surely it was nothing more than a puddle? He continued. Shallow water soaked his clothing. He had to keep his face too near it for comfort.

Then his shoulder banged into the wall. He tried to shift sideways and found he could not. The tunnel was narrowing.

Experimentally he attempted to push himself backward. It was more difficult than moving forward. If he kept going and became stuck at some point, it might be impossible to get out.

And what if there was a grating without a gap under it at the other end?

He realized he was gasping for breath and tried to control his breathing. His clothes soaked, surrounded by the damp, impenetrable darkness pressing in around him, John had the sensation of drowning slowly. When he tried to raise his face away from the water his head hit a hard ceiling.

Then the height of the tunnel was also decreasing.

He had a sensation of suffocation. He forced himself onward. Walls scraped at both shoulders.

Then gray shapes swam in the darkness ahead. Was it a trick of his eyes? He blinked. No. Reaching out he felt vegetation. He pushed through, hearing branches crack loudly and not caring.

He burst out into fresh air, straightening up, leaves and twigs caught in his close-cropped hair.

The builder had luckily considered a grating on the outside sufficient.

John listened in case his noisy entrance had alerted a guard. When he heard nothing he forced his way through thick rhododendrons into a clearing and sought Halmus' artificial cave. He could no longer make out the voice booming down from the column. Had Halmus finished his religious diatribes? Might he appear suddenly in his garden? Or didn't the sound reach back here through the vegetation?

Roosting birds rose in an agitated cloud as he passed below a cedar, a column of darkness rising into the night sky. He dodged behind a clump of rocks artfully arranged to provide, in less drought-stricken days, a waterfall feeding the stream. No one came to investigate what had frightened the birds. He worked his way unchallenged through a wild tangle of shrubbery and closely growing trees until he reached the entrance to the artificial cave.

He could see now what had led to his feeling of puzzlement during his first visit. The dome of concrete stretching back into the surrounding plants was far larger than the cell Halmus had shown him.

There would have been no reason to construct such a large hill for such a small cave.

Pushing away the animal skin hanging at its entrance, John stepped inside. He would have to investigate quickly, given Halmus or one of his guards might arrive at any time. He crossed the cramped space and moved the skin on the far wall enough to peer around it.

What he had expected to find was a comfortable bed, artfully hidden.

Instead he was staring into a large torchlit room with several doors leading from it. A couple of men lounged in the center of the open space honing swords. Neither looked to be of friendly disposition and one, while dressed smartly and sporting an elaborate fibula, had a pugnacious look. The fibula, which at a glance appeared to be shaped like a bird, reminded John of something. Maritza's lament for her allegedly stolen jewelry?

He let the curtain fall gently back in place and escaped the way he had arrived, pausing only to pick up a shiny coin on his way out.

At the place where the stream entered the tunnel he paused. His breathing quickened. Perhaps there was a tree near the wall he could risk climbing and drop down into the street?

He heard approaching voices.

Taking a deep breath, he stooped down and gazed again into the black maw.

You were able to get in, he told himself. You can manage to get out.

Chapter Thirty-six

"Mithra!" John threw the covers back and sat up in bed, shading his eyes against the brilliant light streaming in. The sun was well up and the bucolic scene of fields and meadows, already awake while he was still half-asleep, irritated him.

"Don't fret, John. If you hadn't needed to sleep you wouldn't have." Cornelia appeared in the doorway, fully dressed, carrying a bundle of garments.

John glanced around. "Where are my clothes? I should be working by now."

"Those vile rags you came in wearing last night are out in the courtyard. As soon as I came down to the kitchen this morning I could smell them."

John remembered she had demanded he bathe before going upstairs to their rooms. "I apologize, Cornelia. I didn't think it would be wise to look for a public bath in Megara."

"No, you might have been mistaken for a plague carrier. Here's fresh clothing." She tossed the bundle to him. "As for your old clothes, they might serve as cleaning rags if the smell will come out."

After he pulled on the tunic he followed Cornelia down to the kitchen. As in Constantinople, it had become the central gathering place of the house, quite inappropriately and particularly here where it was not even part of the owner's quarters. But then John had grown up in a modest farmhouse, not a mansion or a country estate, and old habits, as Petrus would no doubt declare, die hard. This morning the sweet fragrance of the herbs Hypatia had hung up to dry mingled with the odors of cooking. The room was already coming to life. John's mother used to say that the kitchen was the heart of a home and as soon as you walked into a kitchen you could tell what sort of life a family led.

He gulped the cup of wine waiting on the table. "Are there any boiled eggs? I can just take a couple with me and eat on the way."

"Oh, John! You're not going back to Megara?"

"No. I have business on the estate this morning."

"You must rest. We haven't had much peace since we got here, and before that—"

"That's over with now."

"You're going to kill yourself!" Cornelia grimaced, obviously wishing the words back.

"You're still convinced I was the intended victim, not Theophilus? If that were true, all the more reason for me not to be wasting time."

She placed a plate of bread and cheese on the table. "Neither of us are as young as we used to be, and who knows what we're facing. The City Defender suspects you or at least has indicated in no uncertain terms that he does. Perhaps he killed Theophilus and hopes to convict you of the crime."

"I'm more concerned about you than myself, not to mention Peter and Hypatia. They chose to accompany us here. They could have remained in Constantinople. I am indebted to them."

"You won't be able to defend anyone, including yourself, if you succumb to exhaustion. Promise me you'll take a few hours off and soon."

"When I'm done with this visit I have to make."

He spotted a bowl of eggs, reached into it, and grabbed one. The shell broke in his hand, spraying yellow yolk on his clean tunic.

By the time he had eaten a breakfast of bread, cheese, and olives, and walked to Lucian's farm, the wet spot on his tunic where Cornelia had cleaned off the egg yolk was almost dry. Not that his destination was a place where he needed to look presentable. Long before he reached the farmhouse the warm breeze wafted to his nostrils the distinctive aroma of swine.

The house seemed deserted. He knocked at the open door and receiving no response went into the kitchen and called out for Lucian. There was no sound except for the flies buzzing around dirty dishes on the table. The room smelled of grease. The white-washed wall behind the brazier was stained an unhealthy yellow.

John pushed open the door leading to a back room with an unmade bed. The window was open and he leaned out.

Diocles was not fleeing across the fields.

He stamped around the house, to alert anyone who might be sleeping.

There was nothing unusual to be seen and no sign that Diocles had been in residence, although John wasn't certain what indication of his presence there could have been. The overseer might well have made off with valuable items from the estate, but John had no idea what exactly had been on the estate to begin with, given Diocles had been careful not to keep an inventory.

On his way out he took another look at the kitchen table but there was no chance of noticing extra tableware. There must have been a week's worth of plates and bowls carelessly piled up, enough for the two men who lived there—or a handful of visitors.

Didn't Lucian employ even a single servant? It seemed not.

The tinny blast of a horn greeted him as he left the house. Climbing the low rise in the direction of the sound, he saw, descending into the boggy depression below, a herd of swine, followed by their immensely fat master, Lucian, wobbling along merrily, now and then blowing his horn.

A muddy, sluggish stream wound through reeds and willows in the bottom of the depression. The swine lumbered forward, each dropping into the first mud it found.

"Good afternoon," Lucian called out sonorously, coming toward John. "The sun is going to be particularly fierce today so I have brought my friends to their afternoon pasture early.

Oh, for a hog's life, to gorge ourselves and wallow in the warm mud without a care in the world!"

"And have our throats cut in our youth," John observed.

"Might it be better then to enjoy our youth and not have to endure the rest?"

John noticed the farmer's face was bright scarlet with exertion. "Tell me, Lucian, have you been wallowing in the mud and neglecting your duties?"

"What do you mean? Is it the fences? I did set my son to righting the matter, but you know how lazy youngsters can be."

"Since Philip is on night duty, he needs to rest during the day so has little time to do the task. I realize correcting the boundaries will take some time, but that's not what I wished to speak about. Where is Diocles? Where are you hiding him?"

"Diocles? But he's gone, has he not? Has someone been lying to you? Who accused me of hiding Diocles?"

"Has he been staying with you?"

"I haven't seen him since he was discharged. You told him to leave the estate immediately."

"You know about that? Then you must have spoken to him before he left. Did he give any indication of where he intended to go?"

The tenant farmer looked around as if seeking advice from his swine. They snuffled and grunted contentedly but had none to offer. "Oh, yes, of course. He was naturally in a hurry. Said he would go to Megara, seek work there. I told him it was unlikely he would be offered any, given nobody wants a dishonest man working for him. Especially one who keeps suspicious accounts."

"A fine sentiment, Lucian, but I happen to know Diocles stayed here after I ordered him to leave. What other activity has he been involved in, apart from robbing the estate?"

"I couldn't say. Isn't that enough? I mean…" He lifted his horn and sent a sour bleat in the direction of several smallish pigs climbing the far side of the depression. As if they understood his message, they trotted back down to their companions.

"Young ones," Lucian said. "Almost time to separate them from their mothers." He lumbered over to a huge hog covered in mud. If its massive sides hadn't moved, John might almost have taken it for a small knoll. Lucian slapped the monster. "Goliath, this is. There's some meals fit for the emperor on him, you can be sure of that."

John decided it would be no use pressing the farmer for information. It was better to give him time to think, and something to think about. "You realize you are a tenant here, Lucian. If I find out you know more than you're saying, or have been involved in some scheme with Diocles, I'll have you evicted."

"Evicted?" The other paled.

"I am not Senator Vinius, nor do I live far off in Constantinople where I can't see what's going on here. I am willing to forgive any transgressions, given how out of control matters were here, provided you make a confession. I am not as interested in theft right now as in finding Theophilus' murderer."

"But surely you can't suppose Diocles was involved, sir? Or myself?"

"Think about what I have said, unless you want to find a new home for yourself and your swine."

John strode away, furious. Lucian was certainly lying. But then, what had he expected? Perhaps Cornelia was right, he needed to rest, needed to clear his mind.

What had he discovered? He wasn't certain the dead man had been the intended victim or who might have wanted him dead or why. His stepfather's illegal activities might offer a clue.

And what if Cornelia's fears were correct and John had been the target?

Now some way from the farmhouse, he was startled to hear running steps behind him.

When he pivoted, Philip was close enough to have stabbed him in the back with the sharpened stave he was waving. "Sir, please, a word with you!"

John's hand had already gone to his blade. He kept it there. "What is it?"

Philip cleared his throat, obviously uneasy. "Sir, I wish to ask a question."

"Ask."

The other looked around and lowered his voice. "It's...it's about your servant Hypatia, sir. I request permission to marry her."

Chapter Thirty-seven

Hypatia and Peter had argued before going to bed. Again. About Philip, again.

Peter had gone to sleep. Hypatia lay awake listening to her husband's wheezy labored breathing, interspersed with fitful snores.

Why hadn't she simply told Philip she was married if she truly had no interest in the young man? That's what Peter kept asking.

Hadn't she, in fact, told Philip? Perhaps not. It hadn't occurred to her that Philip didn't know. That's what she kept telling Peter.

If she wasn't attracted to the youngster then she must be ashamed to admit to him she had married an old man, Peter had pressed on.

But that was untrue. Why didn't Peter trust her? What more evidence of trust could he have than her marrying him?

She enjoyed Philip's attentions, though, Peter insisted. Otherwise she'd put an end to them.

She lay staring upward, watching ghostly reflections flicker across the ceiling. Peter's ragged breathing stopped and started.

Finally she got out of bed, shivering in her thin tunica until she pulled on her clothes. Then she crept out of the room, pausing to move a clay scorpion into the middle of the bedroom doorway to stand guard, just in case.

One of the cats ran under her feet, mewling in anticipation of being fed. She shushed it and went through the courtyard and out the gate.

Philip would be making his rounds. If she took the path to the edge of the property she'd be sure to find him.

There was no point putting the task off any longer.

Night shrouded the landscape. She had not gone very far along the path until the house and outbuildings were concealed by fog rolling in from the sea. Her footsteps sounded too loud. She thought fog would have muffled sounds but tonight it seemed to have the opposite acoustic effect.

She took a rutted trail leading along the ridge overlooking the sea, invisible tonight.

On either side her surroundings vanished into the fog. She might have been treading a narrow track across an abyss concealed from her gaze. That is how it felt living in Megara, going about one's everyday tasks but aware of unseen dangers wherever one turned. A single misstep and you would plunge over the edge.

Out of the house, in the cold, away from Peter's maddeningly loud breathing, she began to realize the foolishness of this midnight walk. Fog swirled and clung with clammy fingers to hair, face, and garments. Trees and bushes swam toward her out of the white miasma, receding behind as she strode forward at an increasing pace.

Could she see Philip under these conditions?

Should she shout for him?

Or would it be unwise to reveal her location?

She stopped and muttered to herself to calm down. Who would be out here aside from Philip or one of the other watchmen?

Apart from whoever had killed Theophilus, or wanted to kill the master, or someone from the city who wished the whole family ill will?

She swallowed and said a prayer to her gods. The clicking and chirping of night insects replied.

A breeze sprang up, momentarily clearing the fog away from a figure crouched beside the path.

No, it was merely a gnarled, ancient olive tree bent away from the sea. How long had the dwarf sat here? Was it part of an unthinkably old grove, long since vanished? Did the ghosts of all who had lived here and cultivated the land through countless centuries haunt the nights?

She thought of demons. The demons supposedly released by the excavations at the temple, the demons called on by imagined pagan worshipers, the demons her magickal clay scorpions were meant to ward off.

She had neglected to bring a protective charm with her.

As the breeze increased it tore rags of mist from the billowing foggy curtain, revealing a stretch of wall, a glint of sea, light from a house.

The blacksmith's house.

Philip was crossing the dirt yard behind the forge.

Hypatia had only a glimpse but she was certain it was Philip. Why would he be going to see Petrus at this time of night?

She started down the hill to the house, hurrying to catch him. Burrs caught on her tunic and thorns tore at her arms as she fought through a thicket that turned out to be denser than she expected.

She emerged from the brush behind a heap of metal rods at the edge of the open space. She smelled smoke. The yard was empty. Weird lights spilled out of the wide archway leading to the forge. She caught a glimpse of an illuminated inner wall. Strange shapes, among them the Key of the Nile, flickered across the wall and vanished.

She ran through the archway, prepared to call Philip's name, and stopped.

Despite the faint warmth radiating from the embers in the forge, she began to shiver until her entire body trembled.

A body lay sprawled in front of the forge.

She bent down and turned the body over.

Not Philip, thank the gods.

The faint glow illuminated the lifeless face of the overseer Diocles.

Before she could decide what to do the owner of the forge appeared. Almost immediately a heavy footstep marked the entrance of Lucian the pig farmer.

The three of them stood there, looking at the body and at each other, all of them equally horrified and mystified.

Or pretending to be.

Chapter Thirty-eight

The City Defender waved a fly away from his face with his stylus and consulted the tablet in front of him before addressing John. "The last time you sat here, you were suspected in one murder on your estate. This morning you are a suspect in two."

"The last time I sat here was because a fish merchant and his friends tried to burn down my house."

"Nevertheless you were a murder suspect, and will remain so as long as you are in Megara."

"How would you benefit from my leaving, Georgios?"

"For a start I'd have fewer criminal matters to worry about."

Today the patch of sunlight John had noticed on his earlier visit reached farther into the room. It felt warm on his back, casting his shadow across the mosaic floor. The head of his silhouette lay across documents near the edge of Georgios' table, a sight that reminded John of a head waiting to be removed with a swift slice from the sword of an imperial executioner.

There was no crowd present, thanks in part to the armed guard at the door. The only others in the room, aside from John and the City Defender, were Hypatia, seated in a chair against the wall and the two guards flanking her, unnecessarily, in John's opinion, considering her ankles were shackled.

Georgios glanced at his tablet again and then briefly pointed his stylus in Hypatia's direction. "This servant of yours—an Egyptian, I understand—was apprehended at the forge of your tenant, the blacksmith Petrus, in the middle of the night. She was standing over the body of the former overseer of your estate, Diocles, who had been stabbed in the back. Your servant's hands and clothing were bloody and she was holding a kitchen knife in her hand. No doubt you have an explanation. I am willing to hear it."

"Perhaps she was possessed by demons, like the fish merchant?"

"More likely consorting with them!"

"It isn't for me to explain, Georgios. She has already told you what happened. She was not involved in Diocles' death. She merely stumbled on the body."

"The people on your estate seem to have a penchant for stumbling on corpses and wandering around after dark. Are these habits you've brought with you from Constantinople? It was my impression those who live there stay inside and lock their doors at night so they won't stumble over corpses piling up in the lawless streets."

"Why isn't this hearing being written down for the administrative records?"

"It is not a formal hearing"

"It is completely irregular."

"In the capital, perhaps. This is the way we work in Megara."

"And it is the way you work?"

Georgios smiled. "Yes. The way the duly empowered City Defender works, along with his armed guards and the support of every citizen." He turned his attention to Hypatia. "You, woman. Do you want to change this fabricated tale you told me?"

Hypatia's eyes smoldered with dark fire. "I told the truth, sir. When I spotted the body I didn't know whose it was or why it was there. There was only the glow from the forge. He might have fallen and hit his head or been intoxicated."

"Surely you noticed the wound in his back?" Georgios interrupted.

"No. There were shadows. I was startled. I rolled him over and saw he was dead. I was afraid whoever killed him might still be nearby so I took out the knife I carry for protection. Since being attacked in the marketplace I felt I needed it. You and your guards don't offer any protection!"

"A perfectly lucid and understandable story," John put in.

"A simpler explanation is that your servant crept up behind Diocles and put the knife in his back, just before Petrus appeared."

"Petrus could have killed the man. It was his forge. Or it might have been my tenant farmer Lucian, who as we have just heard arrived not long after Petrus appeared."

"Neither of them was holding a knife in a bloody hand," the City Defender pointed out.

"Where are Petrus and Lucian?" John demanded. "They should be here to give evidence."

"Don't be so anxious about that. You'll be appearing before a court soon enough. To proceed. Petrus stated to me he heard a sound and went out to the forge and saw the body and your servant there. Then Lucian came to see Petrus on some business."

"What kind of business would they be meeting about at that time of night?"

"Petrus had promised to make a new bucket and repair a few tools. He often does small jobs late at night. Lucian waited until he had seen to his swine and finished the day's farm chores. When he got to the forge he saw the blacksmith, Diocles, and the servant woman. Lucian does not know what Diocles was doing there. He hadn't seen the unfortunate man since you relieved him of his duties."

"So he claims. It's more likely Diocles was staying with Petrus. He hid with Lucian first. Did Petrus also claim he hadn't seen Diocles since I ordered the man off the estate?"

"No. He admitted Diocles stayed with him, just as you say, a few days earlier. It was a simple act of kindness on Lucian's part. After all, they had developed a friendship. Diocles had been a trustworthy overseer for years."

"Not according to the estate records."

The City Defender tapped his teeth with the end of his stylus. "You see, this is what bothers me. You have a grievance against Diocles and he is found stabbed in the back on your estate.

You have a grievance with your stepfather and he also is found stabbed in the back on your estate."

"And I, of course, having served for many years at Justinian's court must be an expert at stabbing my enemies in the back?"

"Ah, so you see the logic of it."

"The master would not do such a thing," Hypatia declared in a loud voice.

Georgios looked thoughtful. "Perhaps not. Perhaps he would have a trusted servant do it for him."

"Are you accusing Hypatia, or me, or both of us?" John snapped.

"I would watch my tone, former Lord Chamberlain. The whole situation is quite perplexing, even you would have to admit as much."

"Yes, anyone on the estate or someone from outside could have killed Diocles for a reason we do not know since he unfortunately omitted to leave a confession. It is very perplexing."

"It is possible. Many things are possible. But there is also the matter of the woman with the knife."

"Who had no reason to kill Diocles," John pointed out.

"Unless she was ordered to or ordered to pretend to have done so. She appears to be quite loyal to you, and why not, considering she is several times removed from her native land and has no friends in Megara?"

There was a rattle of chains as Hypatia jumped up. "Sir, I protest! I—"

The guards slammed her back down hard enough for her head to hit the wall with a thump.

"You need to train your servants better," Georgios remarked. "Another possibility is she might have thought she was killing someone other than Diocles. I note she is fiery as well as beautiful. A romantic intrigue gone wrong?"

John gave Hypatia a look of warning. She remained quiet but tried to burn Georgios to a cinder with her stare.

"My servant would not engage in an intrigue for any purpose," John said calmly. "And considering Megara's port, not so far away from my estate, swarms day and night with foreigners, how do we know the person who attacked Diocles did not come from anywhere ships could bring him?"

"So now I should enlarge my circle of suspects to include most of the population of the empire? I am afraid I do not have the resources for that sort of investigation. In fact, I suspect it would be beyond the capacity of Justinian's entire army of spies." He tapped his teeth again. "By the way, I have learned that you were away from your estate recently."

"I visited Lechaion on business. Is that also considered a crime in Megara?"

"It depends on the business, doesn't it?"

"It appears the most dangerous event happening to a person in this city is to have the misfortune to discover a murder victim. I may be an exile, Georgios, and I may be disliked here but I am a Roman citizen and as such I possess certain rights. And so, I might add, does my servant."

"Of course." Georgios tossed his stylus down and stood up. "And my highest duty is to uphold the law of the empire. Guards, unlock the prisoner's shackles."

He came around the table. "I am releasing your servant to your care until I decide what is to be done."

He touched John on the elbow, urging him toward the open door. John jerked his arm away, but complied.

Georgios bent nearer and spoke in a confidential whisper. "May I be honest? You understand diplomacy, do you not? It is sometimes necessary to negotiate. I could have both you and your servant woman imprisoned immediately and executed within the month. Entirely legally, at that. However, I am aware of your former high standing at court. Like everyone else in the empire I know how Justinian's whims can change. Although I would wager that the longer the time that passes the less likely he is to decide to embrace you again."

"In other words, leave Megara while I have the chance?"

"Not in other words at all. That is exactly what I mean."

◇◇◇

Standing in the sunlight John wondered if the City Defender was telling the truth. He wanted John and his family gone, but he was prudent enough to prefer that John leave of his own free will.

He asked himself the question he had asked Georgios. How would Georgios benefit by John's flight? Would he be gaining something directly, or did he count on being rewarded by whoever would benefit from John's absence? Was he so ready to believe Hypatia would carry out any order John gave her, even murder, because Georgios was prepared to do the bidding of whoever was giving him orders?

Hypatia joined John, limping slightly, bloody abrasions on her ankles.

"Should I hire a cart to take us back?" John asked.

She shook her head, still furious. "No, master. I can walk back. I could run back if need be. I could kick that…that…well…I could kick him into the sea if I got the opportunity! Oh, master, I am sorry to have caused you problems."

"No more than I already had."

They put a short distance between themselves and the City Defender's office, then John directed her to sit on a bench under a colonnade until she felt steadier on her feet.

As she massaged her ankles, John asked what she had been doing at the blacksmith's forge. She explained, hesitating over her words, she had been seeking Philip, about a personal matter, a misunderstanding.

John guessed it must have been connected to Philip's thwarted plans but he thought it better not to the mention the young man had asked permission to marry her.

"I understand why you were outside then, but what made you go to Petrus' house?"

Hypatia paused. "I thought I saw Philip going there. But I must have been mistaken. It was foggy as well as dark." She looked distressed, no doubt realizing the obvious conclusion that might be drawn from her words. "Philip had no reason to kill Diocles."

"I agree. Did you tell the City Defender about seeing Philip? Or, rather, thinking you had seen him?"

"No, master. I…well, it was a personal matter. I didn't want the City Defender questioning me about it."

"Certainly not. You must tell me, though, why you think it was Philip, given the conditions? It could have been Petrus or Lucian, who were both nearby, or someone else entirely."

"It was by the stave Philip was carrying. I thought I saw a stave. It could have been one of the other watchmen."

Or, John thought, anyone who had made a sharpened stave for himself, or most likely, in the dark and fog, she hadn't seen a stave at all but had convinced herself she had, being eager to find Philip, who would naturally have carried one. John had no reason to disbelieve anything Hypatia had told him, and she had no motive for killing Diocles. "Are you sure you're telling me everything? I know Diocles was given to threats. You might have been protecting yourself, or Peter."

"How could you think that?"

He continued his questioning, drawing out every detail of what she had seen as she approached the forge and after she had found the body. "You say just as you arrived the flames in the forge sprang up?"

A familiar voice interrupted. "John, there you are!"

Leonidas hurried to the bench, looking winded. "I heard you were taken to the City Defender," he said. "Thank the Lord you've been released!"

"Temporarily at any rate."

"Word was all over the tax offices and probably the rest of the city by now, so I made haste to catch you. You were leaving the administrative complex when I arrived and the guards delayed me so I lost sight of you."

"I appreciate your concern, my friend. But is it wise, with your home situation…?"

"My apologies for that, John. I don't intend to abandon you. I wanted to know if there is any way I can help. If you need legal assistance, for instance, I can put you in touch with someone, or you might prefer me to contact whoever arranged the purchase of your estate. If it becomes necessary, I mean. If you are prevented. Heaven grant that it won't be necessary."

"Thank you, Leonidas. It's good to have someone I can count on in this city." John reached into his tunic. "I don't want to put you to any trouble, but there's something else you could look into for me. If you find out anything useful I will be in the marketplace tomorrow morning."

Chapter Thirty-nine

Cornelia tossed down her spoon. It rattled off a platter of figs, spun around, and came to a stop against John's bowl of boiled greens.

"The only reason you've been released is so there can be more attempts to get rid of us permanently," Cornelia raged. "We ought to go, John. Fortuna has smiled on you and you've escaped so far, but for how much longer? Neither of those men was worth your life. Why can't we just leave? We could find the troupe we traveled with and join them. They're usually in Alexandria in the autumn. We had nothing then and we were happy."

John put down the beaker of olive oil he had been about to pour over his greens. "We were young. I can't see you leaping from bulls these days."

"Why not? You see I haven't lost my archery skills! Of course, I'd need to get back in practice."

"Broken bones don't heal as quickly when we get older. Besides, what about our daughter and her family? They'll be arriving before long. Where would they go, not to mention Peter and Hypatia?"

"Yes, I suppose I am just dreaming. But couldn't you buy an estate somewhere else?"

"This is the place to which I was exiled. Even if I were allowed to leave, I don't want to draw unwanted attention from Justinian's spies. They would present our flight as evidence of my plotting with enemies of the emperor. After all, I would have plenty of reason to do so."

"They have long memories, these enemies of yours. I hoped we had left all of that behind when we came to Greece. Apparently they took the next ship after ours. And now Hypatia has been entangled in murder. I have never seen Peter so angry and afraid. Estate owners have some protection by virtue of their holdings, but a servant doesn't."

"She has my protection and I have told Peter so."

"As long as you are free. And then what? There is no justice to be had here."

"It was often much the same in Constantinople, Cornelia. Only there were so many people living there it was more difficult to notice that was the case."

A discreet cough revealed Peter at the door. "The blacksmith Petrus, Master."

"You wish to speak to me?" John asked in a weary voice.

"Indeed, sir." His visitor glanced nervously at Cornelia.

"Continue," John told him.

Petrus shifted his feet uneasily and looked down at his leather apron. "I was interviewed by the City Defender, sir, but could not shed any light on the, er, matters involved in his investigation. I thought I should let you know that, as I am certain you would wish to consult me about the topic. For as they say…" He trailed away, misery written on his face.

"I believe I know what you intended to say. A loyal and honest servant is worth a fortune. Is that not so?"

"Indeed!" Petrus brightened. "And I assure you I have nothing to tell you about how Diocles came to be near my forge or who killed him or anything at all relating to the event. I…um… thought you would want to know, sir."

"To save me the trouble of visiting you, no doubt?"

"Indeed."

"You weren't expecting Diocles? You hadn't arranged a meeting?"

"I work hard, sir, and that time of night I am asleep. But a sound woke me. What, exactly, I can't say, being asleep, until I was awake, you see. Once I was awake it was quiet but I went out to the forge in time to see…well…"

"And Lucian's arrival was a surprise also?"

"Just as much. Well, that is, not so much of a surprise as finding Diocles there, in the condition he was in…I mean, dead. "

"I understand. I appreciate your help, Petrus."

"Thank you, sir." Petrus appeared to have gained control of his nervousness. "After all, as I often say, we cannot know what we know unless we first know what we do not know."

As the blacksmith departed, Cornelia stared at his broad retreating back with undisguised consternation. "What does he mean?"

John shook his head. "A clumsy attempt to curry favor, I presume. Petrus doesn't necessarily want me to leave. A new owner might not want him on the estate."

"Unless Petrus is working with a new owner to remove you." Cornelia suggested.

John gave a faint smile. "True enough. One might think you'd spent years at the imperial court."

Cornelia plucked a fig from the platter and chewed thoughtfully. "I know it's impossible but would it be so difficult traveling with the troupe again?"

"It wouldn't be very difficult if we could move freely." John thought she looked wistful and changed the subject. "I see you're wearing a most attractive fibula."

"You noticed! I thought they went well together."

John had a faraway expression. "They? Went well?"

"My fibula and the silver earrings you brought back from Megara." She reached over and put her hand on his. Her fingers were sticky from the fig. "Tell me, John. What are you thinking about?"

He saw her expression was stern. "An elaborate fibula. Possibly two of them. Your jewelry jarred my memory. One of the guards I saw in the room behind Halmus' cave was wearing a winged fibula. It reminded me of something then, and now I recall what it was. Diocles wore a similar bronze eagle."

"And that means…?"

"I've been thinking about smuggling, counterfeiting, illegal weapons, and possibly stolen jewelry. Those fibulas were unusual in design and might have come from the same collection, shared out by colleagues in crime."

"But why would Diocles have any connection with one of Halmus' guards?"

"It might be that Diocles, like the guard, was employed by Halmus. As overseer Diocles had dealt with Halmus. Diocles knew Petrus. He could hardly avoid knowing him given Petrus also lives on the estate and has repaired its farm implements. And don't forget, as Diocles mentioned, Halmus commissioned work from Petrus. Consider, too, as a blacksmith Petrus would have the equipment needed for the manufacture of illegal weapons.

"Look at how the arsonists were armed with spears and swords. They should not even have had access to them. Then there is that iron shipment someone wanted kept secret. If it were all being used for gates and plows there would be no reason to be so mysterious about its delivery. Not to mention Halmus' guards were armed with swords, thus also breaking the law."

"You are thinking Diocles was the intended recipient of the notice the iron had arrived, and he would have arranged to have it delivered to Petrus? It would seem then both of them were assisting Halmus in certain matters he would prefer not be known?"

"Halmus is a fraud. According to Peter, the man lied to me about his supposed pilgrimage. His hermit's cave disguises a much larger area. I believe it's used to store illegal goods, otherwise why hide and guard it? I suspect the coin I found there is a counterfeit. It looked remarkably unused to have fallen out of someone's money pouch."

"And Theophilus?"

John peered down into the bowl of rapidly cooling greens before him but he saw nothing except the tumbling patterns inside his head, glittering tesserae, falling into place, beginning to a form a picture, but one still too full of gaps to make sense. "My stepfather was involved with similar crimes also, as

I discovered while I was away. I have no doubt he was one of those concerned in certain matters here."

Cornelia smiled. "Good!"

John looked at her in perplexity. "What do you mean, good?"

"I mean I would far rather think he was murdered because of a dispute between criminals than that you were the real target."

Chapter Forty

Helen fumbled noisily at the door until Leonidas let her in. She was pale and breathless and burdened with a brimming basket topped with vegetables and a headless chicken.

"You took long enough," she told him. "I might have dropped the basket. I've just seen someone across the street staring at our house."

"Sorry, I was working on my temple to Zeus. You see, I suddenly thought why should Constantinople and Rome have all the glory? That's why I'm building this model of our own claim to fame, and—"

Helen stamped her foot. "Will you listen? There is a man across the street keeping us under observation!"

Leonidas looked out. "I don't see anyone…oh, yes I do. A short fellow. Looks familiar. Now where have I seen him before?"

"I don't care where you saw him, I want to know what he's doing over there!"

"Perhaps he followed you home, hoping that chicken would fall off the top of your overloaded basket? Surely he has the right to stand anywhere he likes? Really, you must not fly away with these notions, Helen. Have you seen him there before?"

She admitted she had not. "But he seemed to be staring so intently."

"Perhaps he can still see that chicken he was hoping to get."

"It isn't funny. There's a look about him I don't like. What if he's one of the City Defender's informants?"

Leonidas continued to stare outside. "We haven't done anything worth informing about, Helen. He's leaving now."

Helen left also, disappearing into the kitchen, emerging before long to flourish a large ladle at Leonidas.

"I told you it was not wise to get involved with your old friend John, and I was right," she continued. "You always laugh, but I have a sense for these matters. John is a different man now than he was when you knew him, Leonidas."

He sighed. "He does not seem so very different from the boy I remember."

"Nonsense!" Helen smacked his arm lightly with the ladle. "He served as Justinian's Lord Chamberlain for years. Men that high up might as well live on Olympus with the old pagan deities. Who knows what enemies he's made or what problems he's brought with him? Problems that could very well come to roost on our roof."

"I don't see how that can be. I took great care to copy the records when no one else was in the archives, if that's what you're fretting about."

"You see? You are being dragged into doing things in secret. Secrecy is almost always connected with dark deeds. Have you forgotten your responsibility to me so that you run off to help a man exiled here? A man you don't even know anymore?"

"I certainly do know my old friend John."

"Do you? What crime was he exiled for? Did he tell you? You have no notion what he might have been involved in. Satan can see Constantinople from his windows and no doubt enjoys its display of sin and murder!"

"Justinian can do what he wants for any reason or no reason. I can't imagine John doing anything illegal—"

"You're thinking of the boy, not the man!" Helen pivoted and stalked off into the kitchen, only to reappear a moment later, a small cloth bag in her hand. "And then there's this!"

She threw the bag at Leonidas' feet. Several gold coins fell out and rolled under the table. "I found it when I went to put the fish sauce I purchased away. What do you think you're doing, hiding money where we keep the fish sauce?"

"I...I...usually I keep it inside the Great Church," Leonidas stammered in confusion.

"A fine place to keep such a sum," she said bitterly, "And you never even mentioned you had it either. Who gave it to you and why?"

Before Leonidas could reply there was a burst of knocking on their door, following by a loud demand to open in the name of the City Defender.

There was a knock on John's door also, although it came in the middle of the night. In Constantinople he might have expected it. Here he was taken by surprise. Warning Cornelia not to follow, he dressed and went out into the tiny entrance hall. He had neglected to pull on his boots and the marble tiles were cold underfoot.

In Constantinople the caller would have been a messenger summoning him to see the emperor, or a pair of excubitors with swords, arriving to escort him to less salubrious quarters.

Here the knocker turned out to be a man with a long sharpened stave.

Philip, escorting a surprising trio: Abbot Alexis, the monk Stephen, and Stephen's mother Helen, the latter red-faced and sobbing.

"My apologies, John," the abbot said. "But Helen came to me for help because I am, if I may say so without appearing boastful, her husband's most powerful and trustworthy friend."

"Indeed," John said.

"That may be," interjected Stephen, "but as Mother explained to me, my father's predicament involves you."

"I will surely help if I can. What sort of predicament is Leonidas in?"

"Ah! As if you didn't know!" Helen cried.

Alexis put his hand on her shoulder. "There, now. Leonidas is an upstanding man. The Lord will look after him." He turned to John. "Our friend has been arrested as being in possession of counterfeit coins."

Chapter Forty-one

Stephen guided his mother into the stark anteroom of the City Defender's office. Helen, sobbing inconsolably, hands over her face, allowed herself to be led to the wooden bench along the wall.

Stephen sat beside her. There was no one else in the room. A bust of Emperor Justinian stared from a corner pedestal, not seeing them. The single window looked out into a featureless gray underworld.

"You were right to come to the monastery, Mother. Abbot Alexis will have everything set to rights before long."

"Your father looked so pale, so worn. Do you think they are starving him?" Helen snuffled.

"He's only been in custody a couple of hours. He told you he hasn't been mistreated."

"Do you think I will ever see him again? What will I do?"

"Of course you will see him again, and before too long. It's all a mistake, I'm sure. Father involved in counterfeiting? It's preposterous."

"It's punished by death. That's what the laws say. Death by burning. Your father told me that himself, years ago. If...if... oh, how could I manage on my own?"

"Well, Mother, hadn't you better think of Father first?" Though his father and the others were nearby there was that peculiarly strong feeling of emptiness that pervades work spaces after business hours.

Helen turned glassy eyes toward him. "You believe I am not thinking of your father, Stephen? How can you say that? It is bad enough that you have no house for me to come to if I am widowed."

"The Lord cares for widows, Mother. You could enter a religious order."

Helen sniffed. "That is your answer to everything. You only joined the church to spite your father. Isn't that true?"

"Mother! You're distraught. Perhaps we should pray together."

Helen ignored the suggestion. "Some sons follow in their fathers' footsteps," she continued, "others do everything they can not to be like them at all. Just because he worked as a tax collector, you had to go into the church where love of money is condemned as evil."

"One of the apostles was a tax collector," Stephen reminded her.

"Your father isn't an apostle. If only he had been firmer with you, then a destitute old widow might have a loving son's home to go to."

"You are not destitute, old, nor a widow, Mother. This is Satan talking, not you."

Helen fell silent. Stephen said a prayer in which she did not join.

"You tried to be so different from your father," Helen continued abruptly. "But you are so very like him. He never kept his mind on his job. His thoughts were always flying off to distant corners of the world. And you, Stephen, your thoughts have flown right out of this world completely. You have locked yourself away from it."

"I thought you approved of my vocation, Mother. As a matter of fact, I would like to see some distant corners of the world myself someday. I intend to undertake a pilgrimage to the Holy Land when the time comes. Halmus dines often with the abbot and I have been occasionally invited to hear him tell remarkable stories about his travels."

"Halmus is a rich man. It's easy for him to travel. How would a poor monk afford it? It takes more than dreaming to live in this world. Look at your father, if he had worked more diligently we would have been able to actually see those places he continually dreamed about."

"Mother! You don't know what you're talking about. I'm not at all like father, pottering away at his miniature world, lost in dreams, and nothing but a glorified clerk all his life. Do you think I don't have responsibilities at the monastery? I'm in charge of the hospice. Abbot Alexis considers me his right-hand man. In fact, he has hinted that I may succeed him when he moves on to a higher office."

Helen began to cry again. In the silence her sobbing sounded very loud. One could almost imagine the mournful wail echoing through the dim, empty corridors and offices beyond. "Perhaps it is the Lord's will I end up in your hospice, a broken old woman, not leading the quiet life your father and I had planned."

"Thank you for permitting John and myself to speak with Leonidas." Abbot Alexis addressed the City Defender.

The four men had drawn up chairs facing each other in the same whitewashed hearing room John had seen before. In the uncertain illumination of a single oil lamp it looked even drabber than it had in daylight, a commentary perhaps on the quality of justice maintained in Megara.

"You answer to a higher authority than I do," Georgios replied. "I would never refuse a reasonable request. Feel free to ask the prisoner whatever you wish as if I were not present."

Georgios had not offered to absent himself.

Leonidas' chair creaked as he shifted nervously. Had he heard the muffled sobs from the anteroom?

"We know you've explained everything to the City Defender, but Alexis and I would like to hear it for ourselves," John began.

Leonidas avoided looking at him.

"What about this bag of counterfeit coins? What were you doing with them?" John asked.

"Working in tax collection, I have a keen interest in counterfeiting. Over the years I've saved examples that have turned up at the tax offices."

"Quite understandable," put in Alexis. "It is part of your responsibilities."

"How is that?" Georgios' tone was curt.

Leonidas swallowed visibly. "I use them to compare to any suspected counterfeits I come across."

"Why would that be necessary?" Georgios asked. "Certainly you are aware of the general characteristics of counterfeit coins. And one counterfeit would not have precisely the same flaw as another."

"That may be. Nevertheless it is…uh…my method."

"One not officially sanctioned," Georgios snapped. "Otherwise counterfeits would be kept at the administrative offices."

"You told us you had already questioned him, Georgios," John said.

"So, one suspect wants to instruct me on how to interrogate another suspect!"

"I am hoping we can clear this up informally. You can't really believe Leonidas is involved with counterfeiters, can you?"

Georgios shrugged. "He's just admitted he stole the coins."

"But, sir, it was no loss to anyone." Leonidas' voice trembled. "They would simply have been destroyed."

"No loss to anyone perhaps but a nice gain for yourself." Georgios leaned toward Leonidas in a threatening manner and his voice rose. "What did you do, pass them off on unsuspecting merchants? A small purchase here and there, who would notice? And quite a nice little side income it must have added up to over the years. Or was it more than that? A lot of money goes through the tax collector's offices. There would be plenty of opportunities to swap your counterfeits for real coins. I'm sure you could describe more sophisticated frauds to me."

"Please," Alexis said, "there is no need to sound so harsh, Georgios. You are not talking to a criminal."

"I'm not?"

Leonidas slumped and folded his arms, as if he were trying to make himself small enough to become invisible. Finally, he raised his face to John and spoke directly to him, avoiding looking at the others. "I suppose I thought of it as a bit of an adventure, collecting all those coins. I mean, who could say where they had been made, in what disreputable places in dangerous neighborhoods or what kind of men might have handled them? The basest criminals, men who prefer to walk in the shadows. When I picked up one of those coins I felt a thrill, my fingers tingled, I could feel the heat of the forge where it had been minted by a swarthy Egyptian, could smell the sea from the deck of the pirate ship transporting it. You understand don't you, John?"

"Of course. Even one who chooses a simple life can still long for a little adventure."

"Longing for adventure is not a legal defense," Georgios pointed out. "A lot of criminals are seeking adventures."

"But as Leonidas has already explained, he was also employing the coins in his work," John replied. He glanced at Leonidas for confirmation.

His friend squirmed and stammered. "Well…I said so…but I was ashamed to admit…well…"

"How did Helen happen to find the counterfeits?"

Leonidas nodded almost imperceptibly. "I became so engrossed looking at them she surprised me when she arrived home. I tried to hide the bag, too hastily. I…I should have guessed she'd buy more fish sauce and put it with the rest." His eyes filled and he shook his head hopelessly. "If only I did not have a taste for fish sauce. What a fate—to have one's life destroyed by fish sauce!"

"Be honest," John continued. "You were looking over those counterfeits to compare them to the one I gave you. Isn't that so?"

Leonidas' eyes widened. "The coin you gave me? What…I don't know…."

"I appreciate you trying to protect me but there's no need." John turned to Georgios. "When I talked to Leonidas in the marketplace after my last visit here, I gave him a coin I suspected to be counterfeit and asked him if he could examine it and let me know if I was right. Was I right, Leonidas?"

"Yes," he said miserably. "The coin is a counterfeit. A very good one."

"And why," John fixed his gaze on Georgios, "did your men happen to barge into Leonidas' home? You couldn't have suspected him. You had someone following me, didn't you? Your man saw me hand the coin to Leonidas."

"No. You're wrong."

"Someone must have told you to go to Leonidas' house."

"We had an anonymous tip. It's no business of yours." There was a threatening undertone to Georgios' voice.

"A man was watching the house," Leonidas said. "Helen told me. I saw him myself."

"That's enough!" Georgios stood abruptly and sent his chair clattering backward. "We've wasted enough time. Guard, escort the prisoner out." He turned his attention back to John. "I shall be interested to hear more about this counterfeit coin of yours."

"You certainly will. Especially where I found it."

Chapter Forty-two

"But you turned my house upside down after you took Diocles' body away," protested Petrus. "I've just managed to get things back in order. Do you really think you missed something the last time you searched?"

"We're not looking for the same sort of evidence this time, as I have already explained." The stark morning sunlight showed dark pouches under the City Defender's eyes. It was obvious he was getting as little sleep as John.

Petrus rubbed his hands on his leather apron. He had already been at work when Georgios and a half dozen of his men, accompanied by John, had arrived. The blacksmith led them across the dirt courtyard and showed them a pile of iron rods. In places weeds had straggled up between them. "Is this a supply fit for an armory?"

"Hardly," John told him. "But it was time for a new shipment, wasn't it?"

"I don't know anything about shipments of iron. I keep enough metal on hand for normal blacksmithing work." He gave John a glare of resentment. "I must protest, sir. You know what they say, if you're capable of submitting to an insult you certainly should be insulted, but I am surprised you would suspect me of wrongdoing to say the least."

"Try not to take it personally, Petrus," John told him. "We're all suspects lately. If you are innocent you don't need to worry about your tenancy."

Petrus merely grunted.

"Your landlord may be in more danger than you are," Georgios told him. "Under the law the estate owner is liable for any illegal activities on his land."

"Not if he reports it as soon as he finds out, which I have done," John pointed out.

"I'm not putting my own neck on the chopping block in order to cost someone else his head," Petrus said. "There's nothing illegal going on here. Search again, if you want. Search twice. I shall continue here in the forge. You're interrupting my work."

"Another commission from Halmus?" John asked.

"No. I'm repairing chamber pots for the hospice at Saint Stephen's. I do work for Halmus from time to time. If your craftsmanship is the best, naturally he hires you. Is it now a crime to work for Halmus?"

"John claims he found an allegedly counterfeit coin while he was trespassing on Halmus' property," Georgios said.

"So I am a counterfeiter now? As if there aren't other black-smiths in Megara or close by."

"Leonidas confirmed the coin was counterfeit," John observed.

Georgios grimaced. "He's accused of crimes himself. Who could be more reliable? And yet here I am conducting a search at the behest of a murder suspect whose servant is also a suspect in criminal activities, not to mention Leonidas, and all three running loose. Never tell me I am not a fair man."

"How could you keep Leonidas imprisoned when the abbot vouched for him personally?"

"Ah, I had forgotten the abbot. Petrus is doing work for him at present. Does that make Alexis a suspect as well?"

Petrus had a copper pot on an anvil and was whacking it resoundingly with a hammer, working out dents and his own anger.

John noticed the motif on its sides was a columned temple. "That's an odd design for a monastery."

Petrus threw his hammer down. "What do you expect on a chamber pot?"

"Do you do much work for the monastery?" Georgios asked.

"A little. I work for churches also. In fact, Halmus occasionally hires me to do church work as a form of charity. Then again there was the birdcage I made to specifications supplied by a woman who did not seem the sort of lady one would expect to keep birds. Some of the iron figures applied to it were remarkably lascivious. I had to instruct the younger estate workers to keep away from my forge while I was working. And what sort of bird goes in a cage so large it needs to be hauled away on a wagon?"

"You've made your point, Petrus. You do a varied business," Georgios replied.

The blacksmith shrugged and sighed. "Mostly it's various farm tools, occasionally plows."

"Is James the fish merchant a client?" Georgios asked.

Petrus rubbed his chin. "I may have done a few little commissions for him long ago. He's a rich man though he doesn't look it, does he?"

"The arsonists who attacked the other night were led by the fish seller, and they were armed with illegal weapons," John said to Georgios. "I realize the law in its vast wisdom has decreed they were all possessed by demons but demons don't supply swords or conjure them out of thin air."

"Demons!" Petrus exclaimed. "They say demons dance in that pagan temple. Oh, I've seen strange lights and weird shadows myself over there at night. Perhaps the weapons James and his criminal friends displayed were forged in the fires of hell?"

"It is about as likely as them being forged by you, Petrus." Georgios said. Turning to John he added, "Just because something is possible doesn't make it so. I don't see what leads you to believe manufacture of illegal weapons is taking place on your estate."

John again outlined how the concealed message concerning the iron shipment had led him, eventually, to suspect such activity.

"You told me this on our way here, but it doesn't strike me as sufficient grounds for suspicion."

John wondered whether the additional information he had learned during his visit to Lechaion would strengthen the case in Georgios' eyes, but thought it prudent to say nothing.

"It all sounds the sort of tale spun by poets and other rogues," said Petrus.

Georgios' men began to straggle back from their assigned search areas, reporting that, as on their previous visit, they had found nothing incriminating.

Petrus had abandoned his work and begun to pace impatiently. "If I had crates of swords hidden away don't you think you would have stumbled across them the first time? Now why don't you tell me you believe I killed Diocles as well as my other crimes?"

A guard appeared and gestured to Georgios, who went over, conferred with him, and returned holding a clay jar he set on the workbench. "What are you doing with these?" he asked, lifting the lid to reveal a veritable hoard of small bronze coins.

Petrus looked puzzled. "Oh, that's just some coins I keep on hand. I clear them out of my money pouch every so often. The whole jarful's practically worthless."

Georgios replaced the lid. He looked thoughtful. "Worthless for buying much, I agree, but useful for making coin molds."

Chapter Forty-three

The City Defender and his men had departed empty-handed and John, returning from the futile search, mulled over the lack of evidence concerning what he was convinced was a web of illegal activities taking place on his estate.

There was certainly a traceable chain of connections between its various residents and criminal activity, he thought as he walked slowly home, but proving it was the difficulty. A jar of bronze coins, like so much of what John had discovered, was suggestive but did not qualify as proof of anything. How could he describe his theories to Georgios if he were asked to do so?

To begin with, during John's visit to Corinth's port he learned Theophilus had been regularly involved in activities that would not bear close scrutiny. His stepfather's criminal associate, during his visit to John's rented room, had indicated Theophilus, among other things, smuggled many goods, including iron. Which would not need to be kept secret unless for the purpose to which it was to be put by the recipient, in this case the man in charge, or in other words, the overseer Diocles. Where could Diocles have sent iron, except to Petrus who worked with it? And Lucian the tenant farmer had been willing to hide Diocles despite John's order the latter should leave the estate immediately. So there were links between all four men, given Lucian would not run the risk of losing his tenancy unless for a very good reason.

Looking further afield, there was what had been established as a counterfeit coin brought back by John from Halmus' artificial cave. Was that only a coincidence? Such coins circulated and this one could have come from anywhere in the district—Leonidas had handled enough at the tax office to have made a modest collection of counterfeits—but it was suggestive one such would have been found in the possession of a man who had business dealings with Diocles.

Admittedly, that was not a strong link, but let it stand for now. John came to a halt at the top of a rise and scanned the glistening sea below. Like his musings, the waters washing at the shore were always in motion, but moved back and forth over the same place.

John thought of Halmus gazing down from his pillar at the citizens of Megara flowing into the marketplace to eddy around its shops and merchants' carts. Strange predilections for a businessman, haranguing the world from atop a column and retreating to an artificial cave to meditate. Denouncing the wickedness of the world might not be considered suspicious, but wouldn't residing in his cave permit him to be in two places at once? While all of Megara thought he was secluded in his garden, he would be free to do business elsewhere without anyone being tempted to pry into his activities.

Was it a fantastic notion? Peter had disputed Halmus' description of the burning bush supposedly seen during a pilgrimage he claimed to have taken. Why lie about such a matter? Unless he had never gone on that pilgrimage, but had been doing something else during his absence?

John resumed walking. The waves whispered on the shore, their message unintelligible.

He considered the mob that had attacked the estate in his absence. Where had their illegal weapons come from? Could the seller of fish have obtained them from the estate or even from Halmus, who as a fellow businessman he must know well? It was possible in Halmus' absences he was making secret sales of weapons, manufactured perhaps by Petrus.

So the circle of suspects returned to the estate, yet the only evidence John had of any of these deductions was a single counterfeit coin, a secret message regarding a shipment of iron, and fraudulent estate accounts.

And none of his theories explained why his stepfather and Diocles had been murdered or if Lucian was indeed also involved and, if so, what assistance he had been contributing.

As he neared home and saw lights glimmering from the windows a thought came to mind. The mysterious criminal web might be hidden in darkness at present but morning would inevitably come and all be revealed in due course in the burning light of Mithra's sun.

There must be more evidence. But with no assistance as would have been the case in Constantinople, finding it would mean another nocturnal journey around the estate.

What John mistook for a puddle in the darkness was a water-filled depression. He suppressed a curse at the shock of cold water rising over his knee as his foot plunged into mud below. Then, thankfully, he stopped sinking. He stood motionless, listening for any sign that someone had heard his blundering. There were only the rasping songs of insects.

Around him, in the hollow, he could dimly make out grassy hummocks and scattered trees interspersed with the shining, featureless black glass of water. Shallow surely? Lucian wouldn't let his pigs wallow where they might drown. Despite the dry conditions there remained a considerable amount of water here, doubtless due to the location containing springs.

He tried to raise his imprisoned foot. The mud resisted. He pulled harder and his foot came loose, leaving its boot behind. He had to dig into the mire to retrieve it.

The air was ripe with the scent of decay and swine. A cloud of mosquitoes followed him as he searched. A lean Greek mostly covered in a tunic was no substitute for a fat, naked hog, but tonight John was all that was available. He waved at the swarming fog, tried to avoid the droning fliers.

Only a fool would search this pestilent pig wallow, which

was exactly why John was here. What better hiding spot than a place where no one but pigs would bother to venture?

A cluster of sickly trees visible against the night sky marked a patch of solid ground near the middle of the boggy area. He made his way to it, clambering over rotting logs, some moss-furred and others slimy. It would be safer but inconvenient to submerge what one wished to conceal hereabouts.

On the island, thorny bushes filled the spaces between stunted trees. John wondered where Lucian kept his pigs at night. Swine could be aggressive, another reason why no one was likely to be trespassing into the wallow.

He didn't relish the idea of waking a monstrous sleeping hog. He took out his knife, though the blade was not long enough to penetrate far into the flesh of a good-sized hog.

Exploring the brush turned out to be noisier than he would have preferred. Finally he came upon the sort of structure he had expected, a crude lean-to, built against a low earth bank. Ducking inside he could make out straw, which on investigation covered shallow pits.

Clearing away straw, his hand encountered iron rods of the kind used as raw material by blacksmiths. Another pit held a bundle of swords wrapped in rags. Most of the swords were of double-edged military quality.

Lucian's role then was to conceal both the weapons Petrus manufactured and the raw materials he used. He had doubtless profited from his cooperation. Diocles had after all allowed Lucian to expand his farm beyond its agreed limits, and he also probably shared in the profits.

Philip was waiting for John when he emerged from the structure.

Placing the fire-sharpened tip of his staff against John's chest to keep him at arm's length and away from John's drawn blade, the young man waited until he was recognized and then lowered his weapon. "I could easily have killed you."

"For inspecting my own estate? I'm pleased to see you are doing the job you are paid for."

"You made a lot of noise, sir. Certainly you have the right to be here, although it puts me in an awkward position."

"You know there are illegal weapons stored here?"

"Of course not. And even if I did I am not going to betray my father."

"You have just betrayed him, Philip. If there was nothing to betray why would you say you would refuse to do it?"

Philip pointed his staff again. "I won't be dragged in as a witness against him, sir. If I should be, I shall deny all knowledge of anything illegal occurring on your land. Besides, I believe the City Defender is being bribed to turn a blind eye."

"Explain."

"Why do you think he released your servant and you are still a free man? Why has so little been done in the matter of Theophilus' murder? I predict the death of Diocles will not be investigated to any great extent either. The City Defender wants as little attention as possible directed at this estate."

"Perhaps your father should not have hidden Diocles."

"Only temporarily. He ordered him to leave. The City Defender is corrupt and also he is not to be trusted."

John realized the allegation also shed light on the release of James, the seller of fish, caught red-handed with an illegal weapon and in the company of arsonists, and his only defense that of possession by a demon. "Your accusation suggests there is something to be discovered."

"I am not clever with words, sir, but I can tell you that it's fortunate the City Defender is corrupt. If it were not so I would kill you to protect my father." Despite the threat, Philip's voice shook.

"And you would no doubt have a story ready to explain my death. After all, you are my head watchman. A mistaken identity on a dark night and an unfortunate accident suggests itself as an easy way to ensure my silence."

Philip shifted his staff. "Not everyone in Megara takes murder lightly, sir. If I were inclined to kill you I would have done it when you told me Hypatia was married to that ancient servant of yours. Please consider, wouldn't it be best for everyone if it was agreed you would not interfere in what is going on?"

John pointed out as owner he was legally responsible for any criminal activities on the estate.

"Indeed," came the reply. "But if nobody knows about any so-called misdeeds, where is the responsibility? You don't have to contribute anything but your silence. That's the only assistance I give. I told father I would not join him and his associates. He therefore tells me nothing."

"Nevertheless, the emperor's laws are being broken."

"I am surprised you would care about the emperor who has exiled you, sir. But as a matter of fact, the City Defender is the law in Megara, not the emperor."

"Only if the emperor allows Georgios to have free rein."

"Besides, I am more concerned with your welfare than the emperor. It would suit us all for you to remain here and for the whole situation to be stable."

"And Peter is very old and may soon leave Hypatia a widow," John suggested.

"I am not ashamed to admit I recognize the truth of that, sir. But, think, your silence would change nothing. Matters would simply go on as they always have, which is what everyone wants. Leave us to live our lives and we will leave you to live yours."

"Stop right there, John. Don't take another step. Turn around. Now," Cornelia continued crossly, "straight to the bath. I'll bring you fresh clothes."

He was sluicing muck off himself when she arrived with a fresh tunic and boots. Cornelia dropped the clothing on a bench and stood by the side of the basin. "You're even filthier than you were after your visit to Halmus. I don't even like to think where you've been this time, although from the smell I would guess a cesspool."

John described his search of Lucian's farm and his encounter with Philip, all the while scrubbing himself diligently.

"Do you think Philip intends to try to reconcile his father and the others with you?"

"Just empty talk, I hope. If he tells Lucian about finding me at the weapons cache...well..." John dipped his head into the water gingerly, to wet his hair and avoid saying anything further.

"It's all very well, unraveling these criminal enterprises, but who killed Theophilus and Diocles? Do you have any notion?"

Chapter Forty-four

"It seems strange Philip would allow you to live given what you had just found out," Cornelia remarked as they emerged into the sticky heat of midmorning.

"For now, perhaps. Of course, I could still be killed and thrown into the sea and who knows where I would be found?" John pointed out.

"I wonder if he is right and the City Defender is corrupt?" Cornelia mused. "Even so, it seems the City Defender does not suspect anyone other than you in the death of your stepfather. Yet I wonder about that. Diocles was killed at the forge and, by what Hypatia said, Lucian arrived not long after she discovered the body. Does this not seem suspicious?"

John paused. "Now you remind me of what Hypatia said about the incident, it strikes me she mentioned the forge was glowing. Why had the blacksmith not dowsed his fire for the night?"

"It seems obvious to me, John. He was doing secret work that could not be done in the daytime in case you made an unannounced visit."

"And either could have killed Diocles or, for that matter, Theophilus. On the other hand, they too had every reason to prevent visits from the authorities to the estate. Is it too much of a leap to make to assume the two deaths are in some way connected?"

"Much is hidden at this point," Cornelia pointed out.

They came to a sagging wooden fence fitted with an extravagant decorative metal gate featuring swirling designs and loops.

"This must be the gate Petrus complained about, the one that caused ill feeling between him and Theophilus," Cornelia observed.

"It's not the one I remember." John pushed the gate open with difficulty caused by vines that had found the fancy ironwork a handy trellis. Looking around, he added, "It feels unfamiliar, changed in some fashion."

Cornelia took his arm. "Does it? Perhaps you are the one who has changed. And now are you going to show me around your old home?"

"It's just an old farmhouse, but there is something I'd like you to see. I thought of it last night." He pointed to a clump of trees just visible from where they stood. "Leonidas, Alexis, and I sometimes camped out overnight among those trees. We pretended to be guarding the empire, represented by that barn. Many a foray we made during the dark hours, fighting off enemies bent on stealing the empire's eggs."

Taking her hand, he led her into the clump of trees he had pointed out. Its canopy closed overhead but the dense growth soon opened out to disclose a clearing where sunlight streamed down over an octagonal kiosk.

"How lovely! And it has a wind vane!" Cornelia declared.

"My father built this at my mother's request. She told me it was a reminder of a visit they took to Athens in the early years of their marriage. She had been particularly impressed by the Horologion. She spent a lot of time here when the work was done. Perhaps it was because it brought back memories of my father. In any event, here it is."

They stood in front of the structure, staring up at the wind vane. It barely moved.

"It was not possible to obtain a copy of the fish-tailed sea god vane or the depictions of the gods of wind they had seen on the original structure, but it is a close enough re-creation to make my mother happy. And as for me, I spent a lot of time alone here reading," John continued.

"A perfect hiding place for a studious boy," Cornelia replied. "Shall we go in?"

"Speaking of which," John said as he followed her into the low-ceilinged interior, "between Leonidas' unfortunate attempt to hide his collection of coins and then the search of Petrus' house for evidence of wrongdoing, I remembered another hiding place last night."

He dragged a short bench away from the wall to the center of the room, stood on it, ran a hand along the ceiling, and pushed one of its planks up and to the side. "My friends and I used to leave messages here for each other, so the grownups wouldn't know. We were spies for the emperor then and our parents were the Persians. But grownups usually do know about their children's secrets. It occurred to me Theophilus might have made use of it."

He groped around in the cavity in the ceiling. "Mithra!" he exclaimed and brought out a flat, circular bronze mold. "Here is definite evidence counterfeiting is being carried out on the estate. It certainly wasn't hidden here when I was a boy. Look, you can see that's Justinian's face." He leaned over to hand the mold to Cornelia. "And there are one or two bags of what feel like coins hidden here as well."

"Theophilus recalled your hiding place after so many years?"

"Of course he did. No doubt he relished the fact he knew our secrets, or thought he did. It must have been a fond memory. He probably enjoyed the idea the stepson who hated him was assisting him in his illicit dealings by handing him such a fine place to hide his own secrets."

More of John's arm vanished into the hole. There was a scraping noise and he moved a short board from one side of the opening to the other.

"Ah, but was my stepfather clever enough to know there is a hiding place behind the hiding place where our real messages were placed?"

His face clouded. "Perhaps he was. There's a box here!"

Stepping down he wiped dust from its plain unfinished wood with his sleeve, cut the cord holding down the lid, and opened it. He lifted out a sheet of parchment and scanned its writing.

Mithra!" he said again, but so faintly it was little more than an exhalation. "I have not searched for my mother, but she has found me." He gave the parchment to Cornelia. "This is her will."

Its few lines left the farm to John, should he return to Megara before her death. If he did not, the land was to go to Saint Stephen's Monastery "in recognition," his mother had stated, "of the godly works they do for the sick, bereaved, and poor."

"She was still expecting you to return," Cornelia said, "and anticipated when you did, you would eventually look here. Your mother intended for the farm to pass from her to you, John. And now you own it, although not by the means she envisioned. You are not going to make this public, are you?"

John took the will back, and stared at it, as if it might hold some undeciphered code. "You're afraid this part of the estate will pass to the monastery because she was dead before I returned? I don't know what the legal situation would be about that."

"We must consult Anatolius about that. But meantime, is there anything else there?"

John sat on the bench with Cornelia beside him. It felt as if a god—the Zeus of Megara perhaps—had reached down and shaken the kiosk, leaving it at a peculiar angle. John had lost all sense of balance. They both stared at the remaining sheet in the box.

"It's not a poisonous snake," Cornelia finally said, plucking it up and thrusting it into John's hands. "Read it to me."

John complied:

> *The repentant sinner John to his dear wife Sophia, greetings from Alexandria. I pray things have been well for you and our son. Many times in many places my thoughts have flown to both of you, yet I was ashamed to follow them. I thank the Lord, believing as I do that John has made both of us proud and did not take to my wandering ways.*
>
> *From this letter you will know that on the day I left I did not commit my body to the sea and my soul to hell, as is commonly supposed in Megara, according to what I was told by a traveler who passed through there. I believed there*

was something better beyond our little farm, but I have learned that whatever paths we travel they all lead to the same destination.

Now that I have nearly reached that blessed ending, the holy father has admonished me to write to you and beg forgiveness as I have already begged forgiveness of the Lord. Give my affectionate greetings to our son. Although I am too weak to write this myself, you will recognize my signature.

John
Written by the scribe Marius in the fifteenth year of Emperor Justinian

Cornelia put her hand on John's. "I'm so sorry, John."

He smiled wanly and continued to stare at the letter. "Perhaps it is a poisonous snake after all. I should have preferred to read that my father planned to return once he'd made his fortune or when he'd had his fill of travel. Anything other than simply abandoning his family."

"He must have been returning home when he fell ill."

"Yes, certainly, Cornelia." John tried to believe her. "He will be dead by now given he was too ill to write himself and this was dictated years ago. More importantly, do you notice when it is dated? After Theophilus married my mother, meaning father was still alive and the marriage was not legal."

His voice almost broke as the words emerged. He had a feeling, close to shame, that his mind should insist on examining every fact, weighing every possibility, and manufacturing conclusions even in the face of such a devastating personal sorrow.

Cornelia squeezed his hand. "It must have been terrible for your mother to hear from someone long thought dead and especially since she had remarried, or thought she had, at least."

John placed the letter into the box, closing its lid carefully. He tried to ignore the stinging in his eyes and the hot flush along his cheekbones. "Theophilus could not inherit the farm since his marriage to Mother was invalid. Therefore it could not have passed to him at her death and so its sale to Senator Vinius may not be valid either. In fact, this document means I cannot be certain who owns the farm. When Mother died before I returned, the monastery should have taken possession. I have to assume she left a copy of her will with Alexis, having made the bequest to his monastery. Why didn't Alexis make his claim?"

"Perhaps," came Cornelia's whispered reply, "your mother is not dead."

Chapter Forty-five

Hypatia sat on the side of the bed rubbing a pungent ointment into the abrasions on her ankles. The sharp odor made Peter's eyes water, but then, in his old age everything made his eyes water—cold, heat, wind, memories of his youth. The cats, one on each side of their mistress, blinked in annoyance but maintained their vigil.

Peter found a place on the bed for himself as far from the black cat as possible. "Those beasts hover about when you don't feel well, like furry vultures."

"Oh, Peter! Cats sense when we're sick and want to comfort us."

"Are you healing well? What else did the City Defender do to you?"

Hypatia replaced the lid on the ointment jar. The cats eyed it warily. "I have told you more than once. I was treated well enough, except for the shackles. Please stop fretting."

"I can't stop worrying when the City Defender's men could arrive to arrest you again at any time. You know he's certain you killed Diocles. You don't think he'll bother to investigate local residents like Petrus or Lucian, do you? Not when there was a foreigner on the scene, and a mere servant at that."

Hypatia looked tense. "I am certain everything will be as it should be. Why wouldn't it be? I didn't kill Diocles. Why would I?"

"I gather from what I've overheard that he threatened the master."

"Don't be foolish!" Hypatia began to nervously pet the black cat.

Peter could hear the cat purring in contentment, a monstrous reaction to the dire situation. "Personally, I think Philip killed the overseer."

Hypatia stiffened. "Yes, you would, wouldn't you?"

Her obvious anger distressed him. "But Diocles was staying with Philip's father when he should not have even been on the estate. It may be there was a quarrel and Philip was settling the score for his father. But the City Defender won't look into the possibility, not when he can accuse—"

"Peter, please stop. You're making me afraid. I've been trying not to think about it."

"Don't worry, Hypatia. I have the solution. I intend to confess to the City Defender that I killed Diocles."

Hypatia stopped petting the cat. She stared at Peter in confusion. "What do you mean?"

"I had the same reason the City Defender will suppose you had. To defend the master."

"But you were nowhere near the blacksmith's forge that night."

"Are you certain? Does it make any difference? I'm an old man. How many years, or months, do I have left? The Lord might take me at any time. Why, I might not outlive those mangy animals you've adopted. You're still young with your life ahead of you. And besides, you will not be burdened with me."

Hypatia leapt from the bed in a fury, sending the cats flying. One of them knocked the ointment jar over and it rolled to the wall. "Don't say such things! I dread the day I am not burdened with you, Peter. I hope it never comes. I won't stand by and let you lie for me. You didn't kill Diocles any more than I did."

Feeling the weight of her wrathful gaze, Peter rose with difficulty until they were both standing. "But it doesn't matter, you see, whether I confess to killing Diocles because I did, indeed, murder Theophilus."

"Sit down, Peter. You're ill. You've been injured, suffered shocks. Your humors are deranged."

"No, that isn't so. The day after Theophilus was found at the temple—after I'd fallen into the pit—well, you see, I couldn't remember anything except approaching the temple, and then waking from a nightmare at the monastery. But it has been coming back to me. First I recalled my dream about the angel standing guard as I lay in the pit. Then more memories returned. I fell into the pit while fleeing from what I'd done."

"I don't believe a word of it!"

"But I do recall walking along and then, suddenly, nothing but air under my feet. I woke with a terrible feeling that I had done something wrong."

"Why would you have killed the master's stepfather?"

"To protect the master, of course. He hated his stepfather. And what was his stepfather doing on this estate at night? Obviously he was up to no good."

"You must have taken a knife with you. Where is this knife? I haven't seen you carrying one."

"I...I haven't remembered that yet. I must have had a knife, certainly. It isn't all clear yet."

"It's clear to me that you want to sacrifice yourself for me and for the master. I won't let you do it. It wouldn't be right."

"The Lord will have to judge whether it is right or not. Tomorrow I am going to confess to the City Defender."

Hypatia took a step forward and grasped his shoulders. Her dark eyes were bright with tears. "I do love you, Peter. I had hoped to escape prosecution so we could enjoy our time together, but if you insist on going to the City Defender I will have to admit the truth. I did kill Diocles."

Chapter Forty-six

Abbot Alexis was sitting at his desk with an open codex before him when John arrived in the early evening. "This is an unexpected pleasure, John. Shall we be talking about pagan religions or reminiscing about our youth?"

His smile of greeting faded as John spoke. "Alexis, please read this. It is my mother's will."

Alexis took the proffered document and laid it down without consulting it. "Yes, indeed. We have the original in our possession."

"There may be some irregularity with its provisions that will need to be investigated but I intend to consult a lawyer I know in Constantinople about that as soon as possible."

"You are talking about inheriting your old family farm?"

"That in due course. I came here today to ask you why the monastery has not claimed it, given it is almost certain my stepfather did not have the legal right to sell it. As I have only just learned."

The abbot closed his eyes for a moment, as if to rest them or to pray. "All things are revealed in due season. Indeed, Theophilus did not have that right, but we discovered the sale too late to stop it. I only learned of the true situation when your mother entered our care. At that time she told me of the marriage that was not. We could not be certain if she was confused or misremembering events and since your stepfather had departed after selling the farm we felt there was no reason to distress her further or expose her to ridicule, so we did nothing about the matter. We did make inquiries and eventually confirmed that what she told us was true."

"And when she died, you would have brought suit to transfer ownership of the farm to the monastery?"

"That was the intent."

"But you have not done so." John said. "Which means one thing only. My mother is alive and in your care and I insist on seeing her now. And then I should like an explanation of why you did not tell me she was here the first time we met again after my long absence."

John insisted that Alexis not accompany him to the hospice. However, he was not to see his mother alone, because Stephen intercepted him on the way.

"May I speak to you, sir? About your conversation with the abbot?"

"You just happened to overhear us?"

John saw Stephen wince in the illumination cast by the church-shaped lantern he recalled from his previous visit. Crosses of light danced on the walls and ceiling as they proceeded down the dark corridor.

"It has proved helpful for me to listen, considering how poor the abbot's memory can be. Not that there is anything wrong with his faculties, but strange and wonderful events that transpired hundreds of years ago are forever pushing from his thoughts the mundane tasks that need to be done tomorrow."

"You are a useful man, Stephen. No wonder he considers you his successor."

"Does he? But never mind. The abbot is not an old man. He will be in charge of Saint Stephen's for many years."

"And you will loyally continue to listen at his door."

They were almost at the hospice. Stephen came to a halt. "Sometimes one overhears things that one would rather not."

"You have something to tell me?"

"May the Lord forgive me for saying it, but the abbot is not above trying to serve both God and mammon. He is well-intentioned. He intends to benefit the monastery and hospice. The fact is, he had questionable dealings with Diocles."

"My former overseer? Why didn't you tell me this before?"

"You and the abbot are old friends. Would you have believed me?"

"No, and I'm not sure I believe you now. I will consider what you have said, provided you can offer proof beyond what you claim to have heard while eavesdropping."

The flickering light from the lantern made Stephen's expression difficult to read.

"What about Theophilus?" John continued. "Did he visit?"

"Often, sir. After he brought Sophia to live here, he came to see her many times."

It was difficult for John to believe. In fact, he admitted to himself, he did not want to believe his stepfather felt any real affection for his mother. Why should he have suddenly begun to treat her in a decent fashion? Wasn't it more likely Theophilus was also visiting the monastery on illicit business? John did not want to think badly of his old friend Alexis, but the man had lied to him about his mother. How then could he now be believed about anything?

"Let us go in," John said.

He stepped into a dismal underworld. The room was long and dimly lit, filled with rows of beds. Most of the occupants lay partly covered with sheets, as still as corpses on biers. A few sat up, fewer still slumped or lolled on stools near their bedsides.

There was a tug at John's tunic. Glancing down, he saw bony fingers with long, black nails fastened talon-like to the cloth. His gaze followed the hand along a skeletal arm and up into a vacant, withered face.

"Hello," the man said in a monotone. "Hello. Hello."

Stephen made shushing noises and removed the hand. "Our greeter," he explained to John.

He proceeded between the beds to the far end of the room, where he set his lantern down on a small table. John followed past the gray faces, hearing an occasional groan, an unintelligible word. The air was heavy with incense that did not quite mask the smell of incipient death.

The ancient woman in the last bed was sitting up, head bowed as she fumbled with cruelly twisted fingers to fasten a red strip of cloth in her white hair.

"I try to give our ladies something to adorn themselves with," Stephen said. "It makes them happy."

Her hair, thinned to a mist, was ornamented with every color. John had the impression of a rainbow rising up from a cloud.

Then she looked up.

The weight of all the years he had not seen her slammed into his chest like a fatal blow on the battlefield, stopping his breathing and almost his heart.

He recognized her looking out at him from beneath her age.

"Mother," he said. "It's John. I've come to see you, as you knew I would."

There was no recognition in the clouded eyes that stared back at him. More like the eyes of a frightened and bewildered animal than the sparkling eyes he remembered.

"She never recognizes anyone," Stephen said in a low tone. "She hasn't for many months now."

John spoke again. "Don't you know me, Mother?"

She gave no sign that she did. The clouded gaze moved away from him, toward Stephen, perhaps looking for reassurance.

"I am too late," John said.

Stephen picked up the lantern. "Perhaps another time, sir. I can tell she is agitated."

John turned to go, determined to walk away without looking back, but he did stop and look around.

Was there a change in her face? She seemed to be gazing at him more intently. Her thin lips twitched, then she said, almost in a whisper, "Mine."

Chapter Forty-seven

It was one of those late-season nights when summer reasserts herself and insists in hot and humid tones she is going to prolong her stay indefinitely. Cornelia lay beside John on the bed, the covers down, waiting hopefully for any hint of a breeze from the open window. His skin next to hers was cool. It was always so. On the hottest days his hands felt cold. He described his visit to Saint Stephen's.

"Why would Alexis conceal your mother's presence?" Cornelia asked. "He should have taken you to her immediately when you arrived the first time. And Stephen must have known who she was, even if nobody else did." Her voice trailed away.

"It was not for Stephen to disobey his superior by revealing she was there. Alexis was extremely upset and begged me to forgive him. He told me he realized it was wrong but he had fallen into the snares of ambition and could not extricate himself."

"Ambition?" Cornelia was incredulous. Churchmen were not supposed to be ambitious, were they?

"Not only for himself, you understand, but also for the monastery." John replied. "The account of the sack of Corinth that Theophilus possessed must have been taken from Alexis' collection of documents. Valuables buried at the temple of Demeter would enrich the monastery, and therefore the church, and would enhance Alexis' hopes of being appointed bishop in due course."

"How did Theophilus find out about this document?"

"As I just learned, he visited my mother at the hospice and not only that, he carried out occasional tasks for Alexis, according to Petrus. No doubt on one occasion he was working in the library, came across the document looking into boxes he should not have been examining, and took it."

"Then Alexis must have read it before Theophilus stole it?"

"Yes. It seemed to him, as well as to Theophilus, the writer was saying the treasure was buried at the temple, so his plan was to wait until my mother died and then produce her will and claim the farm, for that was where the temple was located. For it seems she went to him for advice when she received the letter from my father and realized her second marriage was not legal. He advised her to be penitent and do good works, but meantime to say nothing about what was essentially a private matter. At that time she gave her will into his care. The document I possess is a copy."

Cornelia speculated on whether this advice had caused Sophia to begin preaching in the streets.

"It may have been. I understand she was failing even then," John replied. "When she was reported as dead by Theophilus, she was actually alive and living in the hospice. I suppose it was not exactly a lie, for she was dead to the world and never left the monastery grounds again. But Theophilus had to claim she had died in order to inherit the farm and sell it. The main point is that since Alexis knew the marriage was not valid and the sale of the farm was therefore illegal, the provisions of the will still applied, and if I did not return before my mother died, the monastery would inherit the farm. So he was willing to bide his time."

"Was he? What about the excavations your overseer was making at the temple? According to the slave Julius, Diocles was seeking the treasure but trying to hide the fact by claiming it was necessary work on the foundations. Is it possible Alexis engaged him to direct the estate slaves to carry out that work, given an abbot can hardly go out digging in the middle of the night? It seems to me Alexis has not revealed the entire story."

"There again, Theophilus knew about the treasure and he and Diocles were cooperating in at least one other criminal enterprise. I am thinking here of the shipment of iron."

Cornelia rolled over, putting her arm across John's chest. She could feel his heart beating. "But supposing Alexis was involved and visited the site occasionally to see how the work was proceeding. On one particular night he finds Theophilus investigating the temple. In the darkness he thinks it is you looking around. You stand between him and what he wants, so——"

"You are still afraid I was the intended victim? If I were dead Alexis would still need to sue the estate for the farm on the grounds it had been obtained through an illegal sale, hoping the authorities would side with the monastery, which is not a certainty. That hardly seems a basis to put a knife into someone's back."

"Oh, John! Alexis wasn't thinking as if he was in a courtroom! He wasn't thinking at all! Don't you ever stop thinking?"

"It is true Alexis has extremely bad eyesight," John admitted. "He may have mistaken Theophilus for me, if only because he wouldn't have expected him to be there at that time of night."

"How can you know? How many years is it since you knew him?"

And even then, Cornelia thought, how well do we ever know anyone? She was not even certain what John was thinking most of the time, what turmoil lay behind his tightly controlled demeanor. Why was he lying in bed pondering his investigation when he had just unexpectedly seen his mother, a shade emerged from the underworld? Why, except to avoid thinking about his mother and his past?

"Besides," John said, "my reappearance in Megara might not be permanent. Alexis wouldn't need to kill me. He could hope Justinian changes his mind and has me executed or that the City Defender succeeded in convicting me of killing Theophilus."

"What comforting thoughts! So much more pleasant to contemplate than worrying about you being killed! And it's all very well for you to be searching for a murderer in all this tangle of illegality you've discovered, but who will bring him to justice? Not the City Defender!"

"I am not certain what he would do if he were confronted with inescapable evidence," John admitted.

"John, you simply don't want to admit your old boyhood friend has grown up to be a cold-blooded murderer. You've all but proved Alexis is the culprit. He had a lot to gain, he knew about the hoard, he was already plotting to take ownership of the farm, the monastery is not too far from the temple, and he blatantly lied to you to further his schemes."

"I am afraid you may be right, and yet it's difficult for me to accept that Alexis intended to kill me."

Cornelia leaned over and kissed John's cheek. "So much crime and misery caused by the anonymous writing on that scrap of parchment. Perhaps it is as well your mother has retreated into her girlhood, decorating her hair and knowing nothing of terrible events happening not far from her."

"She is happy, and that is all I would ever wish for her," John replied.

Chapter Forty-eight

"Peter and Hypatia don't seem to be around." Cornelia came back upstairs from the kitchen with a bowl of boiled eggs.

"Is something wrong?" John wondered. "Peter never fails to have breakfast ready." He rubbed at the crick in his neck. Eventually he and Cornelia had fallen asleep in each other's arms, which was good for the soul but hard on the neck, at least at their ages.

Cornelia put the bowl on the table and sat down beside John. "Everything seems quiet. Nothing's on fire. The City Defender isn't at the gate. Maybe Peter mistook the time. It's easy enough out here in the country with nothing going on and no water clock."

"We're fortunate nothing is going on…" John shelled an egg slowly and took a bite.

Cornelia placed her hand over his. "I know this is difficult, John."

"It shouldn't be hard to bring a murderer to justice. You're right, I no longer know this Alexis." He shook his head. "An abbot…then again, the City Defender might not be so ready to see justice done."

"Surely when you explain it all to him…?"

"Unfortunately, I have explanations but little evidence. Granted, once Georgios knows what happened, he could probably find the evidence easily enough with the resources he has, if he wanted to."

"What about the basket, John? Alexis wanted to make the murder look as if it had pagan overtones by leaving that basket at the temple. That's something you could take with you."

"Yes, the sacred basket. Thinking about it reminds me—"

Cornelia interrupted his thought by leaping up and running to the window. "Goddess!" she cried. "I spoke too soon! The City Defender just arrived!"

John met Georgios and a contingent of armed guards in the courtyard. The City Defender looked tired. There were bags under the eyes of the big square-jawed face, and when he spoke it was with bemusement more than bluster.

"You are taxing my patience and my resources," Georgios said. "I don't have enough prison cells for you and your friends and your servants."

"Why are you here this morning?" John demanded.

"According to the confessions I have just heard, that elderly servant of yours, who is apparently more spry than he looks, is responsible for the murders of both Theophilus and Diocles. Your female servant, however, only killed Diocles."

"You don't believe that, do you?"

Now Georgios looked pained now as well as tired. "In part, perhaps, but not all of it certainly. I realize the emperor sent you into exile here but did he order you to bring the crime in Constantinople with you?"

"That's what people feared, so naturally that's what they see. Isn't it obvious my servants are trying to protect me?"

"Or trying to protect each other. The real question is which of you needs protecting? One, or two, or possibly all three?"

"None of us. Neither Peter nor Hypatia is a murderer."

"In the grip of passion we can all become murderers if only for an instant, but an instant is all it takes to drive a blade into a man's back. It is perfectly plausible the old man killed Theophilus. He tells me he was out by the temple that night, and likewise the woman was on the spot when Diocles was killed. Perhaps you ordered these deaths? At any rate, as owner of the estate you are equally responsible."

"You are therefore here to arrest me?" John had noted the guards were blocking his path to the gate. The courtyard penned him in on all sides.

"It is necessary." Georgios' tone was curt.

"I think not. I know who killed Theophilus and Diocles."

Georgios smiled in weary fashion. "If you killed them, of course you would know."

At his gesture a couple of his men drew their swords and stepped toward John.

"I didn't kill anyone, Georgios. But were I to reveal the culprit's identity would you believe me on the evidence I have and act on it?"

"My interest is in maintaining public order in Megara. What is good for Megara is good for me. You have my attention."

"Then allow me to continue my investigations. There is more to be done to ensure justice will be carried out."

The guards who had stationed themselves on either side of John looked away from the man they were supposed to seize and looked toward the City Defender.

"I will allow you one day," Georgios said, "and will leave a few men here with your lady to keep her safe while you continue to look into the matter. Meantime, your servants will remain my reluctant guests."

Chapter Forty-nine

John sensed a chill in Leonidas' house as soon as he stepped through the doorway. It seemed to radiate from the walls themselves. One might imagine that, were Leonidas and Helen to leave, the house itself would remain unhappy in their absence.

Helen, holding a cleaning rag, had stood stolidly in the doorway as if she intended to block John from entering. But she stepped aside and followed him into the room where Leonidas fussed at his work. He was attempting to reattach a small piece of gold leaf to what John recognized as the dome from the Great Church model—only barely recognized, since one side of the dome had been crushed.

Leonidas looked up and gave John a bleak smile. "Earthquake."

Helen snapped her cleaning rag. "A dusting accident," she declared.

John suddenly pitied his old friend. "I apologize for intruding. Do you recall telling me a man was watching the house from across the street before the City Defender's men arrived?"

"Yes. I found it innocent enough at the time but in retrospect I suppose the City Defender was having me watched."

Helen sniffed. "Thanks to you suddenly having high-ranking officials from the emperor's court visiting, since no one paid any attention to you before. Why would they?"

John was silent. Responding to Helen would simply embarrass Leonidas further. Instead he continued to address his friend. "Can you tell me what the fellow looked like?"

"Short. That I remember." Leonidas turned the gilded dome upside down and stared into it as if he might find a memory hidden there. "That's all, John."

He looked so defeated, gazing into the ruined dome of his carefully constructed church, that John regretted ever coming back into his old friend's life, and beneath that regret another, even darker thought tried to force its way forward against John's resistance.

"A gap in his teeth?" John asked. "Does that jar your memory?"

"He was standing on the other side of the street."

"He did have a gap in his teeth," Helen said. "You could see it clearly across the street if you were looking. Well, perhaps not exactly, but there was something wrong with his mouth. I was keeping a close eye on him to remember the face in case it was necessary."

"Thank you. I won't disturb you further."

Leonidas set the dome on the table and started to rise. "You aren't disturbing us, John."

But Helen was already opening the door for his departure.

◇◇◇

At the entrance to the Temple of Zeus John found Matthew lurking as usual.

"Back for further enlightenment?" The self-styled guide greeted John with a gap-toothed smile.

"Indeed. I expect to learn quite a lot from you. Let us go inside this time."

"Alas, I have been barred from—"

John cut him off by showing his blade. "Luckily I have a very sharp pass."

"I would never have taken you for a robber," Matthew grumbled as John escorted him past the towering pillars and into the presence of the god.

Looking down from an enormous height, Zeus' ivory-skinned face shone and his golden hair sparkled in the sunlight against a sky bluer and deeper than the sea. From his neck down to his feet, however, he was a chunk of half-formed hardened clay and gypsum.

John folded his arms, concealing his blade from any who entered the temple. "For a man who has been standing around waiting to regale visitors, Matthew, you seem oddly out of breath. Are you certain you weren't running to get here before me?"

"If you want my money ask for it. Don't mock me first. Perhaps you think learned men such as myself get rich educating travelers? You will see you are mistaken." He started to reach into the folds of his tunic beside his belt.

"Stop!" John ordered. "I know how to use a blade and mine is already out."

Mathew raised his arms slightly from his sides and showed John his palms. "My purse is in my belt."

"I also know you are not a guide," John told him. "You are an imperial spy sent by Justinian to watch me, and perhaps deal with me, if we might put it that way, if and when it suits the emperor's purpose."

Matthew showed John the gap in his teeth. "Don't flatter yourself. Justinian didn't send me to Megara to keep an eye on his former Lord Chamberlain. Naturally, when you arrived, I was ordered to check on you now and then. It was only prudent. My task here is to look into corruption. How the locals divide the spoils isn't typically a matter of imperial concern, but when the malfeasance becomes so widespread that it reaches all the way to the provincial governor, as I believe it does, then the emperor begins feeling it in the treasury."

"You are not alone either, are you?"

Matthew answered the question with one of his own. "How did you guess my identity?"

"At the palace one develops a sense for imposters. Besides, do you really think you could follow me around the city without my glimpsing you?"

"I see. Well, I can't say I wasn't warned about your skills. It is easy to become overconfident and careless spending months in a place full of blind hayseeds."

"Blind and corrupt hayseeds, you mean."

Matthew laughed unpleasantly.

John had positioned himself near one of Zeus' gargantuan feet, some distance from the entrance and facing it, ready to retreat out the back of the temple if any of Matthew's possible assistants arrived. "Were you loitering outside Leonidas' house because I had visited him, or because you suspected him of wrongdoing?"

"Both. After sharing a few drinks at a tavern, one of your friend's colleagues revealed Leonidas' little collecting hobby. He of course considered it just a harmless amusement."

"You were investigating Leonidas because you knew I was an old friend?"

"You'd be surprised what I know about you, my former Lord Chamberlain."

"You can't learn much by pretending to be a guide for visitors."

"Not so. It gives me a reason to be out and about and to be curious about matters, if anyone gets suspicious. I say I'm just trying to find a little local color, interesting events, that kind of thing. I'm planning on writing an account of my travels, you see."

"A believable fable," John admitted.

"Oh, but I am going to write a travel book. I plan to spend my retirement writing. It's remarkable the places I've visited, what I've learned, working for the emperor."

"I don't know how much you've uncovered about the local situation but apparently not enough to start arresting anyone. I can give you information you may not have, but in return, I want assurance that the proper authorities will be given evidence I have relating to two murders."

"In Megara the City Defender is the proper authority," Matthew pointed out.

"I don't trust him to act in the interests of justice."

"I wouldn't be too certain about that. Currently he pleases the provincial governor by turning a blind eye to corruption.

But if the governor is dismissed, the man responsible for bringing order to Megara might well be next in line for the position."

"Nevertheless, I need to be backed by imperial authority."

"Granted, provided you can tell me something useful."

"Thank you. I will explain everything to you on the way to Saint Stephen's Monastery."

◇◇◇

Stephen showed John and Matthew into the abbot's study.

Alexis, startled and annoyed by the interruption, fussed nervously with the manuscripts littering his desk, as if he were unable to quite wake up from his deep studies. "From the emperor, you say? I am honored. If I can serve the emperor in any way I shall be pleased to do so."

Stephen began to leave but John gestured for him to remain. "This affects you also. If it were not for your help we would not be here."

The young monk's expression was so rigidly bland John wondered if he were suppressing a smile.

"So, John, my friend," Alexis leaned forward across untidy heaps of parchment, "I assume you have not brought Matthew to hear a lecture about ancient pagan religions."

"Not exactly."

Alexis had now composed himself. Suddenly the puzzling gap between young Alexis, the prankster, and Alexis the abbot closed and John saw sitting in front of him the same young man who would say or do something utterly outrageous and then smile placidly as if nothing noteworthy had happened at all. The garments Alexis wore, the cross on the wall, the obscure literature, all were part of an elaborate joke. Or was John being unfair?

"Not exactly?" Alexis looked puzzled.

Matthew broke in. "I'm not here for a lecture but I want to know about your involvement with this supposed treasure."

"If John told you about that, he must have explained it's nothing but a legend."

John spoke sharply. "If you believed that, Alexis, why was it arranged for Diocles to put slaves to work digging for it?"

"Diocles? I didn't—"

"You've lied to me enough already. Don't lie again. You admitted your plan was to get possession of my family's farm."

A look of sorrow crossed Alexis' face. "You've been away so long, my friend, you have forgotten who I am."

"I don't think so, Alexis. On the contrary, I was wrong in imagining you had changed."

"And who is it has tried to help you and your family? The only person in Megara who has sided with you? Still, I cannot regret doing what a good Christian should have done. It would have been better for everyone if you had never returned, John."

"Particularly for my family. It was not my choice to come back to Megara!"

Despite the angry retort John realized Alexis was right. He had been correct to avoid his past for so many years, a past he had been severed from forcibly and irrevocably. Now he had grievously if inadvertently injured both of his oldest friends.

And the worst damage was yet to come. Perhaps he should leave matters as they were. Why would he want to avenge Theophilus? He'd wanted to kill the bastard himself.

"Stephen," Alexis said, "light a lamp. I can barely see." A confusion of long shadows had begun to crisscross the room.

Was the abbot delaying the discussion to give him time to think or trying to break the palpable tension?

It was true, Alexis' eyesight was not good. Bad enough to mistake John's stepfather for John at night.

"You surmised the valuables rescued from Corinth were buried at the temple from the contemporary account written on the parchment which Theophilus stole from your collection," John said, determined to say what he wished he didn't need to say. "My stepfather was here often enough and you are careless. One night you went out, in part to see how the excavation was going, but also intending to foment rumors about pagan worship on my estate by leaving a basket associated with the rites of Demeter. You've spent years studying such matters so you knew how it should look and indeed described that very thing to me." John's gesture took in the manuscripts and the scrolls and codices on shelves and in baskets.

"Why do you insist I engaged Diocles to arrange for digging at the temple? Isn't it just as likely Theophilus did it since he knew where to look?"

"But Theophilus did not put a knife in his own back when he mistook himself for me, Alexis."

The abbot had been leaning forward into the dim light. Now he fell back into his chair, vanishing into shadow, his expression hidden. "You are accusing me of trying to murder you?"

"Of murdering Theophilus. It was an impulse. You always acted on impulse. There I was, the one thing that stood between you and the treasure, between you and the post of bishop. Or so you imagined with your terrible eyesight. I'm certain you regretted your action immediately but it was too late."

"John, I can't believe…I always thought you were a rational young man. Perhaps the life you've lived…" His words trailed off into the shadow engulfing him and he might not have been there at all.

"The temple and the blacksmith's forge are not far from the monastery, meaning both are easily accessible to you in the dark. You must have quarreled with Diocles over the excavations. It's occurred to me that since I relieved him of his duties he could no longer assist you. He was desperate. Had he sent for you, looking for a bribe to refrain from exposing you to the City Defender?"

"It all sounds so plausible, John, especially considering how I intended to take advantage of your mother's infirmity, may the Lord forgive me. And, yes, I do admit I wanted the hoard, but as for the rest, I swear I am innocent."

A hazy cross of light slid around the wall and came to rest on the ceiling above Alexis' desk. It reminded John of the description of the angel Peter dreamt had guarded him in the pit and the strange lights resembling the Key of the Nile, Hypatia, a pagan, said she saw at the forge. This led John to think of the decorated basket left at the temple and from that to the strips of cloth tied in his mother's hair.

Stephen sat the church-shaped lantern on the corner of the abbot's desk and John could see his old friend's haggard face, every age line accentuated by shadow,

"Yes, Alexis," John said softly. "I realize now you are innocent."

It was early morning when John knocked on Leonidas' door. It had rained at last during the night, but the puddles he had walked through on the way from the City Defender's office made no impression on him. Nor did he hear the waking sounds of the city or notice the smell of wet earth, encased as he was in a shell of regret and sorrow.

Helen ushered him inside with an expression of mixed fury and terror, as was only fitting, he thought. There was, this time, no slightest sign of welcome in Leonidas' face.

"My friend," John said. "I asked to be allowed to bring the news to you myself. Your son, Stephen, has been arrested for the murders of Theophilus and Diocles."

Epilogue

After returning from Megara, John decided to sit for a while in the triclinium. It was raining again. Through the open windows he could smell the distinctive earthy odor parched land breathes out when it finally drinks in moisture. He could hear the rain tapping at the roof and noticed how the water, trickling down the wall from the leaking roof tiles in the corner did indeed cause the painted waterfall to sparkle realistically.

"What are you thinking about, John?" Cornelia sat down next to him.

"The misery I've caused my old friends. Leonidas is crushed to find out his son is a murderer. And Alexis, though he perhaps did not act illegally, will certainly be removed from his post because of his dishonesty regarding my mother and her will."

"You didn't ask to come here. You couldn't turn your back on injustice. If there were any justice at the emperor's court we would still be in Constantinople."

John continued to stare at the artificial waterfall. "You see now, I was right in avoiding my past."

"Let's not argue over that. How did you come to realize Alexis was innocent? You told me when you got in that you'd been up all night talking with the City Defender and Justinian's spy and I'm sure you're tired of explaining it all, but I'm curious."

John acceded to Cornelia's wishes and marshaled his thoughts, pulling them away from his broodings. "All the circumstances that made it plausible for Alexis to be the murderer applied equally to Stephen. Enriching the monastery might lead to Alexis being promoted to bishop and it would also open up the position of abbot for Stephen. Stephen had easy access to the manuscripts in the library too. He shared some of Alexis' knowledge of antiquities, the significance of pagan ceremonial baskets, for example. No doubt he read the account of the concealment of the Corinth treasure before Theophilus stole it. He knew as much as Alexis about what was going on at the monastery. Anything Alexis didn't tell Stephen, as his constant shadow, Stephen would doubtless have overheard, given his penchant for eavesdropping. He would have known about my mother's bequest to the monastery one way or another. Stephen had just as much opportunity to arrange for Diocles to dig at the temple when the overseer visited on business.

"As for the commission of the murders, quite apart from the fact that I could not see the Alexis I knew as a killer, how likely was it that he would be venturing out into the dark with his terrible eyesight, through fields with half-concealed pits?

"Most importantly there were two things pointing to Stephen's presence at the scenes of the killings. The colored cloths tied to the basket at the temple and the cross-shaped lights that Peter saw while in the pit and recalled as a dream and what Hypatia saw at the forge. The cloth strips were like those Stephen gave my mother to tie in her hair. The strange light patterns were like those thrown by the church-shaped lantern Stephen used when I visited the monastery. Peter, being Christian, saw the lights as what they were meant to represent, while Hypatia, being Egyptian, identified them with the Key of the Nile, the ankh."

"The ankh is more or less cross-shaped," Cornelia agreed. "And we know Stephen was out the night Theophilus was killed because he rescued Peter from the pit. But what was he doing? Meeting Theophilus?"

"He ran into my stepfather by accident. Theophilus stole that document purporting to name the location of the treasure while he was at the monastery to do an odd job or on the pretense of visiting my mother. He returned to the estate to search. Stephen had only intended to leave a pagan ceremonial basket, perhaps to be found by Diocles' excavators. It would certainly cause trouble one way or another."

Cornelia frowned. "He intended to help inflame Megara against us even further, until we fled or were forced out?"

"That's right. But when he came upon Theophilus he realized a corpse would endanger me more than the basket. And it would remove an unwanted competitor for the riches as well."

"Then Stephen didn't think he was killing you?"

"Not according to his confession."

"He has already admitted to the murder?"

"To the murder of Diocles also, as soon as he was arrested. I believe he was eager to tell his story while I was a witness, rather than waiting for Georgios to interview him privately. In which case the questioning might be less civilized."

"Did he say why he killed Diocles?" Cornelia asked.

"Yes, and it was more or less as I had guessed. It seems Diocles had gone to hide with Petrus after Lucian threw him out. He was working on illegal schemes with both tenants. But Petrus didn't want him either. That left the overseer in a hopeless situation. Since I'd relieved him of his position he couldn't continue his partnership with Stephen, using the estate slaves to dig at the temple. Stephen admitted he enlisted Diocles because he couldn't conduct much of a search on his own. Why he thought Diocles would honor any agreement between the two had the hoard been located, I can't say.

"Diocles asked Stephen to meet him at Petrus' forge. He threatened to expose him unless Stephen gave him money. So Stephen, having already committed one murder, had no compunction about removing Diocles."

Cornelia shook her head. "It is hard to believe that Alexis didn't know what was going on right under his nose."

"I have not only pointed out the murderer but also supplied enough information to the City Defender to dismantle a criminal conspiracy. My investigations are finished."

"I'm glad to hear it, John. Will the City Defender actually prosecute anyone, aside from Stephen? He let the arsonist go."

"That was before Justinian's spy, Matthew, came forward. Georgios won't try to cross the emperor."

"Is there really enough evidence to bring all the criminals to justice?"

"As I told Georgios, part of my explanation is as flimsy as a spider's web but remember, the size of the prey those webs catch and hold is out of all proportion to their substance. There is the freshly minted counterfeit coin found in Halmus' secret warehouse, and the fact, as Peter realized, that Halmus was lying about his pilgrimages. No doubt his absences were for less than pious purposes. Diocles was dealing not only with Halmus, but with Petrus, Lucian, and my stepfather. Theophilus and Diocles cooperated in getting iron to Petrus and Lucian hid the illegal weapons the blacksmith made. Almost certainly the arsonists were armed with the products of Petrus' forge. And the coin mold, concealed in a spot my stepfather would have known about, indicates he was involved in that endeavor also, and thus, further linked to Halmus."

"There are enough connections to make a web, but a spider's work can be beautiful in the morning, glittering with dew."

"Not this web. And remember, Matthew has been busy too. I only stumbled over a few of the criminals while looking for a murderer. There are plenty of others in Megara who will be hearing knocks on their doors, including a certain seller of fish."

"And what does it mean for us, John? Will the natives see us in a different light?"

"At least they won't try to burn our house down or stone us in the streets."

"We will need new tenants unless Philip plans to stay in his father's house."

John's expression hardened. "I have told Philip to go. He cannot remain in my employment. I can't trust him. I concealed his father's illegal activities from me."

Peter appeared in the doorway bearing honey cakes and wine. He hesitated as John looked up at him sharply.

"I asked Peter to bring us something to eat," Cornelia explained.

"I'm glad you're here, Peter," John told him. "Please find Hypatia and bring her here."

When Peter departed John pulled a scrap of parchment from the pouch at his belt and handed it to Cornelia. "This is the account of the treasure of Corinth that Theophilus stole from the monastery. Take a close look. You can see it is a palimpsest. Whoever wrote about the matter used an old bit of parchment from which the previous writing had been erased. But not eradicated completely. In a good light you can make out a legal term or two and in the corner, part of Justinian's name. This sheet was probably from a copy of the emperor's Institutes. Just a few years old, in other words. The document is not contemporary with Alaric's sack of Corinth. It's nothing more than a fraud, a prank. It has already killed two people."

Cornelia held the document up to her eyes. "I can make out some of the words underneath, as you say. How were the others deceived?"

"Alexis is half-blind and Stephen, my stepfather, and Diocles were blinded by greed."

Peter returned with Hypatia.

John stood up and addressed them. "I wanted to speak to both of you at the same time. As you well know, much has changed and sometimes in the face of change it is impossible to maintain our lives as they were. Therefore, as of today, you are no longer in my employment."

Peter stared at John in disbelief.

Cornelia jumped to her feet. "John! I know this business with your friends has upset you but—"

"There is nothing to discuss. I have already chosen two of the estate employees as replacements."

Peter finally managed to speak, sounding as if he had a noose around his neck. "I know I have caused problems, master—"

"I am no longer your master, Peter. You and Hypatia were not banished from Constantinople. You chose to come here. You are free to return if you wish. If, as I hope, you would prefer to stay, you may have Petrus' house or Lucian's, whichever would suit you best. I consider your long years of loyal service a fair price for either."

Peter blinked in confusion. "But, but...master..."

Hypatia said nothing. For an instant she locked grateful tear-filled eyes with John's, then pulled Peter firmly out of the room.

The rain was coming down harder now. Hand in hand, John and Cornelia watched it refresh the earth.

Glossary

All dates are CE unless otherwise indicated

ACROPOLIS
Fortified upper district of a Greek city.

ARTEMIS
Greek goddess of the hunt.

ATRIUM
Central area of a Roman house.

BRITOMARTIS
Cretan goddess known as the Lady of the Nets because while fleeing unwanted amorous attention she leapt from a cliff, landing in the net of a fisherman in whose boat she escaped to safety.

BITHYNIA
Roman province in Anatolia.

CHELIDON
Greater Celandine. Also known as swallowwort.

CODEX
Book with manuscript pages.

CONCRETE
Roman concrete was composed of lime, volcanic ash, and pieces of rock.

CORINTHIAN BRONZE

Compound metal also known as Corinthian brass. The method of its manufacture was reportedly lost, thus greatly increasing the value of existing artifacts constructed from it.

DERBE

Town in the Roman province of Lycaonia, Asia Minor.

DEW OF THE SEA

Rosemary.

EUNUCH

Eunuchs played important roles in the military, ecclesiastical, and civil administrations of the Byzantine Empire. Many high posts at the GREAT PALACE were typically held by eunuchs.

EXCUBITORS

Guard at the GREAT PALACE.

FALERNIAN WINE

Considered one of the finest Roman wines.

FIBULA

Brooch or clasp serving to fasten and ornament the clothing of both genders.

GREAT CHURCH

Colloquial name for the Church of the Holy Wisdom (Hagia Sophia) in Constantinople.

GREAT PALACE

Located in Constantinople, it was not one building but rather many, set amidst trees and gardens. Its grounds included barracks for the EXCUBITORS, ceremonial rooms, meeting halls, the imperial family's living quarters, churches, and housing for court officials, ambassadors, and various other dignitaries.

HIPPODROME

U-shaped racetrack next to the GREAT PALACE. The Hippodrome was also used for public celebrations and other civic events.

HOROLOGION

Also known as the Tower of the Winds. Dating from the first century BC, the octagonal structure still stands in Athens.

HYPOCAUST

Under-floor heating by distribution of hot air. The furnace used also heated water.

INSTITUTES

Serving as a textbook for law students, the Institutes formed part of JUSTINIAN I's codification of Roman law.

ISAURIA

Roman province in Anatolia. Isaurians were a notoriously rebellious and warlike people.

JUSTINIAN I (483-565, r 527-565)

Emperor whose ambition was to restore the Roman Empire to its former glory. He succeeded in regaining North Africa, Italy, and southeastern Spain. Other accomplishments included codifying Roman law and an extensive building program in Constantinople. He was married to THEODORA.

KALAMOS

Reed pen.

LORD CHAMBERLAIN

Chief attendant to the emperor and supervisor of most of those serving at the GREAT PALACE. He also took a leading role in court ceremonial, but his real power arose from his close working relationship with the emperor, which allowed him to wield great influence.

MEGARA

Located in Attica, Greece, its neighbors are Corinth and Athens.

MESE

Main thoroughfare of Constantinople, rich with columns, arches, and statuary depicting secular, military, imperial, and religious subjects as well as fountains, churches, workshops, monuments, public baths, and private dwellings, making it a perfect mirror of the heavily populated and densely built city it traversed.

MITHRA

Persian sun god, also known as Mithras. Born in a cave or from a rock, he is usually depicted wearing a tunic and Phrygian cap, his cloak flying out behind him, in the act of slaying the Great Bull from whose blood all animal and vegetable life sprang.

MITHRAEUM

Underground place of worship dedicated to MITHRA.

NOMISMA
Standard gold coin in circulation at the time of JUSTINIAN I.

PAUSANIAS (fl 150)
Author of Description of Greece, which contains extensive information on the mythology, buildings, settlements, and topography of ancient Greece.

PLATO'S ACADEMY
Located in Athens, its curriculum included natural science, mathematics, philosophy, and training for public service.

PRAXITELES (fl 4th century BC)
Considered one of greatest Greek sculptors, his subjects were often taken from mythology.

STRABO (c 64 BC–c 23 CE)
Greek author. His encyclopedic Geography provides descriptions of numerous countries collected during his extensive travels.

STYLITES
Holy men who spent years living on platforms atop columns. They took their name from stylos (Greek column or pillar) and were also known as pillar saints.

TESSERAE
Small cubes, usually of stone or glass, used to create mosaics.

THEODORA (c 497-548)
Powerful wife of JUSTINIAN I. It has been alleged she had formerly been an actress and prostitute. When the Nika riots broke out in Constantinople in 532, she is said to have urged her husband to remain in the city, thus saving his throne.

TRICLINIUM
Dining room featuring a table with couches along three of its sides.

TUNICA
Tunic-like undergarment.

To receive a free catalog of Poisoned Pen Press titles, please provide
your name and address in one of the following ways:

Phone: 1-800-421-3976
Facsimile: 1-480-949-1707
Email: info@poisonedpenpress.com
Website: www.poisonedpenpress.com

Poisoned Pen Press
6962 E. First Ave. Ste 103
Scottsdale, AZ 85251